Scandalous Secrets

A LADY'S DANGEROUS SECRET

HAZEL HAAS

OLIVER HEBER BOOKS

Cover art by Dar Albert at Wicked Smart Designs

Published by Oliver-Heber Books

0 9 8 7 6 5 4 3 2 1

To my husband

CHAPTER ONE

LONDON, APRIL 1816

I *don't want to be here.*
I need a husband.
I don't want to be here.
I need a husband.

Lady Charlotte Tipton, daughter of the Earl of Pulverbatch, braced herself for what she must do. She was at one of the premiere balls of the London Season, because she had a secret.

A terrible secret.

No, a dangerous secret.

Her blue eyes swept over the tableau before her. Hundreds of candles illuminated a gilded ballroom filled with the *crème de la crème* of Society. Bejeweled ladies in their finest gowns batted their eyelashes at preening gentlemen in perfectly tied cravats. Musicians tuned their strings in preparation for a night of dancing. Many would call this scene idyllic. Except Charlotte. All she saw was a means to an end.

She had made haste to travel to London only three weeks prior, due to the *Incident*. Charlotte's entrance into the *ton* had been an abstract thought until now. Her current presence at the Markham Ball and her debut at Almack's Assembly Rooms several nights earlier solidified her fate. She would need to play the role of an innocent debutante in search of a husband, as if her life depended on it.

Because it did.

So much had changed in such a short time. If Charlotte had still been at home, she would have ridden her dappled gray mare astride through the hills of Shropshire with a cool wind whipping across her face. Instead, only hours ago, her lithe body had been forcefully maneuvered into stays that had been tightened without remorse. Then she had been poured into a ball gown consisting of a white satin slip and a silver net overlay embroidered with beaded flowers. Her chestnut hair had been wrangled into a chignon, which offered her the gift of throbbing pain behind her temples. Finally, she had been anointed with a borrowed sapphire parure that was meant to be her *pièce de résistance*, but the jewels only weighed her down. Despite these tribulations, Charlotte was determined to persevere and secure a titled husband as quickly as possible.

She was off to a tepid start thus far. She had been paraded about Almack's as if she were a piece of prized horseflesh, while whispers of her generous dowry spread throughout the crowd. The next day, she had received plenty of flowers from potential suitors, though an air of desperation permeated their notes. She understood desperation all too well, but she did not have much time to spare. Settling for a debt-ridden popinjay would be a last resort.

The distinct pressure of a hand on her upper arm caught her attention. A pair of chocolate-brown eyes bore into her. It was none other than her inimitable and social-climbing aunt, Lady Frances Howe, Marchioness of Hardwicke.

"Damn."

"I heard that, Charlotte." Her aunt's fingers further tightened on her arm. "I did not present you to the Queen to hear you swear like a sailor. Act like a lady."

Charlotte attempted to lift the edges of her mouth into a smile, though all she felt was a grimace. Her aunt did not take note, and with Charlotte in tow, charged into the crowd like a general marching into battle. They approached a group with their heads dipped in polite conversation. Her aunt's face lit up. "Lady Carrington, it has been too long!"

A graceful woman with amber eyes and blonde hair curtsied. "Lady Hardwicke. We're delighted to see you. You remember my daughter, Bridget?"

The young woman, a spitting image of Lady Carrington, stepped away from her mother with downcast eyes and gave a deep curtsy to Aunt Frances, who said, "Of course, this must be your first Season. This is my niece, Charlotte."

The two matrons proceeded to dive into the latest *on-dits* of High Society, while Charlotte and Lady Bridget hovered near their elbows, with Lady Bridget still silent and eyes downcast.

The supposed scandals of the *ton* did not interest Charlotte one bit. Her gaze drifted to two gentlemen engaged in a *tête-à-tête* nearby. These men were oblivious to the women but posed a potential escape from her aunt's idle chatter. Charlotte stared at the men in hopes they would feel her eyes upon them and turn around. Alas, after what felt like minutes of trying, their heads remained bowed deep in conversation, creating an immovable obstacle; meanwhile, guests shuffled around them with jostling elbows and swishing skirts.

One of these skirts belonged to a woman with a hawklike nose, curly red hair, and hazel eyes, who stepped toward them. "Lady Hardwicke, Lady Carrington." She dipped into a curtsy.

Charlotte's aunt looked down her nose at the intrusion and said, "Lady Booth."

Once the social nicety of introductions was over, Lady

Booth took over the conversation. "Lady Hardwicke, I'm *so* glad to *meet* your niece. I heard she is a *diamond of the first water.*" Lady Booth's calculating eyes assessed Charlotte from her chignon to her slippers. "You *are* a pretty thing," she muttered. "I understand this is your first Season. But *why* have you not *come out* sooner?" Lady Booth smirked while awaiting a response.

Charlotte's aunt was unperturbed. "Why my niece is the sweetest young woman and could not bear to leave her dear mother alone in Shropshire. You know how the countess prefers the country."

Her aunt referenced a touchy subject for Charlotte, whose "dear mother" was not so dear at all. Charlotte doubted 'her mother, the countess' had even noticed that her only daughter had suddenly departed for London.

But that was nothing new.

"Luckily," her aunt continued. "Lady Charlotte had no pressure to snag a wealthy husband the moment she left the schoolroom. How are your darling daughters?"

Charlotte flinched. Her aunt's counterattack was commendable.

Lady Booth flushed and pretended to scan the crowd. "Oh! I must be off. There is my dear friend whom I *have not seen* in ages." She turned on her heel and scurried away.

Aunt Frances let out a *harrumph* and turned back to Lady Carrington to continue their gossip. Given that she had no immediate escape, Charlotte merely stood there and plastered a smile on her face. At the ripe age of twenty-one, she had thought she would spend her life in Shropshire as a contented spinster, removed from Society. Instead, here she was as an unexpected debutante with a scandalous secret, navigating the treacherous waters of the *ton* in search of a husband to save her life.

And she was traveling without a soul in whom to confide and utterly alone.

~

I don't belong here.
 I need to find her.
 I don't belong here.
 I need to find her.

Captain James Theodore Adolphus Hughes took a cursory sweep of the Markham ballroom and wished he were any place but there. He could not believe the circumstances that had compelled him to be at this ball. He hated the *ton*. More accurately, he despised them. His blood boiled as he looked at the snobbish, lazy members of the supposed elite who never truly worked a day of their lives for their privileged existence. They sat in their clubs and their parlors, wasting their fortunes in idle pursuits, all the while slandering each other to pass the time. Yet now, he was among them, while accompanying the only person in the *ton* he could tolerate.

His friend, Gabriel Lockhart, Earl of Carrington, tilted his golden head and looked at James with amber eyes. Gabe was explaining his strategy for surviving the first part of the evening, before they could slip away to the card room and not be hounded by the marriage-minded mothers of debutantes. But James could not pay attention to any of the words his friend was saying.

He had to find *her*.

James knew he could not blame his entire fiasco on *her*, but that did not prevent him from wanting to shift all culpability onto the mystery woman.

She was not the reason the ship carrying the shipment of Irish flax to Holyhead had sunk.

She was not the reason he had to placate the textile factory owner for the lost flax shipment with his own money.

She was not the reason he had to stop in Birmingham to tell his childhood friend, Jack Doherty, that he would not be receiving payment for the flax.

But *she* was the reason he was trapped in London waiting for his insurance brokerage to release repayment of his money for the lost shipment.

And *she* was the reason James found himself in a stifling ballroom.

After he had left the insurance brokerage in the kind of rage he had not experienced in some time, he made his way to Gabe's town house and regaled him with his deplorable situation. Gabe offered an exchange. He would use his connections to Bow Street to help investigate the case. In return, James would keep him company at the Season's events, while Gabe did his duty and maneuvered the marriage market for his younger sister, the Lady Bridget.

"Does that sound like a plan?" Gabe asked.

James dragged his hand through his sable hair. "Definitely."

"You didn't hear a word I said."

"Was it that obvious?"

Gabe eyed James seriously. "I will still get my man in Bow Street to look into your problem, even if you don't want to attend these events."

James's mind kept drifting off. His friend was going out of his way to help him, but all James could think about was the lost shipment and how an unidentified woman had ruined the foreseeable future. He needed to focus on Gabe.

"I gave my word. Plus, I know how much you've been dreading marrying off your sister," James replied.

Gabe's mouth curved into a half smile.

James could see why women threw themselves at his friend.

"You have gotten me out of enough scrapes. This is the least I can do." Gabe planted a jovial slap on James's back.

A piercing woman's voice caught his attention. He turned to locate its source. The shrill sound permeated his ears once more, and led him to a raven-haired matron, Lady Hardwicke, who was speaking to Gabe's mother and sister, Lady Carrington and Lady Bridget. Lady Hardwicke had a chestnut-haired young woman in tow, who stood there looking awkward and out of place.

She wore the virginal white dress and glittering jewels of every other debutante, but her expression and carriage perplexed him. She was not all false smiles and youthful hopefulness. Instead, the corners of her mouth deflected downward, and her hands were clasped in front of her, drawing her shoulders forward. A flicker of fear crossed her face, but she schooled her features back into her unhappy expression.

She should be happy. The Season was the highlight of any well-bred woman's life. James could not understand what could possibly bother a spoiled Society miss.

A torn hem?

An empty dance card?

Whatever it was, it was unimportant. The *ton* did not interest James one bit.

CHAPTER TWO

Finally.

Charlotte saw the two gentlemen near Lady Carrington and Lady Bridget had stopped talking. Aunt Frances did not skip a beat and waved at the earl. "Lord Carrington!"

He raised his eyebrows and gave a slight bow as his mother proceeded to introduce Charlotte to her handsome son, who closely resembled his sister. Charlotte realized he was a friend of one of her brothers whom she had only met once. She gave him an obligatory, polite smile with as much gusto as she could manage, which was not much.

Lord Carrington asked her for the honor of the first dance with the insouciance of a practiced aristocrat.

Touché.

The attractive blond earl did not hold Charlotte's interest, and her eyes darted to the black-haired gentleman next to him, but her aunt grabbed the dance card from her wrist before she could take a better look. "Lady Charlotte would love to dance with you, my lord."

Lord Carrington, in his blue, superfine long-tailed coat,

white waistcoat, and white expertly tied cravat, took her dance card and wrote his name for the first dance.

Charlotte pretended to smile as the earl handed back the dance card. "Thank you, my lord," she said, hoping her voice sounded appropriately submissive. She did not know how long she could play the role of biddable debutante.

She took a moment to peer around her aunt for a better view of the other gentleman. A pair of stormy-gray eyes suddenly emerged from behind her aunt's head and caught her gaze.

Charlotte was taken aback.

The combination of black hair and tumultuous eyes made her feel as if she were trapped in a squall and was being pulled out to sea. Despite the danger, she could not break their eye contact, and was swept away in the chaos. The mystery man bowed. Charlotte realized he had been introduced, but she had not caught his name. She did not worry since she assumed he would ask her to dance, as had Lord Carrington, and his identity would soon be revealed.

He was midnight personified, with a black long-tailed coat, waistcoat, and knee-breeches. They were only brightened by the white of his cravat and stockings, like the moon and its reflection piercing the darkness of the night. From the way he carried himself, Charlotte reasoned he must be an aristocrat.

Lord Carrington and this gentleman made a formidable pair of light and dark. Both tall and broad-shouldered, they held their chins elevated in an imperial manner, which had been bred into the *ton* for generations. This mystery man, though, wore a brooding look on his face and was more muscular than his friend the earl. His shoulders were a bit more expansive, his sleeves a bit tighter, and his pants a bit more...fitted.

Charlotte's eyes jumped to the unknown man's face, hoping her perusal had gone unnoticed. The corner of his mouth twitched, and she felt her cheeks redden.

The slight movement of his mouth disappeared in a moment. She wondered if it had happened at all. What was left was a somber visage. He began to address her, "Lady Charlotte—"

"We must be off to fill your dance card!" Aunt Frances quickly clutched Charlotte's upper arm and pretended not to hear the man, before she dragged her away from the group and into the crowd.

Charlotte looked behind her and reentered the stormy eyes of the stranger. She raised her wrist with its attached dance card and held up five fingers, before she was forced to turn around by her aunt's determined walk.

From that point on, Aunt Frances whisked her around the ballroom and ensured she was visible to all marriageable gentlemen. Her dance card was soon filled with eligible, titled suitors. Each time a gentleman was about to write down his name, Charlotte asked him under her breath to leave the fifth dance open. She did not dare to complete her act of subterfuge until her aunt was distracted. That moment came when Aunt Frances ran into her friend who wore a turban with enough feathers for Charlotte to fear there was a live bird attached to her head. This feathered gentlewoman had dire news to tell her aunt involving some elopement to Gretna Green. Her aunt became so absorbed in the titillating story that she left Charlotte unguarded. Charlotte slipped the dance card off her wrist and wrote a name next to the fifth dance.

Lord Silverstone.

A fitting name for a man with eyes the color of silver metal. She let out the breath she did not realize she was holding. Her respite was brief, however, because her aunt finished hearing the entire sordid elopement tale, and was ready for Charlotte's next gentleman cause.

Aunt Frances tapped Charlotte's dance card. "I have reserved this waltz for a very special suitor."

"Oh?" Charlotte said. She had learned to save her breath when her aunt was on a mission.

"Yes, the Duke of Westcliffe will be attending. I have confirmed it with him personally. We have known each other for ages, and he has promised a dance with you. He's in need of a wife and would like to have the matter settled quickly."

They approached the next cluster of smartly dressed ladies and gentlemen.

Charlotte worried her bottom lip while she reasoned through her aunt's words. First, if her aunt had known the Duke for years, that meant he was not young. Second, if he required a wife urgently, that meant he needed an heir. Third—Charlotte paused as the predicament became clear—she would be the perfect wife.

Fear welled inside Charlotte. She needed a titled husband, but she had hoped she could have some say in the matter. Why had her aunt not mentioned this earlier, instead of parading her about the ballroom?

Charlotte could not lie to herself. She knew why.

Her aunt had not become a marchioness by chance alone. It was a carefully orchestrated social move after her elderly first husband, a mere baron, died. Aunt Frances was applying the same tactics to procuring a match for Charlotte. She was moving her across the *ton's* chessboard and filling her dance card with pawns, who would serve as husband reserves in case she could not capture the king, or in this case, the aging duke.

Charlotte did not hear whom her aunt had just introduced, nor did she care, but dipped into yet another obligatory curtsy. Charlotte's gaze remained lowered so that this current group of the *ton* could not see her lips tighten in frustration. She felt helpless, but because of the *Incident,* there was nothing she could do.

❧

James watched as Lady Charlotte Tipton held up five fingers while being pulled away by her aunt and then swallowed up by the swarming *ton,* who flitted from group to group like honeybees collecting nectar.

He turned toward Gabe. "Would you call that a cut direct or a cut indirect?"

"I would say a cut is a cut. But Lady Charlotte seems clearly interested in you despite her aunt. Signaling the fifth dance like that? A scandalous move on her part."

James nodded and tried to find the chestnut head of Lady Charlotte among the guests, but she had disappeared. "She has mettle, I'll give her that," he said. He still did not believe Lady Charlotte Tipton, an earl's privileged daughter, could have any true dilemma that warranted the unhappy expression he had witnessed, but her brief look of fear made him wonder what lay beneath her surface. Then she had surprised him with a touch of boldness when her aunt dragged her away, and she held up her fingers for what clearly was the fifth dance. He was intrigued, and he did not like that one bit.

"I know her brother well," Gabe said.

James grunted in response, not wanting to show interest, but also not wanting Gabe to stop speaking.

"One of her brothers, actually," Gabe clarified. "The Earl of Pulverbatch has four sons, and the youngest child is Lady Charlotte. Her brother Will and I were the same year at Eton. Good chap but always getting into trouble. He's in the British Army now, being a younger son and all. Ashwood, the heir, is a wastrel of the first order."

James did not smile often, but he allowed a moment of levity in response to the start of his friend's diatribe. His cynicism was one of the reasons he liked Gabe. Despite being an earl, he did not take the nobility too seriously, and measured people by their actual worth, not by their title or wealth.

"The second son, Nate, is what you would expect of a spare who has a substantial purse. He is a *bon vivant* and an unrelenting rake." Gabe waved his hand in dismissal.

"After Will, there's Arthur. He's bookish and interested in politics." Gabe paused before he tipped his head in an analytic way. "Then there's Lady Charlotte. I don't know much about her anymore, but I do remember going to High Crest Hall during one of the leaves from school. My mother had taken Bridget to stay with family. I couldn't think of anything worse than being alone with my father, so I made the trip to Shropshire."

Gabe's face became guarded when he mentioned his sire, but he quickly schooled his features. "I remember Lady Charlotte being young, maybe seven or eight years old, and an absolute hellion. I only visited once, so I hadn't seen her in years. During the trip, her older brothers paid her no mind, but she and Arthur tagged along with us. Will was always the most adventurous, and I, of course, could not be outdone by a Tipton. We would compete over anything and had quite the imaginations. One time, we sneaked into the pigpen and had a round of fisticuffs while the massive hog butted us. I stayed standing the longest and won. Another time, we stole some pickled walnuts and saw who could eat the most before getting sick. That one wasn't one of our finer moments, because we could barely eat for the next two days. We always came back for dinner in some kind of mess."

A smile spread across Gabe's face, and he shook his head at the fond memories before continuing. "One day, we were in the woodlands, and there was a grand old beech tree. Will and I obviously had to dare each other to see who would climb the highest."

His smile faded. "I almost became dizzy we climbed so high, but Will climbed even higher. Arthur and Charlotte watched from below, and when we came down, Charlotte swore she could best us. Before we could stop her, she scampered up the tree, wearing pilfered breeches from one of her brothers. She quickly beat Will's height and kept going until it was clear she was the better climber. I couldn't believe how high she went. She was only a speck among the leaves, and we were all worried about her. Finally, we heard her yell that she had won."

James watched the scene play out across Gabe's face.

"I honestly held my breath until she reached the ground. Then the brat smiled smugly. I thought Will would murder her after she scared us so much. He forbade her from tagging along anymore, but she ignored him and continued to try to get his attention throughout the whole leave."

James could not disregard the unfamiliar tightness in his chest that had developed. He never experienced unnecessary emotions, yet he felt for the ignored little girl she had been. But feelings had to be squashed. Lady Charlotte may not have gotten as much attention as she wanted during her childhood, but she was a member of the *ton* and was privileged. She was not on the streets begging for food or selling her body. James knew what it was like to have a less than idyllic childhood, and he had survived with much less than a pampered earl's daughter.

"I'm sure she recovered," James said to Gabe, unable to resist a sarcastic tone.

"You'll have plenty of time to ask her during your dance," Gabe retorted. "The fifth, I believe."

"You think Lady Charlotte holding up five fingers committed me to a dance with her?" James quipped.

Gabe looked knowingly at James. "I think she's a young woman who knows what she wants, and that's to dance with you."

James attempted to appear nonplussed and shrugged. In reality, his perfidious heartbeat quickened at the thought of spinning Lady Charlotte around the dance floor.

"We'll see," James replied, wondering what he was getting himself into.

CHAPTER THREE

Lady Markham opened her ball with a bang by choosing the infamous waltz as the first dance. Charlotte partnered with Lord Carrington, which was not unpleasant. Despite a sad look in his eyes, he was an amiable gentleman, and seemed genuinely interested in what she had to say. He even threw in a quip about her adventurousness as a tree-climbing young girl. The quality of her partners then swiftly declined, and she was subjected to hearing them drone on about their dull interests and accomplishments without once asking Charlotte about herself.

If the fifth dance had not been approaching, she would have gone to the ladies' retiring room to take a break. Instead, the pulse at the base of her throat fluttered in anticipation of dancing with the mystery man. It was to be another waltz, and Charlotte was eager to compare it to her experience with Lord Carrington. The earl had felt comfortable and almost brotherly, especially since he was Will's Eton friend. She certainly appreciated his attractiveness, but in a more scientific manner. Nevertheless, he would be a much better choice than an ancient duke.

Her only concern was if the earl was powerful enough to offer her sufficient protection from the *Incident*. Could she risk it?

A tall body suddenly blocked Charlotte's view of the ballroom. She was by no means petite, but this man towered over her. She slowly raised her eyes from his black jacket and waistcoat to a smartly tied but simple white cravat. Her eyes traveled farther to a hint of stubble on a square jaw, a straight nose, sharp cheekbones, and then...those eyes.

Yes, she had found Lord Silverstone.

He looked down expectantly at her, and a smirk broke through his surly countenance. "You seem to enjoy perusing my body yet again, Lady Charlotte." Charlotte stared at him trying to keep a neutral expression on her face. She had trailed behind her brothers long enough to not be discomfited by bawdy jests.

"Lord Silverstone," Charlotte said, before realizing her *faux pas*. Her hand flew to her mouth.

His brow furrowed. "Silverstone?"

Charlotte stilled for a moment, then squared her shoulders and slowly lowered her hand from her mouth. "I missed your introduction, sir, and I had to hold a place on my dance card," she said without a hint of remorse.

He let out a hearty, baritone laugh, and suddenly, his stormy eyes cleared into a winter sky. Stark yet beautiful.

Charlotte's insides tingled as his laugh reverberated through her body, but she did not have time to analyze this surprising feeling. The musicians started the introductory notes of the waltz, and in the blink of an eye, Lord Silverstone's stern façade returned. He promptly bowed to her, while she prayed he was the titled aristocrat who could save her.

Did I just laugh?

James could not remember the last time he had felt even an ounce of mirth. Now, after only spending minutes in the company of a female member of the *ton*, he had laughed. He assessed his well-being. He must have developed some sort of malady to act with such levity. He performed a cursory evaluation. He did not feel feverish or lightheaded, his stomach was in working order, and he had no new aches or pains. He could not identify a medical reason to cause him to act unlike himself.

Luckily, his self-assessment did not take long, because the next thing he knew, Lady Charlotte was in his arms. Novel sensations overwhelmed him. He almost dropped his hands from her body due to the burning in his fingertips, which was similar to grabbing the pot off the fire before it cooled. He inhaled, trying to calm himself, but a new scent emanated from his dance partner and assaulted his senses.

Honeysuckle and jasmine.

Innocent but spicy.

Who is Lady Charlotte?

"I didn't think I was that boring," a feminine voice challenged. James looked down and fully appreciated the visage of Lady Charlotte for the first time.

Her cornflower-blue eyes danced with mischief. James tried to divert his gaze elsewhere, but it was of no use. Lady Charlotte mesmerized him. She was not the traditional beauty, but her attractiveness could not be denied. Below her striking eyes, dainty freckles smattered her nose. Even he knew they were not fashionable, but on Lady Charlotte, they were perfect. Just another reason she did not fit the mold of a typical debutante. But that was not a bad thing.

She had high cheekbones, and her rosy lips looked like they were just waiting to be kissed. The faintest collection of freckles danced along the Cupid's bow of her upper lip. James wanted to taste each one personally.

He had to stop.

He had never waxed poetic about a woman's appearance in his life.

"I was just observing the scene," he said.

"We're dance partners, so it's only proper you tell me your name," she said.

"I'm not just going to hand it over," he said.

"Fine, we'll have a wager," she countered.

"I thought ladies didn't gamble."

"Lord Silverstone, I am not your typical lady."

James could see her mind working.

"You don't seem like a man who would give up so easily."

How did she do that? She doesn't even know me.

His eyes narrowed. "What is your wager?"

She grinned. "I will ask up to ten questions to determine your identity."

"Five," he said.

Her freckled nose crinkled in a delightful manner. "Seven and that's my final offer."

He let out another unexpected laugh. Was he dancing the waltz with the daughter of an earl in a glittering Mayfair ballroom, or was he heckling for kippers on the docks with a fishmonger's wife?

Regardless of his opponent or any attraction between them, he knew one thing. He had to win.

"Agree. What happens if you cannot guess it?" he said.

"I will not lose."

He had never met any woman, let alone a lady, who was so blatantly confident. He had to admit, it was not as repulsive as he would have thought.

"This is a wager. We must have solid terms before we begin. If you cannot guess my identity, you'll grant me a kiss," he challenged.

"I agree to your terms," she said with a competitive gleam in her eyes.

James would not lose.

Charlotte convinced herself she did not need seven guesses to determine Lord Silverstone's identity. The critical step was to gather as much evidence as she could before her questioning started. Each time they spun, Charlotte caught the salty scent of the sea mixed with an herbal, exotic note. Her brother Arthur, the one with whom she would debate esoteric topics, always pointed out that she did not see the forest for the trees. Nevertheless, Lord Silverstone's scent was critical to who he was. She reviewed in her mind his appearance, including the way he carried himself, and made mental notes.

"I'm ready to ask my first question, and you must be truthful," Charlotte said.

He gave her a sardonic look. "You wound me, my lady. Accusing me of cheating before we've even started?"

"One can never be too sure. I shall start off broadly. Where do you come from?"

Before her dance partner answered, he stared at her in an unnerving manner. Her fingers fidgeted on his shoulder in discomfort. She broke eye contact first. This was not off to a good start. She did not appreciate Lord Silverstone's distraction technique. She could not let him rattle her.

"Birmingham."

Birmingham, Birmingham, Birmingham.

Her mind worked through anything she knew about the city. Charlotte had not a clue what peerage included Birmingham. She felt a tinge of remorse, but nothing her brain could not solve. She cycled through nuggets of information she had discussed with Arthur.

Nothing came up.

The musicians continued to play the waltz in the background, and Lord Silverstone led her across the dance floor. She delved further into her memory to articles she had read in the newspaper, an unladylike habit in which she partook during her mostly unsupervised existence in Shropshire. Her thoughts churned for a bit longer until...the Lunar Society! Charlotte knew she had read about a group of intellectuals and forward thinkers in Birmingham several years ago.

She reassessed Lord Silverstone. He did not strike her as a free thinker, especially if he was an aristocrat. He seemed more of the domineering and inflexible type, which made the Lunar Society comical.

"What are you grinning about? All I gave you was a city," he said.

"I was just thinking of the Lunar Society and picturing you standing on a table, pulling out your hair, and arguing about Plato."

"You have an active imagination," was all he could mutter before he twirled her.

Not an intellectual. More importantly, his response confirmed he was much too serious. She still figured that he was a lord, but could she be wrong? Her aunt did give him the cut direct, but she assumed it was because he was a rake or had some other ghastly reputation.

"What is your father's title?"

"He doesn't have one."

"I see, *Mister Silverstone*." His answer surprised her. There were gentlemen not born into the nobility, but he exuded the arrogance of the aristocracy.

She sifted through other categories of gentlemen and almost

scoffed out loud when she thought of her dance partner standing in the pulpit as a man of the cloth. She doubted he was particularly pious; however, she could picture him scolding the congregation and preaching fire and brimstone. Still, it seemed unlikely. Law or medicine were not good fits either.

What next?

Landed gentry. Charlotte felt she was getting closer, especially because his physique suggested he was not idle. She had the nagging feeling she was missing one more category.

His scent flooded her senses. It was the scent of the sea being carried by the wind.

"The Royal Navy?" Charlotte asked. She had been so deep in thought she did not realize that he had been looking above her head. His eyes darted down to her level.

"What's the question?"

What an infuriating man!

"Allow me to rephrase my query so that you can understand it, sir. Are you serving in the Royal Navy?"

"Yes."

Success! Charlotte's eyes traveled up and down his powerful frame. She hoped to glean any clue as to his rank. Charlotte paused. Why was he not properly attired in uniform? Boney's wars had thankfully wound down, but he just said he was an active member of the military.

Charlotte could not dwell on his attire, and analyzed him further. He was confident—which she had wrongly attributed to an aristocratic birth—and appeared close in age to Charlotte's older brothers. He could have been in the Royal Navy at least a decade and become some sort of officer.

She took a lucky guess. "Are you a captain?"

CHAPTER FOUR

J ames could not look at Lady Charlotte. If his eyes caught her profile for more than a few moments, his mind wandered. The beginning of their waltz was relatively innocent. What would her delectable lips taste like? Would it be like her scent, innocent yet seductive? But as the dance went on, his mind traveled down a darker and more erotic path. Just a glimpse of her elegant neck prompted him to picture her in the throes of passion with her head flung back while he rutted her endlessly.

I need to bed a proper whore, James convinced himself. He had been near celibate for too long. He had avoided the doxies at the many ports of call during the war, worried about contracting the pox. Now that he was in London and had coin to spare, he could rid himself of this pent-up sexual frustration at a fashionable establishment.

"What's the question?" James never missed a word of any conversation. Yet, today, on more than one occasion he was asking others to repeat themselves.

He could only blame women.

First, it was the unidentified woman who had disrupted his

life and forced him to London. Currently, it was the bold and alluring daughter of the Earl of Pulverbatch.

"Are you a captain?"

"Yes," James answered, without divulging any more information. How many questions had that been? Four? Five? He had lost count, but he knew he could not give her anything else. The questions would only become more personal, and he was already starting to feel restless. He thankfully detected the closing notes of the waltz.

It was time to go.

"It has been an honor, Lady Charlotte, but I'm afraid I must take my leave." Captain Silverstone bowed and turned abruptly, before being swallowed by the crowd.

Charlotte stood dumfounded. Had she said something to scare him away?

She let out a huff of breath. The dratted man had left before their wager ended. It was quite unsportsmanlike of him. She would not hold back in reprimanding the cheater, ladylike or not. But first she had to see him again, and there was no guarantee that their paths would cross.

The musicians began the opening notes of the next dance, and she realized she was still standing on the dance floor, appearing thoroughly unsettled. She hurried to the side of the ballroom and stationed herself near the windows. She needed to compose herself.

A glance at her card revealed a baronet's name written beside the next dance. Her partner was only a baronet? Perfect, a dance she could skip. Although the baronet must be powerful or wealthy for her aunt to allow him to partner with Charlotte. But it did not matter. She needed the utmost protection from the *Incident,* and that meant getting to the top of the social hier-archy, where the law could not touch her. The best safeguard would be to wed a duke. Preferably a duke who was not old enough to be her father...or her grandfather. But she may not have that option. How many unwed dukes could there be?

Charlotte crept along the periphery of the ballroom with her back to the towering arched windows and her eyes trained on the goings-on of the guests. She would eventually reach a door to the gardens if she continued her current path. Her feet shuffled along the wall of windows while she tried to blend into the background. What a foolish thought. As if anyone in this ballroom besides her aunt would even notice her.

Speak of the devil.

Aunt Frances and another woman walked arm in arm near the door that was Charlotte's means of an escape from the ball-room. Her aunt always seemed to know everything that was happening, and her sudden appearance further cemented her omnipotence. Charlotte sprang away from the wall and walked straight into the group of onlookers watching the couples glide across the dance floor. There had to be another way for her to find a moment of peace.

After what felt like ages of weaving through the throng of people, she was able to duck out of the ballroom into a doorway. She found herself in an adjacent room, but guests spilled over into the space and clustered in boisterous groups. She walked past them with her head down and continued onward until the din of the music faded. She entered the next room, confident that she had found a place to relax, but she was sorely mistaken.

It was the ladies' retiring room.

Charlotte paused in the doorway, weighing her options. Return to the stifling ballroom and her aunt, or immerse herself in a gaggle of ladies gossiping and fixing their hems? She chose the latter as the lesser of two evils.

She took a few hesitant steps forward, not wanting to agitate the bank of swans before her. Fortunately, the birds in the room barely glanced at her, too busy preening and worrying about their own appearances to take note. She collapsed onto a settee and closed her eyes for a moment.

She missed home.

High Crest Hall had rolling hills, clear skies, and the scent of nature, not masses of people, smoky air, and a persistent reek. Charlotte could not wallow in self-pity though. She was in London, and she had to save herself. She let out a sigh and raised her eyelids.

Two pairs of eyes, one emerald and one blue, stared back at her from the opposite settee.

"You must be Lady Charlotte, the Marchioness of Hardwicke's niece," a poised and striking woman with dark-brown hair and green eyes stated matter-of-factly.

"I am…" Charlotte mumbled. Her attention darted between the woman who had just spoken and her partner, a woman whose light-blonde hair and delicate features epitomized archetypal English beauty. The second woman's blue eyes, lighter than her own, ran over Charlotte's figure in an assessing manner. She caught Charlotte's gaze and leaned back, giving her a lazy grin. "We're absolutely delighted to finally meet you. Your aunt has talked much about your debut."

"I'm afraid you have me at a disadvantage. I don't know either of you," Charlotte ventured, wondering if these women were friend or foe. They were a part of the *ton*, so Charlotte's first instinct was to label them as enemies.

The dark-haired woman sat with perfectly straight posture and replied in a well-modulated voice, "How rude of us. I'm Beatrice Walford…my father is the Marquess of Derby, and this is Eleanor Balfour, daughter of the Earl of Downham."

"A pleasure to meet you," Charlotte responded hesitantly, still unsure as to the direction of the conversation.

Eleanor took the reins. "We feel like we already know you. My older brother, Jasper, is close with Arthur. Your brother has spoken much about you. You seem most unconventional and the opposite of what your aunt has been telling anyone who would listen. We couldn't wait to meet you in person and figure you out ourselves."

If Eleanor knew Arthur, this pair of women had to be friends, not foes. Arthur was everything to Charlotte. He was the only one in her family who truly understood her, and when he went off to Eton, Charlotte had immediately felt the void. Her forced trip to London to find a titled husband would have felt like a death sentence, aside from the fact she would be able to see her beloved brother. He was the only bright spot in this dismal affair, even if he was always busy with Parliamentary work.

Charlotte's face relaxed. "I'm very close with Arthur, so I would trust what he told you."

Eleanor smiled back. "I don't mean to be so forward, but he seemed surprised that you were coming to London. He didn't think you wished to marry, though your aunt has indicated otherwise. Beatrice and I have no desire for our lives to be dictated by a husband or by all those awful rules we must follow, so we thought we had found another lady of the same mindset."

"My aunt made me memorize all of *Debrett's* though I admit, I've purposefully forgotten as much as I can," Charlotte said.

The two other women chuckled then Beatrice added, "I'm glad I still don't have a governess to rap my knuckles or worse for not knowing every ounce of information in that terrible book."

Charlotte smiled at the women and tried to determine what

she could reveal. Although she had just met these two women, she felt an instant connection with them and their forthrightness after she realized they were all on the same side. Yet, trusting too easily had been the downfall of many. "I truly don't want to marry, but a certain situation has forced me to reconsider."

She saw both ladies' eyes narrow. The words tumbled out of her mouth, "I'm not in the family way or ruined in that sense."

Beatrice looked back at her and firmly responded, "Even if you were, we would not judge. We all have our scandalous secrets, and nothing in the *ton* stays hidden for long. The only safeguard is to keep it to yourself or rid yourself of anyone who would tattle."

Charlotte swallowed.

Little did they know that was exactly what she had done.

Charlotte's conversation with the two ladies was halted by her aunt marching into the ladies' retiring room.

Aunt Frances loomed over her. "Charlotte, His Grace has arrived. What have you been doing?"

She lifted her chin defiantly, momentarily forgetting her life depended on the aid of her aunt in finding a powerful husband. She quickly recovered. "I was freshening up to prepare myself for the Duke."

"Come along." Her aunt grabbed Charlotte's arm and yanked her up from the settee. She rolled her eyes toward her new friends before her aunt dragged her out of the room.

Despite dreading a waltz with a geriatric aristocrat, her mood was lighter after meeting Beatrice and Eleanor. She had never had any true friends besides Arthur growing up. High Crest Hall was a vast estate without nearby peers of the Realm whose children would be suitable acquaintances for her. Thus, Arthur had begged their parents to allow him to be tutored at home for as long as possible. When he finally left for Eton, Charlotte would play with the children of the estate's tenants or staff. As she grew older, though, her status as the earl's daughter created a barrier she could not overcome. She assumed the Season too would be lonely, especially because Arthur was often immersed in his governmental affairs and took no interest in Society events. Now, she had a glimmer of hope she would not have to navigate the *ton* alone.

The transition back into the chaos of the ballroom was jarring. Aunt Frances appeared immune and deftly maneuvered them through the crush. Sooner than expected, Charlotte was standing in front of two gentlemen vastly older than her. The first man appeared to be at the start of his seventh decade with a portly figure and thinning black hair sprinkled with gray. The second man looked younger than him and decidedly trimmer. He had sandy-blond hair with a dusting of white in his modest side-whiskers.

"Your Grace," her aunt said, as they both dipped into deep curtsies, then straightened. "Westcliffe, Lord Finch. May I present my niece, Lady Charlotte Tipton.

After Charlotte raised her head, she started to turn toward the stout man assuming he was His Grace.

But the taller man with the athletic frame reached for her hand. "It's a pleasure to meet you, Lady Charlotte." A pair of kind, hazel eyes looked at her. "May I have the honor of the next dance?"

"Yes, Your Grace," Charlotte stammered. The neither frail nor ancient duke offered his arm.

As they walked, she stole a glance at the Duke and his imposing profile. This was not the man she was expecting. He looked to be a similar age as her own father, but that was where the similarities ended. The Earl of Pulverbatch enjoyed the finer aspects of life. Charlotte pictured her sire's protruding abdomen and ruddy face, much like that of her eldest brother, Henry. The two were content sitting about, drinking brandy, and living a life of leisure, only exerting themselves for an obligatory hunt or ride through the park. The Duke, on the other hand, was clearly a Corinthian.

The musicians played the first chords of yet another waltz. Lady Stanhope had really outdone herself. The Duke gracefully positioned himself before he swept Charlotte into his arms. While they moved across the dance floor, he looked down at her with a tender look that seemed like it could be paternal. It was her best guess since her own father never looked at her in such a way. They danced in silence at first, which she appreciated. She needed time to get used to her partner. She felt surprisingly comfortable with the Duke, similar to how she felt dancing with the Earl of Carrington. It was the opposite of the riot of emotions she experienced with Captain Silverstone, though she did not have the luxury to dwell further on that maddening man. She needed a titled husband as quickly as possible. Before meeting the Duke, Charlotte had already crossed His Grace off her mental list of prospects, but now, he was at the top. And time was not on her side.

The Duke broke the silence in his soothing voice, "I'm glad you still had a dance open. I'm sorry for making it to the ball later than anticipated."

Charlotte could not help but genuinely smile at his humble statement. He was neither brash nor arrogant as she assumed was a requirement of his station. "You must be busy with your ducal duties. My aunt made sure I saved a dance for you." Charlotte cringed at her insipid comment but she was sticking to the only subjects she was allowed to discuss: the weather, the gentleman's interests, or the weather.

The Duke chuckled. "I would not call it ducal duties, per se. I have four daughters. Two are married, but the younger ones still live with me. I had to check on them before leaving for the ball."

His eyes were warm with a hint of melancholy she could not quite pinpoint. She would have never thought of any nobleman, especially a duke, giving a second thought about his daughters. Based on her own father, she knew firsthand how a typical aristocratic family functioned. Yes, she had made the right decision in choosing His Grace.

"It sounds like they are lucky to have such a caring father," she replied honestly.

The Duke's shoulders subtly shrugged before he expertly maneuvered them around another couple. "After their mother passed away two years ago, I'm afraid we have all been a bit out of sorts. I do what I can, but I'm by no means a substitute for the guiding hand of a woman. Luckily, I have at least a year before my next daughter comes out." He looked expectantly at Charlotte.

She schooled her face into a neutral expression. Her aunt had failed to mention that not only did the Duke have four daughters, two of whom were older than her, but two had not even come out yet. She would be the worst possible person to introduce the Duke's youngest daughters into Society. That issue aside, she could not imagine enduring another London Season. She wracked her brain. There had to be another duke to consider, even one old and decrepit if that meant she could hide away in the country until presumably he died in short order.

"Do you enjoy London?" the Duke asked.

"I prefer country life. I miss riding in the hills of Shropshire." The truth fell out of her mouth. "The crowdedness and the odors of London are only tolerable for so long."

He chuckled. "I entirely agree with you. Alas, we must

perform certain obligations to return to what we love. I think you would enjoy Kent. I have an impressive stable."

"Your Grace..." Charlotte swallowed. She could not ignore his insinuation of marriage and tip her head coquettishly like other debutantes. "I must be honest. I fear I would be a terrible influence on your daughters. I'm not like the other ladies in this room. Any number of them would be much better suited to introduce your daughters into Society."

The music slowed, providing the Duke with time to formulate his response. He guided her back toward her aunt. But before he deposited her at Aunt Frances's side, His Grace paused. "That's why you would be the perfect woman to guide them. I don't want a simpering miss as my wife. Plus, your Society arsenal would include your aunt, so I doubt you would have to lift a finger." He gave her a wink, then nodded and turned away, disappearing into the crowd.

CHAPTER FIVE

J ames was exhausted.

He squinted against the rare April sunlight that filtered through the clouds on this brisk morning. His body was stiff on his brown gelding as the horse trotted through Hyde Park, not a soul in sight, given the early hour.

The previous night's events ran through his mind. After dancing with Lady Charlotte, his restlessness had increased from her asking him what many would think were simple questions. The ones regarding his father and the Royal Navy felt too personal, though, and had pushed him past what he could tolerate. Consequently, he took his leave and said a quick goodbye to Gabe before disappearing. Although Gabe did not know James's whole past, he knew enough. Gabe had his own demons and understood.

After leaving the ball, James made his way toward the gaming hells in St. James, given their proximity to Mayfair. He thought a distraction, any distraction, would help the restlessness he felt. When he reached the dens of iniquity, thinking he was ready to mindlessly spin a roulette wheel, he could not bring himself to go inside. Being surrounded by smoke and men bent on losing their fortunes was no consolation.

Next, he wandered to *La Nuit Noire*. He entered the high-end brothel, hoping that some quality quim would relieve his needs. Yet, when the scantily clad ladies sauntered toward him with their bodices cut so low the tops of their nipples were visible, he only felt revolted. He desperately wanted to relieve the aching in his cock, courtesy of the infuriating Lady Charlotte, but going through the motions of anonymous sex was not going to relieve his perturbation.

He always had a restlessness inside him that worsened when he felt cornered. Years of childhood abuse had done that, and Lady Charlotte's questioning had triggered the same cornered feeling even further. He had thought the Royal Navy would help quell his uneasiness, but it had not. After years of trying, he still did not know a way to make the restlessness disappear.

He drew his hand from the reins and rubbed his temple. He had made it back to Gabe's town house last night and into his bed, but his head was throbbing from lack of sleep. Despite the discomfort, James could not drop his military training, and constantly surveyed his surroundings. In the distance, he saw a shadow dart into the woods, which he figured was a deer relishing the lack of humans in the park.

Then he heard it.

Thump. Thump. Thump.

His eyes scanned the parkland in front of him before sweeping to the peripheries. Suddenly, in the corner of his eye, he saw movement. James jerked his gaze to the left, and spotted a man on a gray horse emerge from the trees. The man gave his steed its head as it galloped in the distance, the man bent over his mount, his top hat somehow still in place. James stopped his own horse to watch the spectacle before him.

Whoever the man was, he could ride and appeared to have an innate comfort in the saddle, unlike James, whose body was always tense when he rode.

He looked around to see if someone was in pursuit of the rider, given the speed at which he was galloping, but no one else appeared. Perhaps the man had to exercise his horse and sneaked in at an early hour to get in a good ride. Galloping would not be allowed later in the day, when the *ton* congregated on Rotten Row to parade themselves about like peacocks in full plumage. Yet another useless pursuit of High Society.

His musings were interrupted when the man stopped abruptly. Up until this point, the rider had galloped perpendicular to him so that he could only see his side profile. Now, he had an opportunity to get closer.

James clicked his tongue and urged his gelding into a trot. The gray horse in the distance snorted and shook its head, settling down from the morning's exertions. Once he closed the distance and was almost upon the rider, he realized the gentleman was so small his clothes were hanging off him. Before James could contemplate the peculiarity of his dress further, the man turned his horse toward him.

Cornflower-blue eyes stared back at him.

He gaped at the rider before he stammered, "Lady Charlotte?"

A flush crept up her neck and traveled above her surprisingly well-tied cravat. James looked at the figure before him in a new light. Yes, the clothes were loose, but even so, certain features were more pronounced than when Lady Charlotte was in a long, flowing gown. She wore a waistcoat on top of a loose, men's lawn shirt that was tucked into her breeches. Her outfit revealed a thin waist that widened into full hips, which filled out the top of her pants as she sat astride. His eyes grazed over the space between her legs.

A throat clearing broke his ogling, and Lady Charlotte lifted her chin in a defiant manner. "Good morning, Captain Silverstone," she greeted curtly.

Ah, she still did not know his name. He could continue to use this information as leverage. "I see you have been enjoying some morning activity."

"Yes, I prefer to ride early so that Mirabel can get proper exercise. She's used to being in the country."

"And that requires gentlemen's clothes?"

Her head tilted forward slightly. She seemed to look down her nose at him while she sat regally on her horse, as if she were in a Mayfair drawing room. "In fact, it is necessary." She released the reins with one hand and flipped her wrist nonchalantly. "The way to properly ride a horse is astride, and I can't be seen straddling my steed in London."

James let out a choking sound. She must be an innocent to say such a phrase in a casual manner, proving she was truly oblivious to its meaning. He shifted uncomfortably in his saddle.

"You left last night before we could finish our game," she chided.

He felt like a guilty school child, or at least what he assumed one would feel like, and succinctly replied, "I apologize for the abrupt departure, but I had to leave." James was a naval officer. He never apologized. He killed and moved on. Yet there he was, apologizing, of all things, for leaving a fancy party.

"Why?"

Just that simple three letter word, and she had his complete attention. Her eyes stared into his own as she awaited an answer. He had just met this woman, and he would not—no, he *could* not answer. He had been hiding from himself too long to suddenly change course. "It's nothing for you to worry about."

"Maybe it should be."

"No. I appreciate your concern, but trust me, it's better to leave it alone," James responded more forcefully than he had intended.

Lady Charlotte raised her eyebrows. She studied him as if he were a puzzle to solve. "Very well then. In any case, you owe me the answers to a few questions."

"That was last night's game. You can't carry it over to a new day."

"I beg to differ. We didn't discuss this particular rule, so it's assumed that the game will continue until it's completed," she countered.

"Since it was not discussed, the game was interrupted and is now void."

"You make a good point, but you agreed to answer seven questions. If you don't answer the remaining ones, you will be going back on your word."

So Lady Charlotte was trying to badger him into revealing more about himself. He had to admit he enjoyed the banter.

"I would hate to question your honor, sir. I am benevolent though, so I'll propose a new wager."

He felt like a mouse being batted back and forth between the paws of a mischievous cat. "Benevolent? You must be addled."

"Addled? Is that what you call women with a brain? If so, I suppose I am."

James bit back a caustic retort. She did have a point, but he was loath to admit it. "What is your alternate wager?"

"Well, we are both on horses, so we could race."

James took in her measure. She sat comfortably on her horse, as if it were an extension of her body, and rode elegantly. He pursed his lips. He, Captain Hughes of His Majesty's Royal Navy, refused to keep being outmaneuvered by a slip of a young woman who wore men's breeches and rode astride in the middle of Hyde Park. Damn her for getting under his skin, and damn her for noticing his poor horsemanship.

"You are skilled in manipulating a situation, *Lady Charlotte*."

"*Captain Silverstone*, a situation is what you make of it. You can let the situation control you, or you can control the situation. I prefer the latter, and I'm simply moving our situation in a desired direction. If I didn't, we would be here all day arguing. I'll even propose a compromise, since you seem upset. I'll tell you why I know how to manipulate a situation, as you call it, if you answer my question."

James assessed the absurdity of this entire encounter with the brazen and witty Lady Charlotte. As much as he hated to admit it, he did want to know something, anything, about this enigmatic woman of the *ton*.

"All right, I accept your deal. You go first."

"I don't know if I trust your word. You clearly didn't keep it last night. How do I know once I share something about myself that you will honor your commitment?"

"We played a ballroom game last night, a mere frippery. Men die if I do not keep my word. Do not question my honor."

Lady Charlotte nodded with a look of respect. "I'm sorry to have offended you, Captain Silverstone. If you would just answer one of my questions before I share the bit about myself?" She paused and looked at him with widened blue eyes, akin to a dog begging for scraps. "Please tell me your real name. It would make the entire conversation go more smoothly. Unless you prefer being called Silverstone?"

James let out a sigh. This woman was exhausting.

"Fine. My name is James Hughes."

"That seems like a good name."

James continued to hold himself stiffly on his horse. "I would hope so, since one can't choose one's name."

She grinned. "I appreciate you answering my question. As agreed, I'll tell you where I learned to manipulate a situation, or *negotiate* if you will."

Lady Charlotte carried herself like a queen, even in borrowed men's clothing, and had a confidence that he had only seen in a few men throughout his life.

In short, she was remarkable.

He watched Lady Charlotte adjust herself on her horse into what seemed like an even more self-assured position. As he studied her further, though, he realized she was doing it to belie her nervousness.

She fidgeted with the reins and took a deep breath. "My mother was an heiress and an only child. Grandpapa made his money through the Coalbrookdale Coalfield, mining coal and ironstone. My other grandfather, the Earl, needed an influx of money, like so many noble families."

Her mouth tightened and she gave a quick shake of her head before continuing, "My mother and father met at a local ball, and a marriage was arranged. Given my grandparents' trade roots, they were thrilled for their only daughter to marry an earl. After the wedding, my mother's impressive dowry and shares in the mines went to the earldom to save it from ruin. Part of the agreement was that Grandpapa could put men in place who knew how to manage the various assets so that the earldom wouldn't be in financial straits again."

Her face relaxed slightly. "When I was younger, my closest brother, Arthur, and I would go to Grandpapa's office, and like leeches, sucked up every drop of information he would give us. He taught us how to balance ledgers, negotiate, and run a business."

"Lord Carrington told me you had other brothers. You did not include them. Did they not do the same?"

Lady Charlotte let out a bitter laugh. "Lower themselves to

trade? Absolutely not. My three older brothers had a very different childhood than me. From what I have been told, they had a loving and attentive mother, but then two stillborn sons in less than three years slowly destroyed her. She partially came back to life when she had Arthur, who was her angel child. But then an unwelcome seventh child came along."

Lady Charlotte worried her lower lip. "That was me. My mother had nothing left to give, and my parents didn't know what to do with an unwanted daughter. They named me Charlotte after King George's wife, which I assume was the easiest option. I'm the forgotten fifth."

Before James could provide a reassuring word to ease the raw pain that flashed across her face, she shuttered her emotions.

"I would never give up the freedom I had as a child. I had no governess. I sat in with Arthur and his tutors and learned everything a proper gentleman should know. I trailed behind my brothers and had free range of the countryside, whether it was shooting, hunting, or fencing."

She squared her shoulders. "As you can see, I am true to my word." She looked up at the sky, where the sun's rays tried to squeeze through the cloud cover. "It's gotten late, and I must be going before the house wakes up and realizes I'm gone. Good day to you, Captain Hughes." With that, she turned her horse and trotted away.

James did not budge.

Emotions.

He was not used to emotions, and right now, he was experiencing too many of them. Lady Charlotte was a woman of contradictions: brave but vulnerable, confident but insecure. He knew there was more to her, but the pain in his head returned from exhaustion and trying to make sense of this mesmerizing woman. He watched her ride away and wanted to bundle her up in his arms and protect her.

It must be exhaustion making him sentimental.

He needed to return to Gabe's town house to get some rest. Unfortunately, that meant riding his horse. James could not tolerate adding physical discomfort to the disquietude caused by Lady Charlotte's revelations, so he swung himself off the saddle. He chose to walk his mount back. Luckily, the home was just a few blocks away.

As James's boots crunched on the path that led out of Hyde Park, he tried to remove Lady Charlotte from his mind. Yet, despite his efforts, three words stuck out.

The forgotten fifth.

What a sickening sobriquet.

That was what she thought of herself.

He understood.

He was no stranger to feeling unwanted. As much as Lady Charlotte tried to hide it and as much as he tried to ignore her, he saw that she felt terribly, utterly alone.

CHAPTER SIX

Once Charlotte moved out of Captain Hughes's eyesight, she slumped down on her horse. It had taken all her energy to stay poised throughout their conversation.

He unsettled her.

Although he was a man of few words, she felt like he could see beyond the façade she put up to the rest of the world. Though she was with him only a few minutes, next thing she knew, she was pouring out her heart to a man about whom she knew next to nothing.

Charlotte straightened her spine. She would not allow such a lapse of judgement again and let her heart control her mind. She ascribed this atypical vulnerableness to the *Incident*, which was hanging over her head like the sword of Damocles. That must be it, she reasoned, and not that she felt an unexpected connection with the mysterious Captain Hughes.

The only way to control this emotion was to return to reason, as Arthur had always taught her. She took a few deep breaths in and out to calm her mind while she swayed in her mare's saddle.

I have been through a dreadful ordeal and am not acting like myself. I need to return to being the Charlotte of Shropshire, not the Charlotte of London, she insisted to herself.

Yes, the Charlotte of Shropshire would think reasonably and understand that Captain Hughes was a mere distraction who must be ignored. She had a clear path to achieve her marriage goal: marry a duke.

Charlotte nudged Mirabel into the turn to her aunt's town house, and rode to the mews, where she hopped off, handing the reins to the stable boy.

"Did you have a good ride, milady?" Daniel looked at her with the wide eyes of a youth on the brink of adolescence who suddenly was interested in the opposite sex.

Charlotte smiled and gave his hair a tousle. "Mirabel was very happy to have room to run this morning."

He beamed before he led the mare to the stables to wipe her down.

She was thankful she had the foresight to bring along a stable boy from High Crest Hall. While Thomas, Daniel's older brother, was busy running the stables, Daniel was eager to see London. Their family had managed the Earl of Pulverbatch's horses for generations, and she knew Daniel would not tell a soul she sneaked out every morning in gentlemen's clothes for a ride. Moreover, he did not blink an eye when she mounted the horse astride, given she always rode that way in Shropshire. At home, she could ride as she wished, hidden from the prying eyes of London Society.

Charlotte walked through the garden at the back of her aunt's home, pausing to see if any of the flowers had developed buds. Her favorite season was spring, when the natural world awakened from its winter dormancy and came to life for a new year with endless possibilities. At High Crest Hall, she would walk through the gardens each day to monitor the progress of the perennial flowers breaking through the soil, only their tips visible at first. Then, with each subsequent day, they emerged farther from their underground shelter, reaching for the sun and nourishment. She foolishly wished year after year that spring would bring new beginnings for her, but she was perpetually disappointed. It was as if she were stuck in winter while the world around her blossomed into spring.

Charlotte weaved her way through the paths of the garden, noticing the lilac bushes would soon be blossoming. She reached the servants' entrance and sneaked up the back stairs. Before exiting the stairwell, she cracked the stair door open and scanned the hallway. It was empty, so she quickly tiptoed to her room, praying the hallway rug would soften her footsteps. Once inside, Charlotte stripped off her menswear and shoved the piles of clothes into the bottom of her wardrobe underneath a blanket. She put her nightgown back on and rang for her lady's maid, Bailey. Soon her door opened, and a familiar face popped in.

"Lady Charlotte, did you have a nice morning in bed?" Bailey asked in an overly loud voice, making sure the door was cracked open.

"Yes, I have had a relaxing morning lounging about. Can you draw a bath? I'm sure my aunt has grand plans for me today." Charlotte did not trust the staff at her aunt's house and was certain Aunt Frances ordered them to report her every move.

Each morning, she and Bailey went through the same farce of a conversation in case one of the servants was lurking in the hallway. Charlotte adored Bailey, who had been her lady's maid for the past five years. Bailey was the eldest of eight children, so Charlotte appreciated her no-nonsense attitude and the fact that nothing rattled her. More importantly, in Shropshire, she was the only person of a similar age with whom she could talk. Although they had become close, it could not be called a true friendship. Bailey was still a part of the staff and paid to be in her company. In addition, Charlotte could not imagine that a woman of the same age would willingly befriend her. She was the *forgotten fifth*, after all, and entirely uninteresting.

But Charlotte yearned for a connection with others her age. After meeting Beatrice and Eleanor at the previous night's ball, she was cautiously hopeful, because deep down, she was convinced they would soon realize their error and ignore her.

Bailey left the room and collected several servants to haul steaming water up the stairs to the copper tub in her bedroom. Charlotte closed her eyes and lay back on the pillows piled near the headboard of the large four-poster bed. She snuggled under the blankets and counterpane and let out a loud sigh, hoping to convince the servants she was an entitled aristocrat, expecting them to wait on her hand and foot. She had to keep this ruse going if she were to protect herself. After some time, when she listened to the servants filling her tub, she heard the door close. Bailey came over to Charlotte and gently tugged on the bedding. Charlotte's eyes peeked over the counterpane and scanned the empty room.

"Thank you, Bailey, you're invaluable." She pulled back the covers and climbed out of bed.

Her lady's maid quirked her eyebrow. "Life is never boring with you, milady."

Charlotte walked toward the tub. "I'm fine to bathe alone and will let you know when I'm finished. I'm sure my aunt has given you specific instructions on how I'm to look for visiting hours," Charlotte said over her shoulder.

"Yes, milady."

Once Charlotte heard the door close, she undressed and stepped into the steaming water. She sank down into the tub and let the warm water lap over her. She closed her eyes, and immediately her mind drifted back to Hyde Park. She smiled as she pictured the seafaring Captain Hughes uncomfortably sitting upon his steed, with his strong and capable hands tightly gripping the reins.

Suddenly, those same hands morphed into something more disturbing, and bile rose in the back of her throat. A hand wrapped around her neck, depriving her of air. She gasped, trying to take a breath, as her panicked heart raced. A disturbing hue crept into the periphery of her vision and expanded until all she could see was one color: red.

There was blood everywhere.

Charlotte's eyes flew open, and she gripped the edges of the tub. She sat upright, her chest heaving.

The *Incident*.

Charlotte felt like a skittish horse ready to bolt. She trembled as she tried to wrest control of her body from her emotions.

The moment she let her guard down, that fateful day intruded, and wreaked havoc in her entire being. She had tried to convince herself that once she was protected from the law by a powerful man, the memories would stop. Clearly that was not true.

Return to reason, return to reason, return to reason.

Charlotte tried to apply Arthur's mantra to her thoughts, but it was no small task. She could not just forget the worst day of her life. She felt herself panting from fear, and forced her breathing to slow.

She had to stick with her plan.

The one thing she could possibly control right now was snagging a duke. Charlotte pictured the Duke of Westcliffe's kind face, but it was quickly overtaken by a stern visage with gray eyes reminiscent of an approaching storm bent on causing damage.

Captain Hughes.

Drat that man! He was a distraction she could not afford,

especially after revealing too much of herself in a lapse of judgement in Hyde Park. She leaned back in an attempt to resume her bath, but when her upper back reached the surface of the tub, she was jolted by the coolness of the metal. Her ruminations had consumed her thoughts longer than she realized, and the temperature of the bathwater had dropped before she could even wash herself. She picked up the wash ball and quickly lathered the soap on her body before moving to her hair. Her hands massaged her scalp. Despite the cool water, a degree of tension left her body as her hands worked their way down the rest of her hair that extended to her lower back.

Once her hair was sufficiently lathered, Charlotte dipped her head under the water to rinse off the soap. The coolness of the liquid struck her face like someone slapped her and undid any of the relaxation she had experienced with her scalp massage. Her hands pushed off the bottom of the tub to thrust her head through the surface of the bathwater and into warmer temperatures. Her body was covered in gooseflesh, and all she could focus on was the chill that surged through her body. She leaned forward in the tub with her hands resting on her thighs and took shallow breaths.

Her mind was blank.

Before any untoward thoughts could reenter her stream of consciousness, she stood and climbed out, grabbing a nearby towel. After she dried off, she rang for Bailey to help her dress and arrange her hair.

Charlotte was ready to start the day.

Charlotte beat her aunt to breakfast, which was no surprise. Aunt Frances stayed abed late into the morning, and often took a repast in her room. The skirt of Charlotte's white, long-sleeved morning dress floated around her as she went to the sideboard and chose a few slices of ham and a fresh roll to butter.

"A chocolate," she said to one of the servants standing nearby. He nodded and left to gather the beverage.

She situated herself at the table and prepared her roll. She waited for the butter to melt, then allowed the bread to soften in her mouth. Her chocolate was brought in, and she stared at the cup, butter knife still in hand, entranced by the swirling steam that emerged from the warm drink.

Swish, swish, swish.

"Well done!" came a sudden voice from the doorway.

Charlotte dropped her utensil in surprise, the metal clattering against the porcelain plate.

Her aunt swept into the morning room with her lace-trimmed white cap and morning dress adorned with a fichu to mask the low neckline.

Charlotte looked at her aunt suspiciously. Aunt Frances never commended her. When Charlotte was fourteen years old, her recently widowed aunt arrived at High Crest Hall to spend her year of mourning and strategize her next marriage. She was stunned to find that Charlotte was well-versed in gentlemanly subjects, courtesy of sitting in with Arthur and his tutor, yet incompetent in any of the feminine arts. Since Charlotte was an extension of her aunt, and her aunt's main purpose was to rise as high as possible in Society, she set her mind to molding Charlotte into a proper lady.

"Aunt Frances, you've never applauded anything I have ever done."

Her aunt let out a huff. "Charlotte, that is ridiculous. Did you not go into the drawing room?"

"No, I was quite famished so I came to eat breakfast." Charlotte gave her aunt a smile. "What's in the drawing room?"

"Flowers from your admirers, of course! All thanks to my tutelage during your wayward youth."

As much as she resented her aunt for forcing her to endure countless hours of unpleasant comportment lessons, she had to admit they were useful during this unexpected foray into the inanity that was London Society. "I'm glad I've finally flourished. Until now, my life has been meaningless. Thanks to a bouquet of flowers from a dandy I don't know with pockets to let, I have truly succeeded." Charlotte grinned at her aunt.

Aunt Frances shook her head in dismay, but Charlotte thought she caught a hint of a smile. "You were a hopeless cause until I came to High Crest Hall. It is time to put on your brightest face for visiting hours. You have one purpose and one purpose alone: to snag a titled husband."

Although for a vastly different reason, Charlotte could not argue her aunt's point. Aunt Frances sat at the head of the table and requested a tea, before she dove into the lineage, financial status, and reputation of each gentleman who had sent flowers. Her aunt, the woman who rarely left her bed before noon, had gotten up early to catalog the sender of each bouquet of flowers. Aunt Frances rambled on, all the while repetitively lifting her Wedgewood teacup from the table and bringing it almost to her lips before placing it back on the table, too excited to take a sip. Charlotte wondered how long before her aunt became impatient for her to see the flowers.

She did not have to wait long.

"We must go to the drawing room. You've had enough. Come. Come." Aunt Frances stood from the table with grace, her back perfectly straight.

Charlotte shoved the last few pieces of ham into her mouth, hoping her aunt was too agog to notice her poor manners. She rose and followed her to the drawing room. Charlotte stopped in the doorway.

It was an impressive sight.

Every furniture surface and even much of the floor was covered by various shapes and sizes of floral bouquets. She did not think she had even danced with that many gentlemen. She looked over at her aunt. Charlotte had never seen such a look of glee on her face. Aunt Frances swept her hand melodramatically in a wide arc in front of her, to encompass the breadth of the room. "Charlotte, this is all for you. You made quite a splash last night."

"Was it me, or was it my dowry?"

"Does it matter?" her aunt said, moving from bouquet to bouquet. "You need a dowry to wed, and you need one of these bouquets to lead to a wedding."

Charlotte was not ignorant of the fact the hefty dowry Grandpapa had bestowed upon her was unbelievably tempting to many debt-ridden lords. She did not begrudge the gift though, since he included two specific clauses to protect her. It was his way of looking out for her, even after he had passed. He knew how common it was for the *ton* to squander their fortunes in the blink of an eye.

The first clause was that if she did not marry by the age of twenty-five, her dowry would be released to her. The second was that if she did marry, Charlotte retained control of her money. She hoped the *ton* remained in the dark regarding these stipulations because the second one would certainly deter many lords if they knew. Luckily, Aunt Frances had spread the word of the impressive size of her dowry to entice suitors without a mention of anything further. Charlotte would worry about details later.

She walked around the drawing room, weaving through the floral arrangements, looking at each of the cards with superficial notes that reminded her none of the suitors knew anything about her.

Your eyes are the color of a warm spring morning. Charlotte frowned. A warm spring morning could have any color in it.

You have the voice of an angel. She had a terrible singing voice and doubted her speaking voice could be equated to a heavenly sound.

Your hair is the color of sunshine. Her hair was chestnut brown, far from a solar-hued blonde.

As she went through each one, she became more and more disenchanted. Meanwhile, she heard the swish of her aunt's skirts behind her as she double-checked each card with the notes she had already written on a sheet of foolscap.

By the time Charlotte had finally made her way around the room, which took a good deal of time, she noticed one very important suitor was missing: the Duke of Westcliffe.

Before Charlotte could ask Aunt Frances about the omission, she shooed her out of the room to prepare herself for visiting hours in order to have "the most important afternoon of her life."

James waited a while in Hyde Park, not wanting Lady Charlotte to think he was following her. Once enough time had passed, he led his horse along the cobblestone streets that led to Gabe's town house. He left the gelding in the mews, then made his way to the back of the home. The servants were already stirring, and he could smell the scent of bread wafting from the kitchens. Once inside, he made his way up the stairs toward his room to bathe and get ready for the day.

On the second floor, he paused and noted the grim faces of Lockhart ancestors staring down at him from the wall of paintings as if disgusted that a commoner like him tainted their sacred halls. He noticed that Lady Carrington's bedroom door was still closed, and the door to Gabe's chamber was ajar. His friend must have spent the night at the London town house he kept for his mistress, which was a common occurrence. James climbed to the next level and found his room, which was adjacent to Lady Bridget's, due to the lack of other suitable guest rooms.

Gabe had told James he knew he was honorable and would not dare seduce his younger sister, in a politely menacing way only an older brother could convey. James had reassured Gabe he felt more like a second, overprotective brother to Lady Bridget. He tried to repay Gabe's generosity by giving Lady Carrington and Lady Bridget a sense of safety at night with his presence, while Gabe slept elsewhere with his paramour.

James entered his room, which was simply though tastefully decorated in varying shades of blue with rosewood furniture. He took several long strides across the room to snatch up a letter that had been placed on his desk.

James broke the unmarked seal and scanned the contents.

Meet me at two o'clock.

Although it was an anonymous note, James knew it was from the Bow Street Runner Gabe had arranged, Malcolm Morris. He performed his morning ablutions, all the while running through every possible outcome of the impending meeting. He then went down to the morning room and requested a coffee from an awaiting servant, before wandering over to the sideboard, distracted by his thoughts. He placed kippers, eggs, and a roll on his plate, and seated himself at the table. His breakfast was interrupted by the entrance of Lady Carrington, who floated across the morning room, and Lady Bridget, who walked behind her mother with her eyes lowered in a demure fashion.

After the women had ordered their tea, James exchanged pleasantries with them until Lady Carrington dove into talking about the prior night's ball.

She looked at James with concern. "You left early, Captain Hughes."

"I'm afraid I have been at sea for too long and am not used to London balls. It was a crush, and I needed some space."

"That's understandable. How long have you been away from the Royal Navy?" She delicately placed her teacup on its saucer and gave James her full attention.

James shifted in his chair. Lady Carrington asked from a place of maternal concern. "I was injured two years ago in battle, and it took me months to recover. Once I was ready to return to service, the war was winding down. I have been on half-pay since then, but ready to fight again when needed."

"I can see how that has felt like no time at all. Gabriel mentioned that you have been mostly on your own while you travel between ports. London must be quite overwhelming."

James was surprised Gabe had told his mother about his job managing the many shipments of his friend Jack Doherty's Birmingham enterprises.

"Indeed, especially with so many grand events." James hoped that would be enough to satisfy Lady Carrington. She smiled warmly, and then without missing a beat, turned to Lady Bridget to discuss her daughter's hair arrangement for tonight's ball.

James quickened his pace of eating because he wanted to avoid any further interrogation, and also because he had never learned to eat slowly. Between his childhood under his tyrannical uncle's thumb and his career in the military, he had learned to never take a meal for granted. There were no such things as leisurely meals. James excused himself from the table and went up to his room to change into more appropriate clothing for the afternoon meeting.

He opened the wardrobe in his room and pulled out a faded coat, frayed linen shirt, and worn trousers. He did not bother with a cravat or a waistcoat. He slipped on a pair of scuffed-up boots in preparation for disappearing into the sordid masses of London.

James silently closed the door to his room and looked up and down the hallway. Luckily, it was empty, so he hurried toward the servants' stairs and made his way out of the house.

Once he had left the property through the back gate, he picked up his pace and strode through the alleyway until it fed onto the main thoroughfare. He hailed a hackney and hopped in, closing his eyes and leaning back onto the torn squabs.

Finally, he could relax.

James had never lived a life of luxury, and pretending to be a gentleman for the sake of securing Gabe's help was deuced difficult. He was surrounded by suffocating cravats, social pleasantries, and feigned innocence. Even being an officer in the Royal Navy was less oppressive than living among High Society.

Once the hackney neared the docks, the roads worsened. The familiar smell of rotting fish invaded his nostrils and gave him a sense of solace, despite the nauseating stench. As the din of the docks became more audible, the hack slowed, then stopped. James paid the driver and stepped onto the muddy road.

He was home.

He pulled out his simple pocket watch and realized he was early. To kill time, he wandered to the waterfront and watched the organized chaos of men efficiently loading and unloading ships' cargoes. The scene reminded him of worker ants busily marching morsels of food to their queen and returning empty-handed. The water lapped against the great hulls of the boats while they swayed in rhythm to the ebb and flow of the Thames.

James felt a sense of longing for the camaraderie of being a sailor. It was there, with a preordained naval family, that had made him realize how much he had missed in his youth. Although he had loved his mother dearly, his childhood was wrought with unpleasant memories.

His mother had crawled to her brother, the vicar, when she found herself pregnant after the man she claimed was her husband had disappeared a few days after their wedding. James's uncle had taken her in, Christian charity and all, but in fact, he had ulterior motives as a widower. James and his mother lived in an old, two-room building on the parish property in exchange for his mother tending to the vicar's home in the manner of a servant. Once James was out of leading strings, he followed suit serving his abominable older cousin, Herbert. Meanwhile, his uncle fervently believed that James's mother never actually married, and constantly reminded James by calling him a worthless bastard.

James pulled out his watch again. Fortunately, it was ten minutes to two o'clock and time to go.

He walked away from the docks toward the Prospect of Whitby, not far from the riverfront, and entered the drinking establishment. He waited for his eyes to adjust to the dimly lit interior and for his nose to adjust to the stench of unwashed sailors. He had not been on a ship in too long, so the latter was not an easy task. A roar sounded, and he glanced toward the cock-fighting pit. The spectators jostled among one another to get a better view of the fight, money clutched in their hands. This noisy pub was the perfect place to go unnoticed.

He moved around the crowd to the back corner in the usual spot, where he saw a familiar figure sitting with his hat pulled low over his eyes.

James slid into the booth where a tankard of ale awaited his arrival. He wasted no time with small talk, knowing his partner was of a similar mindset. "Any news?"

The gruff voice of Morris emerged from beneath the

shadows of his hat. "Stevens sent word that Roberts is'n' 'is real name. 'E found nothin' bout 'im before two years ago."

James's brow furrowed. Morris's news did not bode well. Roberts was his man of business, and the insurer mandated that he provide the shipping account ledgers in order to receive insurance repayment for the lost flax shipment.

Morris continued, "We looked at the books of the nobs and tradesfolk Roberts managed. Stevens looked at 'em real 'ard and figured out Roberts was fleecin' 'em."

James's mind churned through this new information. "Do you think that had to do with his death?"

"I dunno. We still don't 'ave much. Stevens talked to a maid who worked for Roberts. She was scared and not alotta 'elp, except for one thing."

"What?" James's interest was piqued.

"A woman in a veil came to see Roberts. Mourning or some-thin'. There was a gunshot and Roberts is dead in 'is office, lots o' blood. The woman was gone."

James frowned as his mind conjured an image of a woman dressed all in black. "I went to review my accounts with Roberts earlier that day, but a woman who wore a mourning veil entered his office ahead of me. I didn't want to wait, so I went to see Hann at the Ditherington Flax Mill to let him know about the lost shipment." James paused and shifted in his seat. "When I came back to Roberts's office, he was already dead."

Morris gave a knowing nod. "That was 'er, a Mrs. Gibson, she called 'erself."

"Gibson." James's lips sounded out the name of *her*, the reason for his current miserable existence in London. "I need those ledgers so I can get my money back for the shipment."

Morris shook his head with a solemn look on his face. "Not yet. The magistrate is 'oldin' all the records until they find Mrs. Gibson. It took a lot of *persuasion* to get our 'ands on 'em in the first place. We looked through all 'is books. No Gibson. We dunno where to find 'er."

That was not the answer he wanted. The tension he felt stayed with him. He had to find patience...from somewhere.

Morris continued, "This woman came for one reason and one reason alone, Capt'n. To kill Roberts. Maybe it was for the blunt, maybe it wasn't. Roberts 'ad a lot of enemies. 'E 'ad some funny tastes. 'E 'ad debts from 'Olyhead to Birmingham. Mrs. Gibson could be anyone."

One thing stuck out to James. "Birmingham, you said? Did he owe Jack Doherty money?"

"Oh yeah, 'e was in deep. I 'ear Doherty runs Birmingham. Bawdy 'ouses, gambling 'ells, that sort of thing. Do you know 'im?" Morris raised his bushy eyebrows.

"He's my best friend, and I work for him. Jack is ruthless, but he wouldn't send a woman in his stead as a hired killer."

"'E still may know somethin'. You want to talk to 'im? I 'ave so many leads I need to work for other cases."

"Sure. When I stopped in Birmingham to tell Jack about the sunken flax shipment, he said he was coming to London soon to expand his business."

"Great. I 'ave to be off. I'll let ya know when I 'ave more." With that, Morris slipped out of the booth and snaked his way through the pub's customers, blending into the shadows. He was a man of the darkness, a Bow Street Runner through and through.

James took a sip of his ale as he processed the information he had just learned from Morris.

Mrs. Gibson.

He shook his head in defeat. His life as a captain in the Royal Navy during a war was simpler than his current predicament. There, you knew the enemy. Here, it was all aliases, murder, and secrets.

Who is Mrs. Gibson?

He needed to find her, so he could get the ledgers released and be paid his insurance money. Then, he could leave the *ton* and this awful city.

Before she and Roberts showed up, James had begun to readjust to living on land. Jack had known James needed a purpose, but also that he had restlessness that could not be quelled. Jack had sent James to monitor his shipments at the various ports throughout Britain. It provided James with direction but also kept him moving. Jack's former man of business for western coastline ports was Embry, a heavyset, jolly, middle-aged man whom James had trusted.

But James only worked with him for a short time, because Embry died unexpectedly. Or so Roberts said. Roberts did not waste any time taking over his predecessor's accounts.

James did not know whom to trust anymore.

At least he could speak with Jack. His best friend would never lie to him. They were like brothers, bonded by nightmarish childhoods in Birmingham.

He finished his ale, then made his way toward the door, his height and shoulder breadth preventing a furtive exit like Morris. He squinted in response to the daylight. Once his eyes had adjusted, he stepped away from the pub and then hailed a nearby hack to transport him back to the hellish world of the gently bred. He climbed into the vehicle with his head down and slouched against its squabs in defeat.

James was no closer to finding *her*.

CHAPTER SEVEN

During calling hours, Charlotte was back in the drawing room, adorned in a white-sprigged muslin dress and seated on a cream settee surrounded by suitors. Her aunt hovered nearby in an eye-catching frock, and directed the men as they came in, artfully placing them in proximity to Charlotte based on their title and fortune. For the most part, Charlotte aimed for her best aristocratic smile while the gentlemen tried to woo her by any and all means.

She tried to keep a straight face. She had never thought of how many words rhymed with *blue*. Every poem or sonnet that presented to her attempted to describe her eyes and somehow find a rhyming counterpart. The blue of her eyes was likened to *dew*, *hue*, and her favorite, *coo*, which to her knowledge was a massive Highland cow. For the latter, she could not help but laugh at that particular term of bovine endearment bestowed upon her by a Scottish laird with a gambling problem.

The adventurous ones mentioned her hair, but not one mentioned a word about her personality or anything of substance. Charlotte felt as if she were a painting in a museum, and the gentlemen were standing behind the ropes in a gallery, commenting on her looks from afar.

When these gentlemen attempted conversation, it was the same polite topics that were repeated daily in every Society drawing room or ballroom. It was London, and it was always raining.

Charlotte had just politely put down a cage containing a pair of doves when the room fell silent. For a moment, all she could do was relish the quietness. Then her eyes swept the room until they landed on an imposing figure standing in the doorway.

The Duke of Westcliffe looked dapper in an olive-green double-breasted coat with a cream waistcoat, smartly tied cravat, buckskins, and gleaming, black top-boots. From his standing position, the Duke looked down, both figuratively and literally, at all the men seated throughout the room who were making fools of themselves trying to win Charlotte's favor. She caught the side of his mouth twitch as he raised his eyes from the pups before him and caught her gaze.

She respected His Grace. Despite being kinder than she expected, he still held himself like a duke, with an air of authority that challenged anyone to cross him. She was not the only one present who felt his power. The other men shuffled to the side to make room for him as he parted through the sea of suitors with a bouquet in his hand and greeted Aunt Frances and her.

Aunt Frances ushered the seated dandy off the sofa to make room for His Grace. The Duke positioned himself next to Charlotte. "I thought I would deliver my flowers in person."

Charlotte took the offered bouquet of vibrant pink and yellow flowers. "Thank you, Your Grace. These are beautiful, though I don't recognize them. They seem exotic," she said.

"They're hibiscus flowers," he explained. "Although I don't

come to London often, we have a flourishing conservatory with a very capable gardener."

Charlotte rotated the hothouse bouquet in her hands, so she could fully appreciate their beauty. A few moments passed before her eyes caught movement above the flowers as the suitors left. The last one or two her aunt swiftly shooed from the drawing room, so Charlotte would have a private audience with the Duke.

"These flowers are absolutely delightful, and their bright colors a welcome respite from the dreary weather." She grimaced at the final comment, apparently even she was not immune to using meteorology to fill the silence.

"Lady Charlotte, you don't have to keep up the pretenses. You and I both know you are far more intelligent than to be talking about weather and flowers."

She glanced around the empty room and saw Aunt Frances give her a nod as she walked to the doorway and loudly stated, "If you insist that I'm needed urgently…"

Her aunt slipped out of the drawing room toward an imaginary crisis, leaving the door slightly ajar for propriety.

Charlotte let out a sigh and allowed her shoulders to slump for a moment. "Thank goodness. That was overwhelming." Her eyes darted to the Duke. She knew he had just encouraged her to speak more freely, but she likely overstepped the bounds of proper conversation.

Fortunately, he did not look offended. "I'm glad I was here to save you." He waved his hand dismissively. "They're boys being forced into marriage, either because they need an heir or they need the funds, not because they're ready for it."

Charlotte could not help but raise her eyebrows. "I don't mean to offend you, Your Grace, but my understanding is that you, too, are in need of one of those things."

The Duke of Westcliffe appeared amused. "I see that your aunt has apprised you of the situation."

"Indeed, but I think if we are each clear as to our goals, then we can have a suitable match."

This time, he raised his eyebrows. "You're quite unconventional."

She smiled hesitantly. "I'll take that as a compliment."

The Duke laughed, then said, "Yes, it's most assuredly a compliment. I had the typical Society marriage with my wife, though I did respect and care for her. My daughters are in need of a stepmother, and I'm still in need of an heir. Selfishly, I want a partner I genuinely enjoy spending time with." He paused to shift his body so that he faced her. "I think you would be the perfect match. May I have the honor of formally courting you?"

This request was exactly what Charlotte needed. Being a duchess would protect her from the gallows, and she had to say *yes*. Yet, Charlotte felt a pang of emptiness in the pit of her stomach. Although she had always assumed she would never marry, in her dreams she thought that if someone ever did take notice of the *forgotten fifth*, it would be because of a grand love affair.

Instead, if she were being honest, she was chosen as the vessel for procreation. That pang of emptiness quickly grew into a deep ache as it fully dawned upon her that if she ever did marry, she would never have the love match she had seen in her maternal grandparents. Grandpapa spoke of her grandmother as if she were an angel who had descended to Earth. He would always leave her little surprises: a ribbon, a flower, a tart.

Charlotte dragged herself back to the present and gave the Duke a reassuring smile. "I would be honored, Your Grace."

"Well then, I must call upon your father."

"Oh no, that won't be necessary. You can speak with my aunt."

The Duke looked affronted. "I would think your father would be most pleased."

"No, no, Your Grace." Charlotte felt her cheeks flush in embarrassment. She had just gained the courtship of the Duke... she could not lose it the next minute. "It has nothing to do with you. Of course, he'll be thrilled. I know how busy you are, and I don't want you to feel obligated to go out of your way to call on him."

Charlotte could not let the Duke see how little regard her father had for her and cause His Grace to think that it reflected upon her character. She could not risk anything that would deter the Duke from their nuptials.

"It wouldn't be a bother. I know your father from the House of the Lords. He's an affable man."

Charlotte forced a polite smile on her face. He was so affable that if there was ever a hint of discord, he quickly removed himself from the situation to ensure that affability remained. Her father never wanted to break the cocoon of pleasantness in which he resided.

At this opportune moment, Aunt Frances reentered the room, clearly listening to the conversation on the other side of the door. "Finally! It took some time to escort those gentlemen out of the house," her aunt recounted. "Your Grace, did I hear you mention a formal courtship?"

"You did. I was just saying that I should call upon Pulverbatch."

"Your Grace," her aunt said sternly, "do you think I have not already asked for his permission? I greatly hoped you would court my dear niece, so I already discussed the matter with my brother. He was delighted."

The Duke shook his head in disbelief. "You never cease to amaze me."

Her aunt smiled as if this was the greatest compliment ever

bestowed upon her. "You have known me too long, Westcliffe. You shouldn't be surprised. We will see you tonight at the Sotherton Ball?"

"Yes, I'll be attending for a short time, but then I must leave for another obligation." With that, the Duke of Westcliffe stood, causing Charlotte to rise from the settee.

"We look forward to seeing you tonight," her aunt responded enthusiastically.

"I look forward to seeing you as well," Charlotte said.

The Duke took her hand and placed a kiss on it. He gave her an encouraging smile.

"Your Grace." She watched him leave and told herself it was the right decision. Little did he know, he was the man who was going to unknowingly save her life.

Later that evening, Charlotte rushed down the stairs of her aunt's London home to an awaiting town coach with the Hardwicke coat of arms emblazoned on the side. Aunt Frances would surely scold her for being late, even though she was delayed by the complex coiffure her aunt had demanded Bailey fashion. Now that Charlotte was officially being courted by a duke, Aunt Frances would not let anything jeopardize the chances of her niece becoming a duchess. From hair to slippers, Charlotte's appearance had to be perfect.

Charlotte paused so the footman could open the door of the coach and saw a shadow move behind the equipage before disappearing into the darkness. She figured it was a gentleman who was also tardy for the evening's events. Before she could ponder further, the door swung open, and the footman helped Charlotte inside. She sat opposite her aunt.

Then it began.

Her heart fluttered and her skin moistened with sweat. Her hands flew to her neck in an attempt to thwart the constriction in her throat. She tried to fight the demon that possessed her body, but she could not. Her panicked gaze flew from corner to corner of the coach like a cornered animal.

"Charlotte! Charlotte!"

Her body shook. Silken, gloved hands clutched her upper arms. She continued to tremble until she felt those hands shake her forcefully. The panic partially subsided, and she found her aunt looking at her. Aunt Frances released Charlotte's arms and sat back against the squabs.

"Swooning is one thing, that's why you have smelling salts, but these attacks of the nerves are too much. You are neither the first nor the last woman who must secure a husband."

Charlotte's heart still raced, but the worst of the moment had faded. She unconsciously ran her hands down the front of her dress, smoothing out nonexistent wrinkles while she tried to remain calm. Her hands brushed against her reticule, which contained her pistol, and gave her a degree of reassurance.

She had learned the best way to overcome these episodes was to focus on an object. She found such a target in the ruby pendant adorning Aunt Frances's turban. It fortunately gave the appearance she was looking at her aunt as well.

Charlotte's voice wobbled. "You know how I feel about these things."

Her aunt harrumphed and closed her eyes to rest before her upcoming Society performance. Despite focusing on her aunt's headpiece, flashes of that fateful day and the carriage ride afterward wedged their way into her mind. She continued to stare at the ruby, but the red morphed into blood and her breathing quickened. She scanned the interior of the vehicle and desperately searched for a different object. She locked her eyes on her aunt's diamond necklace, and forced herself to take deep breaths while staring at the sparkling stones.

She remained transfixed on the jewel until sooner than she would have liked, Aunt Frances's eyes flew open. "Have you recovered?"

"I'm ready to be sold to the highest bidder," she quipped.

"You've already been chosen by Westcliffe. He's the catch of the Season. Tonight is your opportunity to shine."

They entered the Sotherton home and joined the other guests in the queue for their names to be announced. Her aunt chatted with those around them until they were finally presented.

The ball was already a crush. Aunt Frances's eyes flicked around the ballroom, searching for the Duke. Luckily, she did not have to look long, given that the Duke of Westcliffe was situated toward the front. It was evident by the female crowd of marriage-minded mothers surrounding him. He stood at least two heads above the throng of women, and saw Charlotte and her aunt. A look of relief washed over his face. He excused himself and sidestepped the swarm of females.

The Duke's long strides quickly placed him before her. "Lady Charlotte, it's a pleasure to see you this evening."

Charlotte could not help but smile. Are you truly happy to see me or are you happy to find an escape from the vultures who circled you?"

"Charlotte!" her aunt admonished.

"No need to worry." He turned his head toward Charlotte. "It is both, of course. Since I have to leave early tonight, may I have the first dance?"

"I would be delighted, Your Grace." He wrote his name on her empty dance card. They engaged in small talk awaiting the start of the dancing.

Soon the sounds of the musicians warming up floated

through the din of the crowd. The attendees found their partners and headed to the area partitioned off for dancing. On this part of the parquet floor, an artist had chalked a night sky that included a full moon, stars, and even a comet. Intricate planets had been placed at the periphery to mark the dance floor's borders.

Charlotte's stomach clenched.

The tableau brought to mind a certain brooding man with hair the color of darkness and eyes that matched a wintry sky. The ornate chalked scene before her disassembled, courtesy of the soon-to-be dancers' feet, much like any hope of a future with Captain Hughes. Her fate had been determined.

"Lady Charlotte?" She did not even realize her destiny was looking at her with a puzzled look. The image of Captain Hughes was swept from her mind in order to focus on the swirling green and gold of the Duke's hazel eyes. He looked dapper in his blue superfine long-tailed coat, white waistcoat, and elegantly tied cravat.

The Duke held out his arm to Charlotte and then led her to the dance floor for a quadrille. Although there was less opportunity for speaking than the waltz, they were still able to exchange light banter throughout the dance. After the final notes sounded, Charlotte genuinely smiled. He grinned back and looked more relaxed than when he was surrounded by the earlier group of women. For that, Charlotte was grateful. Although she could not ignore their age difference, the Duke of Westcliffe was a good man and the best match for which she could have hoped, given her dire circumstances.

He led Charlotte off the dance floor before depositing her with her chaperone, then he looked thoughtfully at Charlotte. "Have you ever been to the coast?"

"Just once, but never to Kent," she replied earnestly.

"I want to show you Romney Castle. It's not too far from the water, and you can smell the salt in the air when the wind blows."

The corners of Charlotte's mouth lifted of their own volition as she pictured herself standing with her arms outstretched on her imagined version of the famed White Cliffs of Dover.

"I would love to visit," Charlotte said. She paused.

A snippet from a recent newspaper article flashed through her mind. She looked at the Duke quizzically. "Is there much smuggling near your land? I understand that the Crown wants to guard the Kent coastline."

The easygoing face of the Duke fractured for a moment before reappearing. "I see you follow current events closely," he replied evenly.

Charlotte's cheeks flushed. She could not scare off the Duke of Westcliffe with her inquisitiveness. She was supposed to know nothing of the world except for the latest fashions and Society *on-dits*. "Forgive me, Your Grace."

The Duke looked taken aback. "You misunderstand me. I'm not deterred by your intelligence. I would hate to spend a marriage with an insipid woman. You bring up a difficult topic. Smuggling is, let us say, *divisive* in Kent." He shrugged his shoulders, attempting insouciance.

"I can't imagine. Regardless, I would be honored to see your home and the coastline."

"It would be my pleasure."

Charlotte studied his face. He seemed sincere.

The Duke turned to her aunt. "You have a wonderful niece, Frances. I must speak with a few House members regarding a bill that's on the table next week before taking my leave. I will see you and Lady Charlotte again soon."

Her aunt beamed and looked around to ensure others had caught the Duke of Westcliffe's flattery.

"I'm quite flushed from such an exhilarating dance with His

Grace. I'm going to freshen up in the retiring room." Charlotte chose this moment to take advantage of her aunt's good humor from the Duke's praise. Aunt Frances nodded her head absent-mindedly, having already spotted another Society matron approaching. Her aunt could not pass up an opportunity to gloat.

Charlotte slipped away toward the door to the gardens on the opposite side of the room. She needed a breath of fresh air, and wove through the elegantly dressed guests, avoiding a silken hem here and a polished men's shoe there.

A murmur spread through the crowd before she could reach the doors to exit. She followed the gazes of those around her to the front of the ballroom.

Even from a distance, Charlotte could see the tall figure of Lord Carrington perusing the scene before him in an amused manner. Next to him, an equally imposing man stood, with silver eyes sweeping over the crowd, lips pursed and face grimaced.

Charlotte bit back a gasp.

Captain Hughes was dressed as an officer, and he was absolutely breathtaking.

The blue coat of his Royal Navy dress uniform hugged his broad shoulders, and was fashioned with two golden epaulettes. The white waistcoat underneath glowed in the candlelight and matched his form-fitting white breeches and stockings. He was every bit the imposing naval officer and exuded power. There was something about a man in uniform, and this particular specimen was magnificent.

Captain Hughes already haunted Charlotte's thoughts, especially when she lay alone in her bed at night. How could she think of anyone else ever again?

The Captain flinched as throngs of mothers and debutantes descended upon Lord Carrington and him. He shifted on his feet uncomfortably. Instead of feeling sorry for him, Charlotte felt a different sensation.

Is this jealousy?

She was baffled. When she saw the same group of matrimonial predators around the Duke, she empathized with him, but felt no resentment. Now, she wished she was the one in front of Captain Hughes vying for his attention.

It is jealousy!

Charlotte pushed that startling conclusion aside. She had to marry the Duke of Westcliffe to save herself. There was no other choice. She turned around and hurried to the doors leading outside. She needed to escape before any other untoward thoughts entered her mind.

James felt cornered by the marriage-minded mothers and their giggling debutante daughters who encircled him. This agony was why he never wore his uniform in public. Alas, Lady Carrington had insisted, and he could not say *no* to her. James tried the tactic of ignoring the young women thrust before him by looking over their heads at the crowd.

He looked down to see several mothers simultaneously tap his forearm with their fans to draw his attention. It felt as if a flock of birds had descended upon him and were pecking his arm in hopes of finding a plump worm. He clenched his teeth and used all his restraint to keep a placid look on his face while he continued to ignore them. He told himself he was scanning the guests gathered in the ballroom in order to avoid interacting with the women, which was true, but there was more. He searched for a blue-eyed beauty whose wit and intelligence intrigued him. James knew he had no right to an earl's daughter, but he could not stop thinking of Lady Charlotte.

There.

He saw a chestnut head making its way toward the balcony. He was not surprised to see her escape the crush of the ball. He gazed down at the women looking up expectantly at him and said in the same commanding voice he used for his sailors that brokered no argument, "You must excuse me."

He emerged from the group then swiftly walked to the doors leading outside, the revelers parting and making way for his imposing form. He felt the eyes of the *ton* boring into his back but resisted the urge to turn around. Fortunately, the music started for the next dance, which provided them with a diversion and allowed James to escape.

CHAPTER EIGHT

J ames stepped outside and felt a stark contrast between the stuffiness of the ballroom and the cool night air. There were a few lanterns placed around the balcony, which overlooked the stately home's gardens. At first, James did not see anyone, but as his eyes adjusted to the darkness, he realized there was a shadowy figure at the far end of the terrace.

He spotted a white and sea-blue ball gown embroidered with flowers that caught the flickers of lantern light.

It was Lady Charlotte.

An almost full moon shed a hazy glow on the scene. He approached quietly, trying not to disturb her. He could see the side profile of her face as she looked out over the gardens, her hands resting on the balustrade for support. Lady Charlotte looked like an empress gazing out on her domain.

James paused...she was gorgeous.

And lonely.

Illuminated by moonlight, he could discern a haunted look cross her face while she remained lost in her thoughts. A new realization struck him in that moment. He wanted to wipe all of Lady Charlotte's worries away.

No, he chided himself.

Although not a typical simpering miss, she was still a young lady of the *ton* who was beyond privileged, a group who lived with excess and who never had to wonder where they would find their next meal or if they would have a roof over their heads that night.

James purposely made noise as he approached her. She startled and whirled around. For a brief moment, a look of surprise and then perhaps amusement appeared on her face. Before James could blink, it was gone.

"Captain Hughes, I didn't expect to see you out on the balcony."

"Oh?"

"You seem to have many admirers in the ballroom."

James studied her further. He did not yet know every nuance of Lady Charlotte's intonation, but he swore he detected a hint of jealousy in her voice. "I needed to escape. It's why I typically avoid my uniform at these events, but Lady Carrington cajoled me into wearing it."

"I suspected as much. You looked as if you were being marched to the gallows. I have to admit, though, you are quite dashing, Captain." Her eyes widened as she realized what she said, then they darted downward in an embarrassed manner.

"You find me dashing, Lady Charlotte?"

"Given that you're always so grumpy, I can't tell if you're teasing me. That's quite impolite."

He took a step closer to her so that he was almost touching the skirt of her dress. "When have you ever worried about politeness?"

Lady Charlotte lifted her head, and instead of her usual bravado, James was met with a frown and a blue stare.

"Since I realized I must marry the Duke of Westcliffe to save myself," she whispered.

James stepped back in surprise. A duke? Save herself?

He assumed Lady Charlotte was on the hunt for a husband for the same reasons as every other lady of the *ton*: titles, heirs, and spares. Yet, she truly seemed troubled.

"What do you mean *save yourself*?" He felt the protective urge to strangle with his bare hands anyone who threatened her.

Lady Charlotte just shook her head, and her shoulders slumped, which tugged at James's heartstrings. She was the most strong-willed woman he had ever met, but to see her crest-fallen made him want to fix whatever had her so upset.

"I can't tell you why, but the Duke of Westcliffe, has asked to formally court me. We'll be married soon." Her voice was laced with resignation.

James could not help himself and grabbed both her arms. He looked into her eyes earnestly, "You can tell me anything."

"Captain, I'm sorry. I can't say." She tried to square her shoulders, but failed. "He seems to be a kind man. It's just…"

"What is it?" James asked.

Her voice came out softly, "I don't love him."

Without thinking and with his usual sense of honor nonexistent, James stepped closer and pulled her into his arms. His lips connected with hers, and he immediately began to devour her like a starved man. He felt Lady Charlotte's initial shock as her body tensed, but swiftly she pressed her lips back. He wrapped his arms around her back, and he felt her breasts push against his chest. She twined her hands around his neck, and her fingers pulled at the collar of his jacket. He angled his face so that he could kiss her more deeply, all the while flicking his tongue into her mouth to test her response. After a few attempts, her tongue hesitantly engaged.

She must be an innocent.

James's self-control could only last so long, innocent or not. His tongue pushed deeper into her mouth and danced with hers. She quickly picked up the rhythm, her tongue matching his, thrust for thrust. Despite her inexperience, James would not expect anything less from this vivacious woman. His mouth left hers, and he started to trail kisses down her neck to her collarbone. He felt her pulse beat rapidly. She was as aroused as he was. He lifted his head for a moment, his chest heaving.

He knew he should not have touched her, but he could not resist the invisible force pulling him toward her. He had always prided himself on his honorable actions, yet with her, he could not walk away.

James's kiss ignited a flame inside her she never knew existed.

And what a kiss it was!

When she was younger, she would overhear her brothers and their friends talking about their exploits with the opposite sex. Charlotte had been curious, and convinced Thomas, who was just a stable boy at the time, to kiss her. It was a brief, perfunctory interaction, and Charlotte was underwhelmed.

"Come with me." James grabbed Charlotte's hand and led her down the stairs to the gardens.

"Do you know where you're going?" she asked.

"No, but that has never stopped me before." He pulled her down a path past rosebushes not yet in bloom.

Charlotte could see her breath, given the earliness of the season, yet she did not feel cold at all.

She burned inside.

They passed a fountain and continued deeper into the gardens, making a turn down a narrow, overgrown path. Charlotte soon found herself in an alcove under latticework covered by vines. There, a small stone bench was placed under the arbor. James sat and pulled Charlotte onto his lap.

Even though she knew it was wrong, it felt so right.

For the first time, she was at eye level with his silvery gaze, which was cast in shadows from the arbor. Moonlight filtered through the vines and latticework, speckling his face. Despite the darkness, Charlotte could see that the storm normally in his gaze was absent. Instead, there was a hunger she had not witnessed before.

"I can't stop touching you. Please tell me to stop," he said as he stared at her.

"I can't," she responded.

He shifted and she felt a rigid form pushing against her thigh. From what she had gathered from following her brothers and their friends, she understood what that meant.

Charlotte wanted him, too.

If she was going to be forced to spend her life with a kind but fatherly man, she would never have a chance to experience passion like this. She may be innocent, but she knew the fire between them was something special.

He captured her mouth again and thrust his tongue inside, seeking more. She responded with the same fervor, wanting all of him. She wrapped her arm around his neck and pulled him closer. Their tongues intertwined at a frenetic pace. His hands wrapped around her waist, urging her closer to his body.

His lips left hers, and she felt a sudden void as the cool air danced around her tingling mouth. She quickly forgot about this loss of connection when his lips trailed down her neck again, this time descending lower. Her head tilted back to expose more of her chest, and she let out a moan she could not control. She felt his hands leave her waist and move to the front of her dress.

He tugged down her bodice, exposing her left breast and nipple to the night air, causing it to pucker. He dipped his head down, and his warm breath relieved the chill. His lips wrapped around her nipple, and his tongue ran circles around the nub, stimulating it further. He caught the nipple slightly with his teeth, sending a jolt of pleasure from her breast to her core.

Charlotte gasped in response.

He lifted his head and gave a devilish grin. "Do you like that?"

Before Charlotte could respond, he diverted his attention to her other breast and sucked and nipped just as much as its partner. Her bottom wriggled against his lap and searched for more.

"Dammit, Charlotte. You're going to make me spend in my breeches."

He called me Charlotte.

Through her sensual haze, the thought crossed her mind. She liked the sound of her name in his gruff voice, stripped of all formality.

James lifted his head. Her chest heaved as her insides coiled in anticipation of what was to come.

"Give me more," she begged, wanting to ease the tension in her core.

A chill surrounded her legs. The skirt of her gown was bunched at her thighs, and James's hand snaked its way up her leg, past her stockings and garters. His mouth returned to her nipple, distracting her. Suddenly, his hand was between her folds. Charlotte clutched the back of his head and tugged on his hair to counteract the sensations that overwhelmed her.

His finger grazed her entrance. He paused and lifted his eyes. "You're so wet for me."

Charlotte could not answer.

She was flooded with a deluge of new, pleasurable feelings. His finger moved through her folds, coating itself in her juices.

"I want to watch you," he murmured.

His finger slowly entered her, and her breath caught as her eyes flew toward the heavens.

"Charlotte, look at me." She lowered her gaze and stared back at him, desire pulsating through her veins.

"I want you, James." He let out a choking sound before he withdrew his moist finger and brushed two digits over the most sensitive part of her womanly area, her pearl.

"More!" Charlotte demanded, surprised by her outburst.

"James, I want more," she pleaded. His name sounded so right on her lips.

"I want you looking at me when you find your release."

"Yes," was all Charlotte could say. His words caused the flame in her core to burn even hotter. She looked into his hooded eyes. His fingers sexually tormented her again and quickened their pace. Charlotte's hips unconsciously rocked, trying to ride his hand. James switched to stimulating her pearl with his thumb and then thrust two fingers back into her cunny.

Charlotte heard mewls she realized were coming from her. Her hips found a rhythm that matched that of James's fingers. A pressure built deep inside her core, and she chased a sensation she did not understand.

"Let go," James commanded. A look of raw desire simmered in his gaze. Charlotte did not comprehend what he was saying. Her body was fighting a rising feeling she was trying to control. Her brows furrowed while her hips continued to thrust.

James's voice softened. "Let your body take over. Allow me to pleasure you," he coaxed.

The intensity in his eyes broke her concentration, and all of a sudden, the pressure released. Charlotte felt an explosion in her body, and her vision was momentarily shrouded in darkness before stars flashed behind her eyelids. Her entire body convulsed.

James's fingers flickered over her pearl and thrust in and out of her cunny. His voice broke through the sensations. "Look at me, Charlotte. Look at me."

Her body shook, but she was able to pry her eyes open. James's mouth covered her own to muffle the staccato of screams. His fingers continued to work her, allowing wave after wave of pleasure to roll through her body. Her hands tightened around his neck. She never wanted to let go.

The pulsations lessened. Her body collapsed from utter exhaustion. Charlotte dropped her hands and rested her head against James's chest, where she heard the racing of his heart. She felt all was right in the world, a sentiment she had never experienced.

Distantly, she noticed James's arousal still throbbed against her leg. He slowly removed his hand from underneath her skirt and kissed the top of her head. His arms wrapped protectively around her body, and she felt safe in his cocoon. She lifted her eyes to look at him, and though there was still desire, there was also a tenderness she had not seen before.

"Charlotte! Charlotte!"

"Good God," James muttered at the sound.

The moment shattered.

Charlotte's head whipped toward the direction of the voice.

"Oh no!" Charlotte jumped off James's lap. She pulled down her skirts and tugged her bodice in place as best she could. Her hands flew up to her hair and tucked wayward strands back into her chignon.

"My aunt."

Her bloody aunt.

James was having the most remarkable experience of his life, and it was ruined by her blasted chaperone. In addition, his arousal remained unabated, to add insult to injury. He watched as Charlotte slipped out of the alcove, her shoulders back and her head held high. He had kissed many women. Hell, he had sunk himself into many as well, but he had never felt anything like what had just happened with Charlotte.

Charlotte.

He could not think of her as Lady Charlotte of the *ton* anymore. No, she was bold, vivacious, and witty. After feeling like a shell of a person following the war, and well, even before the war, she was a breath of fresh air.

Charlotte made him feel alive.

All he wanted to do was sequester the two of them somewhere far away where he could make her scream his name over and over again.

But that could only happen if she were his wife.

A shrill voice broke through his thoughts. "Charlotte, what are you doing out here? Were you having a dalliance? Your dress is wrinkled!"

"Of course not," Charlotte replied evenly. "You saw how I looked in the carriage. I believe I'm ill. I danced with the Duke as is my duty, but then I felt faint. There wasn't anywhere to sit on the balcony, and I was afraid I would swoon. I came to the gardens to find a place to sit and just breathe."

James listened intently as Charlotte seamlessly concealed their liaison from her aunt. He knew deep down that hiding it was for the best, but he could not deny a part of him wished they were caught.

He would do the honorable thing and make Charlotte his wife.

James's stomach dropped and his arousal vanished as their reality reemerged. A marriage between them was impossible. He could never force Charlotte to be tied to a nobody for the rest of her life. She was destined to become a duchess.

James's fists curled from the futility of it all. Being near her and knowing he could never have her was torture.

James waited on the garden bench until Charlotte and her aunt left, then he returned to the ballroom. Once inside, he wore a look of indifference, but that did not deter the marriage-minded mothers. Soon, he was surrounded by eligible ladies yet again. This time, he signed up for as many dances as he could. He needed a distraction from what had just transpired with Charlotte, and knew that because of his sister, Gabe would have to stay for a while.

Dance after dance, James peered down at beautiful, accomplished debutantes who would be the belle of any ball, but none compared to the fiery Charlotte.

Gabe and his mother and sister were finally ready to leave, so James joined the women in their carriage back to their town house, while Gabe left in a separate carriage to attend to his mistress. The women chattered excitedly about the ball and with whom Lady Bridget had danced, while James listened in the corner, feeling frustrated.

Once they arrived home, James went to Gabe's study. The room was dark, aside from a banked fire. The servants knew the master of the house rarely slept at home, but always had his study at the ready, just in case. James poured himself a glass of his friend's finest brandy, settled in a wing chair near the fireplace, and stared at the specks of embers. He knew he did not deserve Charlotte, yet he could not stop thinking of her. He took a gulp of brandy, hoping it would numb the pain. It did not work.

His thoughts shifted to Charlotte's unnamed suitor, the Duke of Somewhere. James knew he could never compete with a duke and that he should not interfere with the life that was being planned for her. Yet, this realization did not dampen the frustration and hopelessness he felt at never being able to truly be with Charlotte.

James never liked to lose control but tonight was an exception. One glass of brandy became two, two became three, and so forth. He drank until he could drink no more, and stumbled up to his bedroom for a night of fitful sleep.

CHAPTER NINE

James awoke the next morning just as dawn broke, and felt his head pound and his stomach churn as much as it did after a grueling battle. He pulled himself out of bed, still in his clothes from the night before. He shuffled to the wash basin and splashed cold water on his face.

Fresh air.

He needed fresh air before he cast up his accounts. Being out in the open would clear his head. He washed and changed into fresh clothes before leaving the town house from the back.

James reached the mews while the sky slowly illuminated the sky. The stable was quiet at this early hour, and he saddled his horse. He mounted the gelding and rode to Hyde Park. The freshest air was at sea, but in London, a horse ride in the park would have to do. However, the tension he held in his shoulders was exacerbated by the stiff way he rode, causing him to regret his choice of early morning activity.

Not one to quit, he continued to the park. Once he made it through the gates, James nudged his horse into a trot, and soon a canter.

A canter was not enough.

He urged his horse into a gallop, despite his poor riding skills. He wanted a bruising ride with a sense of danger to make him feel alive and forget the toll the hangover took on his body. The wind whipped across his face, and his muscles flexed in exertion. On and on he rode, deeper into the park.

Then he saw her.

Suddenly, he pulled back on the reins, and the emotions that had been disappearing rushed forth once again.

"You," he growled at the familiar figure on horseback.

"James? Whatever is the matter?"

"Nothing."

Charlotte's brow furrowed in consternation. "Something definitely happened. What is it?"

"You should be getting ready for duchess duty. I am not the man for you."

Irritation flashed across her face.

"I told you...I must marry the Duke. I have no choice."

"But what if you had a choice?" James challenged.

"You're asking me about a hypothetical situation."

"It should be an easy answer if last night meant nothing," James said. He knew he was being unreasonable, but he wanted to know how Charlotte felt.

Charlotte took a deep breath and looked up at the sky, as if searching for answers from the heavens. Finally, she lowered her gaze and fixated on James. "Last night was everything. I felt a fire inside of me I didn't know existed. But my fate has been determined."

"I want you to come to Gabe's town house tonight."

Charlotte looked taken aback. "Are you fit for Bedlam? With his mother and sister there?"

"No. His other town house. I'll make sure he's not using it. It would give us one night together before you marry the Duke."

Charlotte worried her lower lip, turning the proposition over in her mind.

If only she knew what that thought did to him.

Her eyes refocused on his, and her chin tilted stubbornly. "I'll come. I want to experience something that is my choice, not something laid out for me before I'm forced to become a wife."

"I'll meet you by your aunt's mews at midnight."

Charlotte nodded. Without another word, she turned and rode away.

James was dismissed.

Charlotte went through the motions of the day: visiting hours, social calls, and idle conversations, all while wondering what the night would bring. She was a mix of emotions ranging from angst and guilt to anticipation and excitement. She had bolted from Hyde Park after accepting the foolhardy proposition from James. She had acted with her heart, not her mind, and she had a terrible inkling it would lead to trouble.

Return to reason.

Charlotte, the *forgotten fifth,* had been noticed for who she was, not just a dowry or a broodmare, and she could not deny the heat between them. She told herself their liaison would assuage the flaming desires between them before her marriage to the Duke; thus, helping the union in the long term. Men behaved improperly all the time with no recourse. She, a woman, deserved one cherished memory to carry with her into a marriage of convenience.

Charlotte told herself, *it is a perfectly reasonable plan.* A nagging feeling in her gut told her it was wrong, but she chose to ignore it.

After she completed the afternoon's forced social obligations, she slumped into the upholstered chair in her bedroom, ready for a break. Just as she leaned back and closed her eyes, a knock sounded on the door, and Bailey entered and walked briskly toward her.

"Milady, your aunt ordered me to dress you for your ride in Hyde Park with His Grace."

Charlotte groaned. With so much on her mind, she had already forgotten about her outing with the Duke.

Bailey looked at her apologetically. "Lady Hardwicke would like you to wear your new riding habit."

Charlotte reluctantly raised herself from the chair, and Bailey proceeded to dress her in a green woolen skirt accompanied by a tight-fitting jacket with brass military-style buttons, which glistened in the daylight filtering through the window.

"A riding habit befitting a duchess," her aunt had crooned in the modiste's shop.

Charlotte wished she could dress Aunt Frances in these ridiculous costumes and have her go in her place. Her aunt truly enjoyed being on display, and a ride down Rotton Row with the Duke of Westcliffe would suit her perfectly. Charlotte shook her head, picturing her aunt stuffed into her petite outfit, smiling obscenely and waving to the *ton* from her seat next the Duke.

"Lady Charlotte?" Bailey said.

The vision evaporated. Alas, this was her own fate, and she had to do whatever was necessary to marry Westcliffe. She sat at the vanity with resignation, her shoulders curled forward. She was in no mood to be paraded about with the Duke, but she had to prevail. Her life depended on it.

Bailey tugged at her hair, which forced Charlotte to straighten her posture.

Yes, I can do this, she coaxed herself.

Bailey rearranged Charlotte's mane into a low chignon that accommodated a matching, jauntily set chapeau. Like her aunt, it included a dramatic flair with a feather proudly fastened to the fabric.

Her lady's maid arranged the hat and gave it one final tug. Bailey stepped back to appraise her handiwork as Charlotte looked at herself in the mirror and saw a stranger. She was still not used to seeing herself adorned in the latest fashions like the rest of the ladies of the *ton*. In for a penny, in for a pound, as they say.

"You did well," Charlotte said.

Bailey curtseyed and left the room.

Charlotte took one last look at her alien appearance.

I can do this, she repeated to herself and went downstairs. Her aunt must have been impatiently awaiting her arrival, because she immediately swept into the entrance hall.

"I knew this riding habit would fit you the best!" Aunt Frances clasped her hands together, pleased with herself.

A rap sounded on the front door.

"Robinson, wait a moment," her aunt said.

She marched over to Charlotte and grabbed her upper arm. Her aunt tugged her away from the door. "You must be in the drawing room. You cannot look as if you're hovering near the door in anticipation."

Charlotte let herself be dragged into the drawing room and positioned on a settee. There was no sense in fighting her aunt. She just wanted to be free of her talons as quickly as possible.

Aunt Frances sat in a nearby chair and then shook out the skirt of her gown so it fell naturally around her legs.

"Sit up straight, Charlotte. You must always look impeccable." She pushed her shoulders back in acquiescence. Her aunt gave one last apprising look before she plastered a placid expression on her face, as if she had been whiling the day away in a field of flowers.

Aunt Frances's skills were endless.

"His Grace, the Duke of Westcliffe," Robinson announced. Charlotte and her aunt stood and greeted the Duke.

"Wonderful to see you both. Lady Charlotte, you look lovely today."

"Thank you, Your Grace," Charlotte responded politely. It was not the Duke's fault he was not James, but it was still hard for her to muster sufficient enthusiasm for their ride in the park.

Her aunt had no such problem. "What a splendid day for a carriage ride."

"Indeed, it is. I admit, I'm looking forward to being back in the country where the air is truly refreshing."

Her aunt smiled and the Duke offered Charlotte his arm. They walked out of the drawing room and outside, where the Duke led Charlotte to his awaiting curricle. He helped Charlotte into the carriage himself. She could not help but note the gorgeous, matching black horses that would lead them for their ride. The horses' coats possessed a healthy sheen and shimmered in the hazy daylight.

The Duke climbed in beside her and took the reins. He made himself comfortable while Charlotte straightened the skirts of her riding habit.

"You have a beautiful curricle, Your Grace," she commented with a sense of awe.

His mouth quirked up on one side. "Lady Charlotte, I may be older than you, but I'm not on my deathbed. I still enjoy a proper ride."

Although she knew he was teasing, she could feel her cheeks flush. "I would never imply such a thing. You appear quite hale and hearty."

He chuckled and then snapped the reins. They engaged in some idle chitchat about the weather so the Duke could concentrate on driving to the park. Even in Mayfair, there could be a cart or errant pedestrian suddenly in the way of the carriage.

Fortunately, their drive was uneventful, and they promptly found themselves on Rotten Row. The Duke expertly maneuvered the carriage down the treelined bridlepath. It was refreshing to see some greenery in the midst of the filth and grayness of London. Rotten Row was replete with aristocrats on horseback and in equipages, moving slowly to ensure their presence was noted by those around them.

"I'm counting the days until I can return to the country," the Duke admitted. He frowned at the carriage in front of them, which had stopped abruptly so the passengers could speak with a couple traveling in the opposite direction.

"I echo your sentiments, Your Grace. I've missed Shropshire and its openness."

Gentlemen on horseback facilely moved around the stopped vehicle, and the Duke's attention was consumed by nodding to other members of the peerage. Charlotte observed the deference they gave him when they passed.

Soon, the Duke eased the curricle forward, and he returned to their conversation. "There's plenty of land around Romney Castle for riding. It's not just the sea. You'll have free rein over it all."

"You seem to already know me well, and what I would like." She could not help but warm up to the Duke of Westcliffe, even without feeling an ounce of passion.

"Don't think me impudent, but is it safe to be out riding with the...transport of goods in the area?"

The Duke shook his head, grinning in amusement. "I believe we have already established that smuggling exists around my land. I try to keep myself removed from it. I have more important things to focus on than the transport of goods, as you just called it," he said, and shrugged his shoulders nonchalantly. "You don't need to worry about safety. None of the smugglers would dare approach my family. My daughters walk by the water. They're chaperoned, of course, but I never fear for their well-being. You'd have a degree of freedom as a married woman."

"That's good to hear. I imagine there may be less smuggling anyway, now that the war has ended."

"Smuggling is like the tides. The tide comes in and goes out no matter what's happening, but sometimes it changes in size. Although the tide may not be as strong, it never goes away completely," the Duke said. He cleared his throat. "My late wife's mother was French, and I'm afraid my daughters and I became accustomed to certain French luxuries. I'm glad they'll be more accessible again."

Charlotte smiled. He truly was an amiable man, yet stormy gray eyes flitted into her mind.

She forced herself to focus on the present conversation. "I'm sorry about your wife."

"We had an amicable relationship." The Duke's face was unreadable as he looked straight ahead while steering the horses.

He left it at that, and Charlotte saw a melancholy enter his gaze, even more so than when they initially met. She had learned the Duke was an easy conversationalist. For him to suddenly appear tight-lipped, she assumed there was more to the story.

They rode in silence for a few minutes, aside from greeting others who passed their curricle. Charlotte could tell the Duke's mind was elsewhere, likely consumed by thoughts of the duchess.

"Westcliffe, how are you this fine day?" They were stopped by a gentleman on horseback who appeared a decade younger than the Duke. The man pulled on the reins of his steed.

The Duke gently eased their horses to a halt. "Brockton, it is a wonderful day. It's good to see you. Lady Charlotte, this is Lord Richard Norman, Viscount Brockton. Lady Charlotte Tipton is the daughter of the Earl of Pulverbatch."

"A pleasure to meet you, Lady Charlotte." He paused for a moment in thought. "You are Arthur Tipton's sister?"

"Yes, my lord. He's the youngest of my brothers, and the one I'm closest with."

He made a sound of approval. "Brilliant man. He has a great future ahead of him in politics. He just needs to loosen up a bit."

Charlotte smiled—that was Arthur to a T. "He would be happy to ponder solutions to problems all day and night, if possible. I have rarely seen him while I've been in London, because he is so passionate about making changes for society. I haven't been able to coax him to any events."

"There is still time. The Season is young. Hopefully, he'll attend one social event before it's over. Westcliffe, I'll see you later at the club?"

"Yes, we can talk further."

Lord Brockton gave as best a bow as he could muster from atop a saddle, and nudged his horse down Rotten Row. After Charlotte's eyes left the viscount, she caught the scowls of a mother and daughter in a carriage. If only they knew she did not wish to play this game. Despite liking the Duke, she would readily hand him over in exchange for a certain captain.

But she could not.

If these women were any indication of the feminine sentiment toward Charlotte now that the Duke was courting her, she would send a note to Beatrice, Eleanor, and shy Bridget to go to a tea shop with her. She needed allies.

Before long, they left the park, and the Duke pulled up to her aunt's town house, and his face took on a more serious look. "I hope this afternoon has been to your liking."

Her heart fluttered, though not from excitement, but nervousness. "Yes, Your Grace. I've had a lovely time."

"As you have seen, I don't like to beat around the bush. I have greatly enjoyed your company and would like to set a date for the wedding."

Her stomach dropped. This declaration was exactly what she needed to save herself, but instead of relief, she felt panic.

"I'm honored you wish to do so. May I make a small request to wait a few days more? I feel as if it has been such a whirlwind."

"Of course. I don't want you to feel overwhelmed. Due to my need to be at the House of Lords, I'm not leaving London imminently. I thought we could marry before the end of the session, so you could return with me as my wife."

"I'd like nothing more. Thank you for understanding." Charlotte smiled as best she could after the lie fell from her lips. Her insides were in turmoil both from her dishonesty with the Duke and the implications of their marriage.

I need to protect myself. I need to protect myself. I need to protect myself.

"It's been a wonderful day, thank you," she said.

The Duke nimbly dismounted from the curricle, not noticing her smile had faltered, and helped her down. He escorted her to the front door, which the butler had already opened.

"I have Parliamentary business at the club tonight, but I'll call on you tomorrow. Until then." He lowered his head and kissed the air just above her gloved hand.

"I look forward to it." She stretched her facial muscles back into a smile.

The moment she stepped inside her aunt's entrance hall, her face fell. She trudged up the stairs to her room. After what felt like eons, she entered her chamber and locked the door.

Charlotte threw herself onto the bed and sobbed uncontrollably.

CHAPTER TEN

James climbed into a hackney that would take him near Lady Hardwicke's town house. He peered out the window and noted the illumination of the streets from the moon. While the vehicle rattled along, he wondered if Charlotte would even meet him, and cursed himself for being a selfish, pompous arse by tempting her, an innocent, with his proposition.

When James was around her, he lost all good sense and could not get enough of her. She was like an opium addiction, and he kept crawling back for more. She was a hard habit to break.

The hackney stopped at a side street not too far away from Lady Hardwicke's home, and James hopped out. He paid the driver half the fare and instructed him to wait. Once approached the alleyway behind the town house, he heard a man's voice slice through the stillness of the night.

"You bitch! I finally found ya, and yer gonna rot in 'ell!"

James quickened his pace and pulled out the dagger he kept handy.

"I'll kill you!" shouted a woman's voice.

An eerily familiar woman's voice.

James swiftly approached the source of the sound and moonlight filtered into the alleyway.

There stood Charlotte with her hair askew, pointing a pistol at a man on the ground who grasped a dagger. The look in her eyes was hard to read, but she must be frightened.

"You won't do it," the man snarled. James froze, not wanting to cause a misfire by surprising Charlotte.

James recognized her look—he had seen it in some of his men. It was a past trauma suddenly reemerging, causing a person to freeze.

James jumped into action at the same time the man realized Charlotte was frozen. The ruffian sprung to his feet, clutching his dagger. James gave a warrior's cry while running toward the two of them.

The rogue held his dagger at her throat and eyed James. "Who are ya? One step and she's dead."

Charlotte's eyes widened. The blade dug into the front of her neck, and a trickle of blood dripped down her throat.

James met her gaze to give her a look of reassurance, though he was not optimistic with only a dagger in his hand. Then, out of the corner of his eye, James spotted the pistol Charlotte had dropped.

"I don't know this wench. Why don't you just blow the grounsils with her? No need to waste such a pretty thing," James said, and relaxed his arm that was wielding the blade. He had to outsmart this bastard, and there was only one thing he thought would work.

One terrible thing.

The man contemplated what he had just said. "No, this chit 'as to die. She tried to kill me."

"Why can't we have a little fun with her? If you won't, I want a turn before you finish your business," James taunted.

"What do you 'ave to do wit' anything? I'm the one who gets 'er."

James shrugged his shoulders nonchalantly. "You don't seem to want her."

Charlotte flinched. The knife at her neck had moved while the man was thinking. James used all his might to not move and rip the blade out of the bastard's hand and give him the slow and painful death he deserved.

"I'm gonna fuck this strumpet."

"I'm glad you grew some bollocks. You get her on the ground, and I'll hold her for you. I don't want her screaming."

The scoundrel pushed her onto the ground. She landed with an *oomph* that shattered James's heart. He could not make any mistakes.

He sprung toward Charlotte's pistol.

"You son of a bitch!" Charlotte screamed. As James had hoped, she fought the man tooth and nail, though he had not expected the litany of expletives with which she verbally thrashed him.

James reached the gun; it was primed.

The blackguard had foolishly turned his back on James in order to straddle Charlotte. James wanted to shoot him in the back. The bastard deserved no honor, but there was a chance the bullet could pass through him and hit her.

James quickly maneuvered so that the man could see him.

"You'll never dishonor another woman again," he said.

The blackguard paused his bungled attempt to lift Charlotte's skirt and looked up at James. His eyes narrowed after he saw the pistol trained on him. "You—"

James yanked the man off Charlotte with his free hand and threw him to the ground.

Boom.

The man crumpled, and James turned away, cold and unfeeling.

Charlotte stared at him with a mix of disbelief, fear, and shock on her beautiful face. Blood trickled down her neck.

"Damnation! Are you hurt anywhere else?" he asked. He quickly ran his hands over her body, which was mostly covered in a cloak, and then looked at her throat. He knew the wound was not deep; she was still breathing, and the blood was not spurting from the vessels in her neck. From what he could tell, it was in fact a shallow cut. James searched Charlotte's face, and he saw an empty look in her eyes.

Shock was setting in.

James reached underneath her dress. His hands rummaged around until he felt her petticoats. He ripped off a strip of fabric and pressed it to Charlotte's neck. He lifted her hand to the cloth.

"Hold this," he ordered. She left her hand in place and stared blankly ahead. James was used to her sharp tongue, which made the silence unsettling. A stirring in the mews caught James's attention. The gunshot had likely awoken the stableboys. James needed to get Charlotte out of there.

He scooped her up, suddenly realizing her lightness. She had such a bold personality that it often made James forget she was quite small in comparison to him. With her clutched to his body, James rushed down the alleyway and back toward the hackney. He reasoned that the best place to take her was their original destination: Gabe's mistress's town house.

He knew Charlotte was alive, but her silence caused his mind to play tricks on him and doubt her wellness. He reached the hired carriage and maneuvered inside and positioned her on his lap. He shouted the address and added, "Go! Quickly!"

To James, the hackney could not move quickly enough. He had never been the religious sort, what with his life seeming like an endless hell, yet now, his curses were intermixed with prayers for Charlotte's safety. He would go to church every day and twice on Sunday if it meant the woman he loved would be well.

James pressed her closer to his body, and his heart skipped a beat as he felt Charlotte tuck her head into his chest. Her hand still held the fabric at her throat. Maybe there was a God after all. He would take any improvement in her condition as a sign of hope. The gravity of what he had just thought wormed its way into James's mind.

Love? Did James really tell himself he loved Charlotte? The hackney made a turn, and he instinctively pulled Charlotte closer to his body.

It could not be.

She was being courted by a duke, and for James to think there could be anything between them was futile. He was a lowly naval officer, who was a bastard per his uncle and did not deserve to be within five feet of Charlotte.

But he could not deny what he felt, especially after seeing her in that glorious rage with a pistol trained on another man's head.

Guilt surfaced.

It was his own fault she was put into this situation. She was bleeding from her neck and in shock. If James had not proposed this late-night tryst, she would never have been out near the mews.

But one question nagged at James. Was the ruffian there by chance or was this a targeted attack? Charlotte seemed to be running from something, and he had a gut feeling it was no coincidence that a nefarious man lurked outside her home.

Mayhap he should not feel guilty and instead feel thankful he was there to save her. The shock on Charlotte's face before she could pull the trigger was undeniable. James was glad he could do the deed himself. He had never been innocent—his uncle swore he was born in sin, after all, so what was another death on his hands?

It was nothing.

James's ruminations were broken when the hackney slowed down a few streets away from Gabe's town house. Despite the urgency of getting Charlotte inside, he had to make sure no one saw her; otherwise, she would be ruined. If James did not deserve her before, he certainly was not worthy of her now, and could not risk her being forced to marry him. James gave the driver his payment and hurried along until they reached Gabe's property.

James opened the rear garden gate and made his way to the back of the house. He had to ensure there would be no cause for tongues to wag. He eased open the door as quietly as he could while supporting Charlotte's body with his other arm. Gabe had told him his staff was tight-lipped and loyal to a fault, all necessary characteristics when housing a member of the *ton*'s mistress.

James hurried up the servants' stairs from the basement to the ground level. The butler appeared.

"Dawson?" James said.

"Yes, Captain. We've been expecting you." Dawson did not bat an eye while James held a limp woman in his arms.

"I need water, clean rags, bandages, brandy, and some cheap alcohol. Lady Charlotte has been injured." This time, there was a flicker of emotion on the butler's face before he smartly turned on his heel to retrieve the requested items.

James addressed a maid hovering nearby, "I'm taking Lady Charlotte upstairs." The maid's head bobbed, and she grabbed a chamberstick to lead him up the central staircase.

James strode behind her. His arms finally started to feel tired, his body knowing they had reached their final destination.

He took a deep breath and made his way up the stairs for one final push. Once he reached the unfamiliar landing, the maid paused and looked at him expectantly.

"To Lord Carrington's chambers."

The maid showed him to a nearby door, and then lit a candlestick near the bed once inside the room. A fire already burned, providing additional light. James could make out dark green drapes and upholstery in the masculine space.

A voice from behind him echoed into the room, "I have the items you requested." Dawson stepped around James and into view. The butler laid the supplies on a table between two upholstered chairs near the fireplace. There were already two glasses and a decanter of brandy set up. James asked Dawson to wait outside the door in case he needed anything else. He brought Charlotte to the massive four-poster bed and eased her on it. He said as softly as he could, "You're safe, Lottie, I'm here to take care of you." James would do everything in his power to protect her, even if she was promised to another.

Mine, flashed through his mind while he waited nervously for her to respond. He suppressed the unwelcome thought. She could never be his.

Charlotte lifted her head slowly and stared at him with owlish eyes and blinked, still in shock. At least she was alert and not injured too badly. James would take any small mercies.

He gingerly removed the strip of petticoat that was now stuck to her neck from the blood drying and removed her cloak to ensure he did not miss any other injuries. The cloak was streaked with dirt from her scuffle with the ruffian. James threw it to the ground in disgust. He scanned her body once again and found no additional wounds, then walked over to the fireplace and poured a glass of brandy before he headed back to the bed.

"Lottie, drink this. It'll help you when I look at your neck more closely." She stared at James blankly. It broke his heart to see his brazen beauty in such a state. She was usually so vibrant.

He lifted the glass to her lips and tilted it gingerly, hoping she would open her mouth. When the strong drink reached her lips, they parted ever so slightly, and he could ease the liquid into her mouth.

He thanked the God in which he did not believe. He had no idea what he was doing and was not skilled at comforting someone. Although his mother had shown him love, the cruelty of his uncle throughout his childhood overshadowed any maternal warmth, leaving James with a cold indifference. This lack of emotion helped him in war, but left him unprepared for helping a lady he did not deserve.

Charlotte drank a sufficient amount of brandy to hopefully numb the pain from the wound, so James retrieved the water, rags, and cheap alcohol. She was in a simple gray dress that was wrinkled from the night's events. James inspected the strip of petticoat he had removed from her neck. The fabric was bloody but not drenched.

"Well now, let's see what we have here." Although Charlotte remained motionless, speaking to her helped calm the fear that crept into him. He had never needed any support when he tended to his wounded men, but this was different.

It was Charlotte, and he cared too much. But that had to stop.

He cleared his throat and grabbed the candlestick, examining the wound under better lighting than the alleyway.

He gave himself a stern warning. No terms of endearment, no tender gestures. She was destined to become the Duchess of Westcliffe. He was a mere commoner, unworthy of breathing the same air as she.

"Charlotte, I'm going to clean your skin." He dipped a rag in the water and gently rubbed the damp fabric over her wound.

She flinched, which was a good sign. She had an inch or so gash running horizontally along the bottom of her throat. It was not too deep and not too wide, so he thought stitches could be avoided. From being at sea during the war, he had sewn up many of his men when in a pinch, but Charlotte's delicate neck did not deserve his clumsy attempt at stitching.

He finished cleaning the wound and her surrounding skin with water. She stared straight ahead with a lifeless look in her eyes. He called for Dawson outside the closed door. The butler approached the bed with a well-trained, emotionless demeanor.

"Lady Charlotte's wound needs to be cleaned with alcohol, and she might jump off the bed."

"Yes, Captain. Shall I call for the surgeon?"

James let out a scoff. "Certainly not. She doesn't require stitches. I'll clean the wound myself."

"Of course, sir."

James paused, sensing the butler hovering behind him.

"Is there something else, Dawson?"

"Captain, if I may be so..."

"Out with it. I don't need the formalities. I'm not a bloody lord."

"Yes, sir, I mean Captain," Dawson stuttered, likely never having been so flustered in his life. He cleared his throat. "Lady Charlotte may need a change of clothes."

James furrowed his brow as he assessed Charlotte's appearance. He had noticed her dress briefly, but had been more focused on her wound. He neglected the bloody neckline of her wrinkled dress. "Can you procure a nightdress from the, erm, mistress of the house?"

"Yes, Captain." Dawson turned and left the room.

James lifted her hand off the bed and was jolted by the iciness of her skin. This would not do...she had to be warmed. He did not want to dirty the sheets and tuck her into the bed in her current state, so James rubbed her hand and forearm and then switched to the other side. He felt brutish, because his large hands easily encircled her petite arm while he moved them up and down her limb to generate warmth. The chill from her skin was profound and seeped through his calloused fingers and palms. He moved to Charlotte's legs and eased up her skirt and petticoats in order to remove her half boots. In any other situation, he would have felt a rush of desire to view her exposed, delectable, stocking-clad ankles; however, all he felt was guilt that this traumatic event was his fault. Her feet were also cold, so he vigorously rubbed them.

A moan escaped from her, and his eyes flew to her face. Was she starting to recover?

"Charlotte?" He stood and put his hands on her shoulders instinctively. She flinched. "Dammit, I didn't mean to jostle your neck." Her blue eyes flitted to his face, which was a morsel of reassurance James devoured.

"What happened?" she murmured, her eyelids fluttering.

James gulped. "You were waiting for me by the mews, and some bastard attacked you." He wanted to skirt around the truth to ease his guilt, but he had to be honest with her.

Her eyes widened. He tenderly grabbed each of her hands and rubbed his thumbs on top. "I'm so sorry."

She crinkled her nose. Her inquisitive mind churned despite the shock.

"There was a gun," she whispered.

"Yes, I believe it was yours. It felt quite small in my oafish hand." James gave a half smile after his attempt at levity.

She took a big swallow, and her hand flew up to her throat. "What happened here?"

"The man threatened you with a dagger at your neck and pressed a bit too hard." He did not want her to realize she had frozen in the midst of the altercation.

"Where is he?" she asked softly.

"Dead."

"Good," she responded definitively.

Her answer surprised him. Despite everything that had happened, she was still fighting. His heart swelled, then quickly deflated as he reminded himself she could never be his.

A knock on the door preceded Dawson, who walked into the room with a nightgown. James nodded to the far end of the bed.

"I'm going to use alcohol to clean your wound before we get you ready to sleep," he said.

She warily eyed the bottle of cheap alcohol on the bedside table. James poured another dram of brandy. "Please drink this. It'll help with the pain."

He offered her the glass.

Charlotte grabbed it and drained it in one motion, flinching again with the jostling of her wound. She looked at him. "Captain Hughes, you're going to catch flies in your mouth."

He closed his mouth and grinned, relief washing over him. She remained pale and admonished him in a weaker voice than usual, but she seemed to be on the mend. "I see you don't mind the taste of brandy."

"I stole it from my brothers all the time. Clean the wound and be done with it."

"Of course, my lady," James responded, and fought a smile from her bossiness. "Dawson is going to hold your arms down. There'll be a bad sting."

"I was always scraped up as a girl. I'll be fine. Dawson, no need to restrain me."

Dawson stepped back, but remained nearby in case he was needed.

James was not used to his orders being challenged...ever. But this slip of a woman had just put him in his place, and he did not care. He adjusted the candle on the bedside table to provide optimum light before he poured alcohol on the rag.

"On the count of three. One...two...three." He cleaned the wound with the alcohol-drenched fabric. She let out a hiss but did not jump up like some of his men.

However, he caught several select words he had last heard on his ship.

"You have quite the vocabulary," he teased.

"You'll be hearing a lot more if you don't hurry. I had four brothers to learn from."

He poured additional alcohol onto the rag and quickly cleaned the area once more.

Charlotte clenched the counterpane in her hands, but she remained stoic throughout the ordeal.

"All done."

She let out a whoosh of air and closed her eyes. She opened them and stared directly at him.

"Thank you, Captain," she said evenly.

He was impressed. Charlotte really was a remarkable woman. Grown men had cried hysterically when James tended to their wounds, but she, an earl's daughter, released nary a tear nor a sob.

She was made of sterner stuff.

CHAPTER ELEVEN

A knock sounded on the door.

"Come in," James said.

After cleaning Charlotte's wound, he had loosely tied a bandage around her neck and now collected the remaining supplies. The maid entered.

"I'll leave you to change out of your soiled clothes." He reluctantly left the bedchamber and grabbed the bottle of brandy on his way out. He went downstairs in search of Gabe's study to collect his thoughts. Once he discovered the room, he put down the brandy and collapsed into a wing chair near the fireplace. He did not care that the fire had not been lit. The coolness of the room was refreshing. The night's events bounced around his mind haphazardly.

A glass and decanter sat next to the chair. He lifted the lid and passed the vessel underneath his nose. The smell of tobacco and caramel assaulted his senses, and he knew this was a better spirit than the brandy he had just given Charlotte. It was likely the cognac Gabe reserved for himself. James needed a bracing drink, so he poured himself a glass without hesitation. He would ask for forgiveness later.

James took a sip and savored the flavor. He closed his eyes and rubbed his hand across his face. The whole night was his fault. His honor had flown out the window, and he had proposed a salacious tryst to Charlotte.

How could I have done such a thing?

But he knew.

Charlotte intoxicated him, despite being his better.

Just like in the backstreets earlier in the night, his mind argued with his guilt. The blackguard must have been lurking outside Lady Hardwicke's town house, irrespective of anything James had done, and it was actually a good thing he was there to save her.

James clutched the glass more tightly. That bastard was dead, but he must not be acting alone. Charlotte was hiding something from him, and he could not fathom what she had done that would warrant a price on her life. Anger unfurled inside him that anyone would dare touch a hair on her beautiful head. Although he was not good enough for her, he would never let any harm come to her.

James sipped his drink and mulled over the supposed atrocities a lady of the *ton* could commit.

Was the cutthroat a hired assassin by a jilted lover or the angry wife of a paramour?

No. James could not believe those scenarios. Charlotte seemed like an innocent. She definitely kissed like one.

Theft?

Although he did not pay much attention to the *on-dits* of the *ton*, Charlotte did not seem impoverished.

Murder?

She did not seem like a killer. Moreover, he could not imagine a situation that would arise in her cosseted life where she would take the life of another.

James was stumped. He looked down at his glass and realized it was empty.

Right.

Time to check on the enigma that was Charlotte.

"Come in." Her voice permeated through the closed door after James's knock. She still did not sound like her usual self, though he could sense strength in the tone of her voice. He cracked open the door, noting that the maid had left. He saw a bundle tucked into Gabe's massive bed. Although he would have to spirit Charlotte back to her aunt's house before dawn, there was yet time for her to recover more before she had to leave. She would stay put in this bedroom while he slept in a guest chamber.

He walked into the room and closed the door softly behind him, treading lightly on the plush Axminster carpet toward the bed. He took a moment to assess her. The maid had unpinned her chestnut hair, and it fanned out gloriously over the pillow. She stared up at the ceiling, and James noted a hint of color in her cheeks. The ruffled neck of a white nightgown encircled her elegant neck and peeked out from beneath the counterpane.

James reached the side of the bed. "How do you fare?" He reflexively lifted his hand to reach out to her, but then pulled it back, knowing she was not his to touch.

"Better enough. Thank you for saving me," she answered in a soft yet steady voice.

"Nonsense. I saw you holding the pistol. If I had not shown up, I'm sure you would have taken care of the ruffian."

More white nightgown fabric emerged from under the counterpane. She shrugged her shoulders. "Perhaps."

Charlotte pushed herself up and propped her back against the headboard. As she maneuvered herself, the counterpane slipped from her shoulders to her waist.

Good Lord, the ruffled neck was deceiving. The fabric was

completely translucent. James should not have been surprised—she borrowed the nightgown from a courtesan, after all.

Before he could divert his eyes, James caught a glimpse of two darkened circles on her chest beckoning for attention. His member twitched at their sight, so he quickly focused on Lady Charlotte's face. James swallowed, realizing she had no idea how much of her he had just seen. More importantly, she did not know what just a glance of her delectable body did to him.

He cleared his throat. "We can talk more after you have rested. I'll come back to wake you early to leave for your aunt's house so that she is none the wiser. I wouldn't want you to suffer a scandal."

Charlotte worried her lower lip before responding, "Thank you."

He could not get the fleeting image of her breasts from his mind. It was a tantalizing tease that made him want to explore more of what the transparent nightgown was barely concealing. James chided himself. She had just been through a traumatic experience that was largely his fault. He was an absolute bounder for thinking of what it would be like to tear the barely-there fabric from her body, worship every inch of her, and then sink his cock to the hilt inside her cunny.

He shook his head, trying to vanquish the desire from his mind and his body.

"Are you quite alright?" Cornflower-blue eyes stared back at him with concern, and she thankfully pulled the counterpane to her shoulders unassumingly.

"I was just clearing my head." Heat rushed up James's neck in embarrassment. "I bid you goodnight, Charlotte." He abruptly turned from the bed and walked briskly toward the door.

His hand reached for the doorknob, but Charlotte's voice floated through the air, "Wait."

He paused and closed his eyes. He rested his forehead against the door and willed control over his body. "Yes?"

"Stay with me." A pleading note laced her voice. James took a deep breath and turned away from the door. She looked fragile and vulnerable buried in the massive bed. Gone was the bold woman he had come to admire. James knew the honorable course of action would be to leave the room, but how could he say no to her distraught face?

"Of course. I'll sit by the bed."

He walked toward the fireplace and lifted one of the wing chairs with ease. After his time in the Royal Navy, he could sleep in any situation and in any position, including sitting up. Before he could reach the bed, Charlotte's voice carried across the room once more.

"Can you hold me?" Her voice was now desperate. "Please?"

James paused and looked toward her again, truly appreciating her youth and innocence as her wide eyes begged him to comfort her. Her wittiness and bravado always made James think of her as much older, but there she was, scared and alone, battling demons he did not understand. He placed the chair down in the middle of the room and walked to the bed.

"I'll hold you, but I'm staying above the counterpane." He wished there was an ocean between them. Hell, he would even take a moat, just anything to keep his baser urges at bay. Instead, a piece of fabric would have to do.

This is a terrible idea.

He removed his dirty boots before climbing onto the bed. Charlotte moved her pillow around and scooted herself closer to him then positioned herself on her side. He extinguished the bedside candle and curled behind her, before he draped his arm over her. Even though the counterpane separated their bodies, her hair remained unbound and flowed over the pillow. The scent of honeysuckle and jasmine invaded his senses, bringing him back to their first dance. A protectiveness surged through him, and he became lost in her scent, tugging her close to him. James heard a sigh escape from her as the tension in her body eased. After a few minutes, she breathed more slowly, and James allowed himself to relax. Before he knew it, he fell into a deep slumber.

James awoke abruptly to screams and a thrashing body. He jerked himself upright, ready to smother the danger that was beside him. Luckily, the glow of the fireplace illuminated the source of the disruption, and he stopped himself from attacking.

"No! No!" Charlotte clutched her neck and screamed while kicking her legs and punching into the air. "Don't kill me!"

James's heart rioted at her suffering. He wanted to wake her but knew from his experiences with his sailors that it could make it even worse.

He watched helplessly as Charlotte thrashed. After what felt like hours but was only minutes, her movements slowed. She opened her eyes with a panicked look on her face.

"Charlotte, it's James. You're safe."

"James?" she questioned, staring at him.

"You were having a nightmare."

Her gaze dropped, and she nodded. "I know," she whispered.

James needed to find out the full truth from Charlotte, but now was not the time. Nevertheless, if talking about her dream would help, he would lend an ear.

"What happened?" He asked softly, and gently held her hand.

Charlotte shook her head vigorously. "I can't tell you."

"You begged someone not to kill you," he said more harshly than he intended. He would personally murder anyone who threatened to harm her.

"Ow!" Charlotte squeaked.

James did not realize his grip had tightened around her hand. He loosened it and turned her body so that she looked directly at him.

"You don't need to tell me everything, but you have to let me in, just a little. Someone tried to kill you tonight. I need to know who's after you so they never lay a finger on you again."

Charlotte felt a warmth develop inside her. James was willing to fight her demons. She had never experienced someone taking care of her like this. Yes, Arthur protected her in a brotherly fashion and would defend her honor if required, but he was the bookish sort. She could not imagine him physically fighting for her; it was simply not in his nature.

James, though, was a different story. Charlotte had gotten a taste of his unleashed strength when he accidentally tightened his grip on her hand, and she was utterly intrigued. It distracted her from the nightmare she had just experienced.

"Please tell me who's after you," he pleaded.

Charlotte closed her eyes to collect her thoughts, but that was a mistake.

It all came rushing back.

Dark, beady eyes glared at her while her wrists were shoved against the wall and held in place by a surprisingly strong, masculine hand. A stab of pain jolted through Charlotte's body, and her head jerked painfully against the wall. The door was kicked shut with a thud and then locked with a key in the man's free hand. His lips widened into a snarl, exposing yellowed teeth and fetid breath.

"You have pushed me too far!" His fist thumped next to Charlotte's head for emphasis, which caused her to flinch.

"Do you know what happens to chits who anger me?" Charlotte winced from spittle that landed on her cheek. Her eyes darted around the room and searched for an escape. She twisted her wrists, but they were still pinned to the wall and did not budge.

"You didn't answer me, you worthless nob! I'll do it for you." The pressure on her wrists increased, causing Charlotte to fear they would be crushed.

"They die," her tormentor hissed.

Charlotte reacted with the first action that came to mind and jerked her knee upward into his manhood. He let out a shriek and clutched his crotch, releasing her restraint. Charlotte bolted to the door. The doorknob rattled as she frantically tried to open it.

"You bitch! You're not going anywhere until I'm done with you!" Charlotte glanced over her shoulder before she futilely tugged on the doorknob some more. She saw the man run to his desk and yank the drawer open. Charlotte searched again for an escape and found nothing. She looked back toward the desk, only to find the barrel of a gun moving closer to her.

"Don't kill me!" Charlotte screamed.

She floated in the world of the in-between. She thought she was awake but could not leave the past. The horrific scenes of the *Incident* intruded into her thoughts and would not let her escape.

Her eyes flew open. In the dim light, eyes of silver looked at her with concern.

"Lottie, you're safe. You screamed again about someone trying to kill you."

"Who's Lottie?" Charlotte had to distract herself from the nightmare that was her mind.

"Why you, of course." James looked back at her with a crooked grin on his face that looked oddly familiar. When James was not scowling and did not have a storm brewing in his eyes, he was quite attractive.

"No one has ever called me Lottie. Arthur calls me Charlie, but that's the only nickname I've ever had." She shrugged, trying to ignore what was left unsaid. She did not want to focus on the fact she had never had the chance to be close to anyone besides her brother.

"Well, I've called you Lottie," James replied warmly.

His eyes bored into her, and she thought it was caring she saw in them, and not the pity she was dreading.

Could she confide in James?

She had told Arthur the story of the *Incident*, but no one else.

It was too damning.

Arthur had thought through her predicament and given her a logical solution: marry a man with a title for protection, preferably a duke. This was Arthur's way of comforting her, but it was not enough. She still felt as if she carried an insurmountable burden. Maybe, just maybe, she could tell James about the *Incident*.

He collected her hands into his own and looked at her imploringly. "Someone did something terrible to you. I beg of you, tell me who it is so that I can make sure they never hurt you again."

There it was once more. James was offering her ultimate protection from the past. Charlotte opened her mouth to tell him everything, but before she could start, an image of blood trickling across the floor clouded her vision. Her body tensed.

"What is it?"

Charlotte shook her head, trying to dislodge the picture from her mind. "I can't tell you. I can't tell anyone." The only person she could trust in the world was Arthur, and even that was taking a risk.

One slip of the tongue, and she was headed to the gallows.

No one else could learn of the truth, especially because Charlotte knew in her heart that the man outside her aunt's town house was no coincidence. One day's missteps had enmeshed Charlotte in something bigger, something scarier than she could ever imagine. There was only one thing she knew for sure.

Someone was out to get her.

CHAPTER TWELVE

F our whole days.
 Charlotte was trapped in her bedroom and restless.
After the jarring episode near the mews and her brief stay at
Lord Carrington's town house, James had helped Charlotte
safely back to her aunt's abode. She was able to slip in unnoticed
before the household awakened.

When Bailey came in the morning after the cutthroat's
attack, her lady's maid immediately saw the bandage around
Charlotte's neck. The two decided it would be best to tell her
aunt that Charlotte was ill.

Charlotte now knew the best way to keep Aunt Frances's
attentions at bay. Her aunt had not personally checked on her
once, fearing she would become sick. She had a busy social
schedule to uphold, after all. Due to these necessary obligations,
she instead relied on reports from Bailey.

At first, Charlotte was relieved to have a respite from her
aunt's nagging, but after four long days of confinement, she
would have welcomed her aunt's badgering. She had written
notes to Beatrice, Eleanor, and Bridget, inviting them to visit a
tea shop with her, but she had to cancel with a vague excuse

after she was attacked. Without any sustained distractions, she had too much time to think about the *Incident* and its related events, which made her more anxious about her future. To make matters worse, a certain sable-haired man, whose gray eyes changed as quickly as the wintry sky, invaded her thoughts each time she tried to plan the grand Society marriage she would have with the Duke of Westcliffe.

Charlotte felt her cheeks flush while she sat at the escritoire in her bedroom as she recalled the way James's fingers had deftly brought her to an earthshattering release that evening in the gardens. But Charlotte knew he had not shown her everything. There was more.

She had once asked Arthur what happened between a man and a woman, but his cheeks had flushed just as much as hers, and he would not give her much information. Instead, she had to piece it together by eavesdropping on her brothers and their friends and by reading a lascivious book left behind when they went off to Eton. Yes, there was a whole lot more.

Charlotte tried to banish the Captain from her thoughts and stared at the letter she had avoided opening. She recognized its seal as that of the House of Westcliffe. Charlotte's body was tense while she broke open the wax. She was worried that someone had seen her with James and told the Duke.

Her heartbeat quickened at the thought of the consequences of Westcliffe rescinding his attentions. Her hands trembled while she unfolded the foolscap.

Charlotte skimmed the contents. She had always been a quick reader and let out a sigh of relief. The Duke apologized for missing the past few days' social events due to a family matter.

She was safe.

For now.

A knock on the door sounded.

"Come in," Charlotte called out curiously. She had not seen anyone but Bailey these past few days. Her lady's maid had fortunately procured endless books and even a chessboard to help abate her boredom. Bailey must have thought of something else to occupy Charlotte's time.

The door flew open and three well-dressed ladies marched into her bedroom.

"What a surprise," Charlotte exclaimed. Beatrice, Eleanor, and Bridget surrounded her bed and promptly assessed her condition.

Beatrice, who seemed to be the leader the group, spoke first. "Although we only met briefly, something seemed off in your note canceling our trip to the tea shop. We were all excited to get to know you better. Just as I thought. You're not in fact ill." Her eyes focused on the bandage around her neck.

"Just a minor mishap. All is well," Charlotte responded, trying to sound nonchalant.

"Captain Hughes was right." This time, it was the voice of Bridget. Charlotte shifted to see the timid woman standing with her shoulders back just behind Beatrice. Her voice was bolder than Charlotte expected, given her behavior at the Markham Ball, though it still had a soft, melodic quality. Charlotte tucked away the fact that Bridget seemed more comfortable in an intimate setting with only women present.

"Captain Hughes?" Charlotte asked innocently, hoping she could hide her interest at the mention of his name.

"He's staying at our home as a guest of my brother. When it was mentioned that you were ill, he seemed worried and suggested we check on you. He suspected it wasn't contagious."

"His guess was correct." Charlotte tried to draw them off any scent that would suggest James knew more about what had happened to her.

"Now Charlotte," Eleanor began in her silky voice that held

a constant sense of aristocratic insouciance, "we all have our own secrets. Bridget told us Captain Hughes seemed very concerned about how you fared. Is there anything between you?" She waved her hand dismissively. "We'll not judge."

Charlotte tried to hide the guilty look on her face as the three ladies gazed at her. She knew she did not have to tell them everything about what had transpired with James, but there seemed to be an unspoken expectation that Charlotte reveal at least a tidbit of information. Confiding in these women would perhaps help them all become friends.

Friends?

Charlotte had never had such a relationship with anyone, yet she thought these three ladies who showed concern for her well-being could potentially be called such, if all went well. Charlotte's heart warmed, and she realized she had to trust them if they were to become friends and be considered one another's confidants.

While Charlotte was making the decision on how much to tell the other women, Bridget broke the awkward silence. "Captain Hughes was most insistent I deliver this personally to you," she stated in her unthreatening voice. She procured a letter from her reticule and placed it on the bedside table.

The interlude gave Charlotte enough time to gather her courage and show a degree of vulnerability to them.

"Captain Hughes saved me from some trouble." Charlotte pointed to her neck. "I believe I owe him a great deal."

"Is that all you feel? Gratitude?" Eleanor asked pointedly. She looked at Charlotte with her deceptively lazy eyes.

Charlotte swallowed. She had not revealed much of anything.

Trust.

She had to trust these women. "Perhaps not. To be honest, I don't know what I feel. I can't stop thinking of him. And I have to forget about him, but it's so hard. My betrothal to the Duke will be announced soon."

The ladies nodded with understanding etched on their faces. They too were unwilling female cogs in the constantly spinning wheel of the *ton*.

"Bridget, can you thank Captain Hughes for his concern? I'll read his letter in private so that I can pen an appropriate response. I have to be polite, but then I need to move on."

Charlotte did not trust herself to read the letter in front of the three women. She was afraid her emotions were too muddled at the moment and would be written across her face.

"I'll tell him," Bridget responded. She grinned, which transformed her visage from the sullen look Charlotte had witnessed at the Markham Ball. If one could ignore her sad eyes, Bridget really did have the most angelic appearance.

"There's one additional reason we came to call," Eleanor said.

"Oh?" Charlotte hoped the conversation would shift away from her personal affairs.

Eleanor eased four invitations out of her reticule with a mischievous look in her eyes. "Lady Stanhope's masquerade ball is in three days. It's a deliciously scandalous event that occurs each year during the Season, where all propriety is left at the door. Beatrice and Bridget have already agreed to attend. We thought you'd like to be included as well."

She pulled a separate piece of foolscap from her reticule that was dyed black and had no writing on it. Eleanor smirked, then made eye contact with each of the other ladies in the bedroom. "But it gets better. I haven't told anyone yet that I received a coveted invitation to the black door."

Beatrice and Bridget gasped, and Eleanor's face broke into a triumphant smile. Charlotte eyed them with consternation.

"Um...Eleanor, if you wouldn't mind explaining the *black*

door?" Charlotte's voice hitched at the end, feeling self-conscious and naïve.

"It's absolutely glorious. Only the truly depraved get to cross the black door," Eleanor replied gleefully. Charlotte did not know how to react. She had much more important matters to address, namely the *Incident*, and did not think crossing some forbidden door would be of much help. Charlotte's eyes darted to the two other women to gauge their reactions. Bridget looked down at her feet uncomfortably while Beatrice had a determined look on her face.

"Although Eleanor has procured invitations for all of us," Beatrice explained, "she only has one for the black door. She may be able to get one or two of us past the guard, but not everyone."

Charlotte pondered the invitation. She was soon to be a married woman—a duchess, of all things. Even though she should not take her focus off the *Incident*, it was probably her only chance to attend a masquerade ball. But she had to be careful.

"Thank you for including me. I'd love to get to know you better and attend the masquerade ball. I'm more than happy to avoid the black door and leave the spots open for the rest of you. I have enough scandal I'm fighting at the moment."

Beatrice answered first, "That's very kind of you." She paused. "I may need Eleanor to get me through that door."

Bridget spoke next, "I'll stay at the main masquerade ball with Charlotte. I don't think I have use of the black door either." She seemed as if she was reassuring Charlotte just as much as herself.

Eleanor clapped her hands together. "Wonderful! What fun we'll have! The theme is ancient Greece. I've already put together costumes for Beatrice and Bridget. I can make an outfit for you in no time." Eleanor looked at Charlotte in an assessing manner, mentally making measurements. "Do you have a choice of Greek goddess?"

Charlotte responded with the first one that came to mind. "Persephone."

Eleanor's brows furrowed. "That's a bit depressing, don't you think?"

"I'm being forced into a certain life against my will, just as Persephone was thrust into the Underworld. I think it's an entirely appropriate choice," Charlotte replied dryly.

A worried look crossed Eleanor's face. "I see. I am sorry, Charlotte. I'll make you look like the most beautiful Queen of the Underworld," she offered.

"Thank you. I look forward to it." Charlotte lifted the corners of her mouth in an attempt at a smile, trying to ease the tension she had caused in the room.

Beatrice moved the conversation forward. "Eleanor's grandmother will chaperone the group to make it as proper as possible. Unless you would like Lady Hardwicke to come along."

Charlotte scoffed. "Definitely not, but I appreciate the thought. If my aunt got wind of me attending this ball while being courted by the Duke of Westcliffe, she wouldn't be pleased."

Bridget shrugged her shoulders. "She may understand. I think it's a rite of passage before being married off. My mother asked outright if I was going to be sneaking off to attend, knowing that it always occurred around the same date. When I told her I was considering it, a glazed look came over her face as she remembered her time at the Stanhope Ball while she was a debutante."

The ladies then chitchatted about their costumes for the ball and some Society gossip before the trio said their goodbyes.

The moment the bedroom door closed, Charlotte hastily

opened the letter from James. Her stomach dropped after she read the four words printed in his masculine scrawl.

Same time, same place.

Charlotte penned a response without a second thought.

Yes.

She summoned Bailey to deliver her note to Bridget before she left her aunt's home. Although Charlotte's emotions roiled inside her, she knew she had to see the Captain. She could not get him out of her mind, and she needed some sort of closure before she married the Duke.

She hoped this rendezvous would be enough.

CHAPTER THIRTEEN

James peered into the alleyway behind Lady Hardwicke's town house. He arrived early to ensure all was safe. Even so, he questioned his sanity. He was asking for another catastrophe to happen, but James could not help it.

He had to see Charlotte.

When Lady Bridget mentioned at the breakfast table that Lady Charlotte was ill, he knew why. He prayed she was hiding away to give the wound time to heal; however, he worried she had developed an infection. He needed to know she was well, so he encouraged Lady Bridget to visit her, his letter in tow. He was relieved to learn Charlotte was on the mend.

James had never felt such strong emotions before, and it was entirely unsettling. He fretted constantly about Charlotte's safety and wished he could be with her always for protection. It was not just for her safekeeping though. He wanted to see those cornflower-blue eyes alighting with happiness or her freckled lips smiling in response to something he said.

God, he had even thought he *loved* her.

What a ridiculous notion.

It was a moment of weakness when he was scared she was gravely injured.

For a reason Charlotte would not reveal, she had to marry the Duke of Westcliffe to save herself. James's fists curled. If only she would trust him, he could find a way to assuage the mysterious burden she carried and prevent a forced marriage to the Duke.

Then she could marry me.

He chided his traitorous mind. Even if she was freed of her commitment to the Duke, he would never be good enough for her.

The creaking of the iron gate that led out of Lady Hardwicke's garden broke James's ruminations. He had been so lost in his thoughts of Charlotte he did not even hear her approach him. He had never been this careless in his life. A slip of a woman was making him lose the instincts he had honed from years at sea.

A cloaked figure emerged from the gate, shadows hiding any features.

"Charlotte?" The figure quickly looked from side to side, and then the hood fell back, revealing chestnut hair loosely arranged in a chignon.

"James!" Charlotte walked toward him and threw her arms around his neck. She buried her head in his chest. He was taken aback, but in a pleasant way. He was convinced that she would never want to lay eyes on him again. But here she was, in his arms, and he did not want to let her go. He murmured sweet nothings and rubbed her back tenderly.

She lifted her head to look at him. "I missed you."

He removed his hands from her back and traced her cheekbones. "I've only thought about you. How do you fare?"

"Like I've been locked in my room for four days."

James chuckled. "Your neck is healing?"

"Quite well. Bailey made her mother's poultice, and it has worked wonderfully."

"I'm glad."

"Thank you." She smiled, and he felt for a moment as if he was the luckiest man in the world, until reality reared its ugly head.

"I should have better protected you." His voice came out gruffly while he tried to hide the emotions swelling inside him.

Charlotte's chin lifted in a defiant manner he recognized too well. "Don't blame yourself. I'm not yours to defend."

"But what if I want you to be?"

"I'm afraid that's not possible." A forlorn look crossed her face.

James's gut clenched. He could never compete against a duke, even if he knew a way to get Charlotte out of her bind. If there was no chance of a future between them, he just wanted one night. One night where they did not have to think about Society marriages or criminals or what could never be. One night where they could acknowledge the irresistible pull between them. One night where it was just her and him.

He rubbed her back again. "I know. I just want one night."

Charlotte's eyelids lowered and fluttered. She softly said, "Me, too."

He clasped her hand. "Come with me."

"Oh! Now?" She pulled her hand back and looked up at him.

The side of his mouth quirked up. "It's now or never, Lottie."

"I choose now," she said without a moment's hesitation.

He grabbed her hand and led her through the backstreets to an awaiting hackney. Her hand fit perfectly into his own, just like they were meant to be together.

But they were not.

It was just one night.

Once the driver deposited them near Gabe's home, he led a hooded Charlotte down a few streets until they reached the back of the house. Soon, they were standing before Dawson, who was awaiting their arrival.

"Captain." He bowed his head as if it were entirely normal for him to appear in the town house of Gabe's mistress with an unescorted and unwed lady yet again.

"We're in a much better state than the last time we were here." James attempted levity, which was not a common occurrence for him. Yet, having Charlotte with him made the dismal world suddenly seem brighter. The butler's face remained placid. No, there was a slight twitch at the corner of his lips.

"Your chamber has been prepared."

"Thank you, Dawson."

James led her upstairs to a guest room at a sedate pace, trying not to drag her up the stairs or throw her over his shoulder as he wished to do. They entered and he unclasped her hand. He felt a chill in his core at the sudden loss of contact.

"Does this suit you? I thought we should be in a different bedroom." He looked sheepishly at her, realizing even being in Gabe's town house may be traumatizing. He was sure he would muck something up again. Her eyes swept across the room several times as if to reassure herself. He held his breath.

"It's perfect. I barely remember the house, I was in such a state."

He let out a sigh and took a step closer to her. He did not want to miss a moment. Desire burned in her eyes, much like what he felt. Her tongue ran across her delectable bottom lip nervously. He let out a groan as his cock twitched to life.

"What?" Charlotte asked, suddenly tentative.

"Lottie, you don't understand what you do to me. I want all of you." He took another step closer, so that her cloak brushed up against his trousers. He did not know himself anymore. In the past, his honor would have forbidden him from ever suggesting such a tryst yet again, but she had broken through all his restraint.

She gave a hesitant smile. "We must not waste any time then." He unbuttoned her cloak and helped her out of it. The heavy fabric dropped to the ground with a thud.

"I need to see more of you," he said.

He hastily pulled the bodice down her shoulders. He was so focused on getting her naked that he barely saw her mouth drop open. He spun her around and feverishly undid the ties at the back of her dress. He cursed his hands, which were typically agile, because they felt like blocks while he fumbled with the laces. After what felt like forever, he pivoted her around and took a step back to admire his handiwork. She stood in her short stays and chemise.

Not enough.

He needed to see more.

His patience for another set of laces had entirely dissolved, and he was about to rip open her stays. Before he could pounce, she took a step forward, grabbed his forearms, and gave him a good shake.

"James!"

Suddenly, her face came into focus. Her brow was crinkled, and she looked at him worriedly, the bandage tied around her neck. The bloody wound that was all his fault.

"Are you well?"

"Perfectly well." He ran his hand through his hair. James had never believed in witches, but he wondered if they did exist. He had felt possessed when he frantically disrobed her, unable to control his urges. He never lost control. It was as if she had cast a spell on him. His honor had flown out the window.

"I thought..." Charlotte worried her bottom lip.

"What did you think?"

"That I could see some of you first? Before all this is gone?" She waved her hand at her remaining clothes.

She was an innocent whom he had harmed, and all he wanted to do was ravish her. He knew he was destined for hell—his uncle had reminded him often enough—but even this was low for hm.

"The least I can do is give you what you want." He shrugged off his jacket and dropped it on the floor. Charlotte's eyes followed each of his movements, then focused on his neck. He lifted his hand, trying to understand what drew her attention.

Ah.

"Do you want help?" she asked.

He nodded in response. A grin spread across her face, and she stepped toward him. Charlotte swiftly undid his cravat and threw it to the floor more forcefully than necessary.

"I've been dreaming of unraveling you."

James let out a hearty laugh he did not even recognize. "Is that all you've been dreaming about? *Unraveling* me by taking off my cravat?"

"You're so stuffy all the time!" She paused and tilted her head. "Are you mocking me?"

"I would never. Your innocence is endearing."

A determined look crossed her face. "I'm not as sheltered as you think. Take off your shirt and breeches, so I can look at your cock."

James raised his eyebrows.

"Now," she demanded imperiously.

"Yes, my lady." He lifted off his shirt and stopped before removing his bottoms. This was the Charlotte he knew. She was bold and commanding. An empress presiding over her domain. James wanted little to do with the ruling class, but Charlotte was an exception. An exception that aroused him when she used her haughtiest voice.

An exception to whom he would submit any day.

~

James was glorious.

Charlotte had been intimidated at first, but now she was simply in awe. He stood proud like a statue, though comparing him to a lifeless figure would be a disservice to his beauty. Without a shirt, his shoulders multiplied in size and revealed a well-defined chest, dusted with dark hair. If he lay down, she was sure she could balance a glass of wine on his muscular abdomen. Below his navel, a trail of dark hair led to his nether regions, which were frustratingly still covered by his breeches. She had clearly ordered those to be removed, but she would demand he continue disrobing in a moment. First, she must finish perusing what was available. Ah yes, she had not inspected the strong arms that had apparently carried her the night she was attacked.

She found his right hand, which gripped the top of his breeches, apparently awaiting her command. It was an extension of a sinewy right arm that must have developed from his years at sea. His left arm—

The warm feelings that had coiled in her most private area abruptly disappeared.

His left arm had been behind his back, but now it rested at his side. And it was hideously marked. This arm was marred by thick, fibrous scars that left dark-brown markings over its entirety and gave it the appearance of a gnarled tree trunk.

Her eyes darted to his face. Gone was the brief glimpse of levity she had witnessed when he had teased her, and back was his customary scowl. His gaze was unwavering, and she knew he dared her to dwell on his injuries.

Now was not the time.

She licked her lips and forced her perusal to resume. She would have to come back to those scars later, though she hurt for him and the pain he must have endured. She needed to distract herself. Her attention was captured by the hungry look in his eyes, which had replaced his challenging glare. It gave her a sense of power she had never experienced before—to be desired.

"Off," she ordered, and pointed to his breeches.

He raised his eyebrows and smirked. "You're awfully demanding."

She lifted her chin and responded in her most supercilious tone, "James, I will not ask *twice*."

His smirk spread into a full grin that lit up his stoic face. He was breathtakingly handsome when he allowed himself even an ounce of lightheartedness. "I'll remove everything as you command, but I need to pleasure you first."

"Oh?" Charlotte replied before she could continue her domineering persona. She tried to understand what he meant. She thought her experience with him in the gardens had been an aberration. Whenever she overheard her brothers and their friends talk, no one ever mentioned pleasuring the woman. Before he could answer, she stepped toward him and dropped to her knees and reached for the fall front of his breeches.

"This is what's supposed to happen first," she stated with bravado.

James's strong hands gripped her wrists and stopped her from proceeding.

"No, you're a lady." He pulled her to her feet, causing her to lose her balance. She fell into his chest and her fingers splayed out on his bare, muscular skin to catch herself. His chest hair tingled her fingertips.

"It's my duty to pleasure you." His head dipped down, and he captured her mouth. He kissed her with such fervor that she could only open her own mouth in response. His salty, sea-breeze scent enveloped her. His tongue tangled with hers. After the initial shock, she eagerly responded to his passionate kisses. She stood on her toes and wrapped her hands around the back of his neck, trying to bring him closer. His mouth paused their ministrations. She was about to object, but then she felt his lips move down the non-bandaged portion of her neck. His evening stubble heightened the sensation.

His hands had been rubbing her upper arms tenderly, but now, his right hand reached down to her buttock and pulled her closer. She felt his straining member pushing into her abdomen, causing her to squeeze her thighs together as that odd, tingling feeling she had also felt in the gardens heightened.

He lifted his head for a moment and murmured into her ear, "Hold on to me." She tightened her grip around his neck, and he effortlessly scooped her up. She wrapped her legs around his hips for support and let out a squeal while he strode over to the bed. Giddiness swept through her, and her heart raced in anticipation.

Wanton.

She felt wanton, but in this moment, she did not care. He gently placed her down on the counterpane. Time seemed to slow as he carefully unlaced her short stays, savoring each moment, his frenetic actions gone. She wiggled her shoulders to help him ease her out of the stays, leaving her covered in just a chemise. His eyes intently scanned her body, darkening with desire. She sat up and moved onto her knees, never breaking eye contact with him. She raised her arms, and he lifted the chemise over her head.

Charlotte heard his sharp intake of breath from beneath the fabric. When she emerged, she found him looking at her as if he were a starved man seeing food for the first time in days. Her nipples puckered from the chill of the room and the longing in his eyes. She was stark naked, but instead of feeling vulnerable and exposed, she felt treasured, and most importantly, safe.

"You're the most beautiful woman I've ever seen," James said with reverence. She was even better than what he had dreamed.

And he dreamed of her every night.

The frantic need to strip her bare had subsided, and he had allowed himself to relish each moment of removing the rest of her clothing.

He only had one night, after all.

And Charlotte calmed him.

The restlessness that plagued him was at bay when she was near.

His empress knelt on the bed, waiting for him without a stitch of clothing. Her hair was restricted in a chignon, but he would fix that. He took in the rest of her perfection.

He winced. Almost perfection.

His stomach dropped as his gaze flickered to the bandage around her neck.

He swallowed and focused on the rest of Lottie. His eyes found her freckled lips, swollen from his ravishment, which were waiting to be attended to once again. He had imagined where else Lottie had freckles, and he was not disappointed. Light ones dotted her shoulders, which he had glimpsed when she was dressed in her ball gowns. But there were more, and they were in the most delectable of places. His mouth watered as he stared at the freckles that dotted the areolas of her well-shaped breasts. He wanted to suck those nipples until Lottie came apart in his arms. His eyes traveled to her trim waist that widened into sensual hips, and then the thatch of dark curls that covered his ultimate destination. He climbed onto the bed and placed his arms on either side of Lottie.

"You're mine," he said.

"Yes," she responded, then licked her tempting lips. James crashed into her mouth yet again. He oscillated between losing all control around this woman, and having a sense of calm. He pulled back and yanked the pins out of her hair, throwing them onto the floor. Her wavy, chestnut mane fanned out over the pillow. He took a handful and twirled the silky strands around his finger.

"Magnificent." He released her hair and dipped his head over her breast. His tongue circled around her already hard nipple. With each swipe of his tongue, it hardened further. Lottie let out a moan, and his cock strained against his still-fastened breeches. Her bottom wiggled against the bed. She was restless.

He was going to fix that.

CHAPTER FOURTEEN

C harlotte was overwhelmed by sensation. Shocks shot from her nipples to her core, leaving a needy urge in their wake that begged to be alleviated. She jerked her hips toward James and sought the release she had experienced in the gardens. She had always been unsure of herself, but tonight she was pushing all those insecurities aside and focusing on the present. This was the only night she had with him. She wanted to cherish every minute of it so she could recall these sacred memories when she was lying alone in her bed as the Duchess of Westcliffe.

James's lips moved from her breasts down to her abdomen. His calloused fingertips massaged her hips, heightening the feeling. He paused at her navel and tickled it with his tongue for a moment. She shifted her hips even more. The wretched man was teasing her. He needed to go lower.

"Eager, are you?" James taunted with mischief in his eyes.

"I want more," Charlotte hissed through her teeth. Once he had started to ravish her body, any thoughts of trying to pleasure him first had fled her mind and all she could focus on was finding the same release as the gardens.

"Can you be more specific?"

"Lower," she demanded.

"You nobs get so upset when your orders aren't obeyed." His lips brushed below her navel, then hovered just above her curls.

"Lower, dammit!"

His eyebrows shot up and a boyish grin crossed his face. "You're insistent, my little empress, but I still need more guidance. Do you want me to touch your cunny?"

"Yes!"

"I want to hear you say it."

Her hips writhed underneath James. "Touch my cunny, now," she demanded.

"With pleasure."

James spread her folds and slowly licked her most private area. His pace quickened. The pulsation in her body intensified with each lap of his tongue, and tingling burrowed deeper inside her. Involuntarily, her hips thrust up toward his mouth, seeking more pressure. Her moans were a mixture of pleasure and frustration. After the tryst in the gardens, she had replayed the night over and over again in her mind. She reasoned that the earth-shattering explosion she felt in her body was in fact *the little death*. And she was chasing that same elusive feeling once again.

"I want you to look at me when you come undone." She whimpered as his gray eyes lost their teasing glint and instead stared back at her with wicked intent. Seeing him gaze at her with his mouth hovering over her sex was the most erotic image Charlotte could ever imagine. It made the pressure inside her build more quickly until she was almost bursting. But it was not quite enough. Something was holding her back. Her chest heaved as she looked at him, her breasts rising and falling rapidly.

"Relax. I'm going to finish you." He ducked his head into

her curls once more and found the nub at the top of her folds. He rapidly swirled his tongue on the most sensitive part of her sex and inserted two fingers into her wet entrance. Before she could overthink what was happening, the pressure inside her reached its peak and everything shattered.

Charlotte's vision went black, and stars flashed behind her eyelids. Her whole body tensed up as ripples of pleasure cascaded from her core to her extremities. She let out cry after cry, as the most wonderful sensations pulsated through her. She distantly felt his tongue lick her pearl while waves of ecstasy continued to overwhelm her body. She lost all sense of time. When the sensations finally subsided, her body went limp, and her mind became blissfully blank.

She remained in repose and savored the feeling of being absolutely spent. When she eventually opened her eyes, James lay on his side, head resting in his hand. He looked at her adoringly. "How do you feel?"

"Amazing," she responded serenely. His face lit up in a genuine smile. With his chiseled chest bared and his right arm muscle on full display, he was stunning. His left arm was conspicuously draped behind his back.

"I'm not done with you yet."

"Oh?"

Left arm forgotten, James hopped off the bed and opened the fall of his breeches with both hands. He slid them off, leaving him in his smallclothes. He then shimmied out of them and threw the undergarments on the floor. He stood at the side of the bed for her perusal.

Her heart fluttered and her cheeks flushed as her gaze traveled from his defined abdomen to his enormous, straining member. It protruded from his body proudly with its veins pulsating. With the scars on his arm and his hulking size, he exuded power and strength. He looked like a virile, ancient god ready for battle. A throbbing reemerged in her core as her eyes remained fixated on his cock.

She wanted him to plunder her.

James climbed onto the bed and crawled toward her. He then positioned his body on top of hers. His lips touched her own, and she could taste the salty and musky flavor of her own juices. As he tenderly kissed her, she felt the hardness of his cock near the entrance to her folds.

"You're so wet for me," he murmured. He took his member in hand and rubbed it at her entrance, coating the tip in the fluids that rushed from her sex.

"Yes," she moaned. She pushed her hips farther toward him. She understood the general idea of what would happen next. His face appeared tense, and the muscles strained in his neck as he held himself over her, waiting to enter. She wanted him so badly, though she did not know how all of him would fit inside her. She was not a petite woman, but nevertheless, he seemed so...big.

"Are you ready?"

She nodded, not able to speak further. She was awash with anticipation.

"God, Lottie, I love you," James confessed, and thrust his member inside her. She let out a cry as pain suddenly shot through her body, and the muscles of her sex clenched down.

He stopped moving abruptly and his eyes widened. "You're a virgin?"

Charlotte grimaced while her muscles tried to dispel him from her body. "Yes. Of course, I am."

"But you were going to suck my cock," he responded, as he held his body still.

"So?"

"Dammit, Lottie. I didn't mean to hurt you." He withdrew from her body and hovered above her.

"I still want you." Although there was an initial stab of pain when he penetrated, she felt a worse void after he pulled himself back. Her body was still screaming for him.

"I'm sorry," he mumbled, and looked at her imploringly.

"Take me properly," she said definitively.

He kissed her again. His tongue slipped inside her mouth, dancing with her own. He toyed with her nipples and caused them to peak. He then took his time tracing his hands over her body.

"Are you ready?" he asked gingerly.

"Yes," she said.

He closed his eyes briefly as if saying a silent prayer then opened them, searching her face. Seeming satisfied with what he saw, he eased his member into her sex gently and kissed her lips. He pushed farther. She felt a twinge of discomfort as he continued, but also a sense of fullness. It made her feel that he was the piece of her life she had been missing. Once he was to the hilt, she let out a sigh as her body adjusted to his girth. Her legs instinctively wrapped themselves around his hips to accommodate.

"You feel so good."

"Is this it?" she asked, confused.

He smiled against her lips. "We're only getting started, love."

He withdrew, and she whimpered in protest. He pushed forward and repeated the motion, silencing any of her qualms. Instead, she let out a gasp as new sensations assaulted her core. Her hips moved in rhythm with James's, seeking a deeper connection. He thrust more vigorously. He cupped her buttocks to deepen the penetration, and she let out a cry as he found a spot of pleasure she never knew existed.

"James," she moaned, unable to form any other coherent words. Their slick bodies moved together in a rhythm as old as time, while the moisture from their heated passion formed lubrication at her pearl. As James pulled her hips toward him, his thrusts stimulated her pearl while continuing to drive into the pleasure spot in her sex. A deep pressure built inside her core, and this time, she was so overwhelmed she did not even try to fight it. Suddenly, she shattered and screamed his name while her body shook in ecstasy. She felt her sex clamp down on his member, and she trembled. Her back arched, and her heels dug into his back as waves of pleasure reverberated through her body until her voice became hoarse from yelling.

"Lottie!" James shouted in the background. Her body had calmed, and her eyelids fluttered closed. He fiercely removed himself from her sex. The orgasm had wiped Charlotte of all her energy. She watched in a detached fashion while he released a warm, white liquid onto her thigh. She did not even flinch.

Her mind felt blank and muddled at the same time. She blinked several times, trying to fight the drowsiness that had overtaken her. He sat on the edge of the bed with his back to her. His hands rested on his thighs to support his body, and his shoulders rose and fell quickly, surely trying to catch his breath.

She had never experienced something so amazing in her life, despite the confusion regarding her virginity. She would think about that later. Her brain slowly started to work again and fought against the sleepiness. Three words dug their way into her consciousness.

I love you.

James had said he loved her. Was that what she was experiencing? Was love not wanting to ever let someone go? Was love a deep and inexplicable connection one felt with someone else?

It must be.

But love was not for her. Feelings were fickle and could not be trusted. They would not save her from the gallows.

Only one man could.

And it was not James.

James turned to face Lottie as his breathing slowed. Her compelling eyes were glazed over, their lids heavy with satisfaction and exhaustion. His mouth quirked into a smile. He had just had the most magnificent night of his life. Although he had tried to be careful while in the Royal Navy, he had had his share of women before tonight. Nothing could equal what he had just shared with her. All of his other sexual experiences paled in comparison. Those times were simply the joining of bodies for pleasure. With Lottie, it was the joining of body, mind, and soul.

James did not know how he could ever let her go. One night was not enough. He wanted Lottie forever. He had also just taken her virginity, bastard that he was. He'd thought her an innocent, but when she got down on her knees to suck his cock, his mind questioned this assumption. That kernel of doubt was enough to justify his jaded mind he could take her. And yet, somehow he did not regret it. He thought he had honor, but when it came to Lottie, he could not control his overwhelming need to possess her. Emotion furled within James to think of any other man ever touching his Lottie. He would never let that happen.

"Come here," he coaxed. He eased himself onto his back and held out his arm. He scooped Lottie into his body. She rested her head on his chest and snuggled into his side.

"I don't want this to ever end," he whispered, and rubbed her back lovingly. She let out a sigh.

"Let's rest for now," he said. He kissed the top of her head and inhaled the smell of honeysuckle, jasmine, and sex, hoping to commit it to memory for the rest of his days. Once he raised his head, he looked down to see that Lottie had already fallen asleep. He closed his eyes, and within seconds he fell into the deepest slumber he had ever experienced.

Some time later, he awoke to find Lottie with her hands on his chest, looking around the room in a dazed manner. Her silky locks tumbled over her body in the most delightful way. She caught his gaze and averted her eyes while a sheepish smile emerged on her face.

"Hi," she said in an embarrassed tone. His cock twitched to life while he took in her beauty. All he wanted to do was repeat their passionate lovemaking, but he had never bedded a virgin before. He was afraid Lottie would be sore. Plus, there was something he wanted to talk to her about, and he would need all his willpower to focus on the task at hand. She distracted him entirely too much.

"Are you in pain?" he said.

She caught her bottom lip with her teeth and a thoughtful expression crossed her face. "A little, but it's not too bad. It's just...different."

He rubbed her back. "I'm glad." His brow furrowed. "I'm sorry. I didn't realize you were a virgin."

"I don't understand why you thought I wasn't."

He ran his hand through his hair nervously. "At first, I was sure of it. You kissed with such naïve abandon. But then you went on your knees, and I questioned that. No innocent miss should know such things."

Her mouth opened in the most adorable O. "I have four older brothers. I would always tag along behind them, even though the older ones would ignore me. I overheard a lot." Lottie's cheeks flushed. "I thought the kneeling part was what a woman did to a man before they, um, joined."

He felt the weight of Lottie supporting herself on his chest and chuckled. "It's something that can be done between a man and woman, but it's usually a doxy. I would never expect it of a lady."

The flush now traveled down her neck and her shoulders. "Oh! But you had your mouth...down there." Lottie sat back on her knees and waved her hands toward the lower portion of her body.

He shrugged. "I suppose I did, but I wanted to pleasure you. And it was not entirely selfless. I dreamed of licking the juices off your cunny."

"Oh!" she exclaimed again with a slap on his chest. "You scoundrel!"

"But did you like it?" he teased.

She bit her plump, lower lip and released it. He almost exploded with desire. "Well, yes."

"Then it was entirely worth it."

She shook her head in disbelief. "You're incorrigible."

He rubbed Lottie's back once more and thought how to broach the subject he had been trying to avoid.

He cleared his throat. "There is something I wanted to talk to you about."

Lottie moved off him and sat up, awaiting the news. Except she had forgotten she was stark naked. He swallowed and took in her pert nipples and intimate hair. God, he could even see her pearl.

"You distract me." His eyes swept over her bare form.

"What...oh!" Lottie scrambled underneath the counterpane. She propped a pillow against the headboard and sat against it while tucking the fabric under her armpits to provide coverage. She nodded once she was settled.

"I'm in London, because I work for my childhood friend, Jack Doherty. He has a business empire in Birmingham, and I oversee shipments at different ports in England and Wales. One of our flax shipments from Ireland was lost at sea, and I had to come to London to receive the reimbursement from the insurance company. I stopped in Shrewsbury to talk to the mill owner and to meet with our man of business in the west, Roberts." He saw Lottie's eyes widen in response to his story.

He continued, "I needed to get a copy of the shipping account ledgers to bring to the insurance company." He paused. Lottie was a lady. He should not share the next portion of the story, but he felt as if he needed to warn her. She was made of sterner stuff than other women of the *ton*. "The day I went to retrieve the documents, Roberts had been murdered in broad daylight by a woman who said her name was Mrs. Gibson."

Lottie let out a gasp. He took her hand to reassure her before he went on. It was ice cold. He had hoped she would be less affected by his story, but it was understandable that she was shocked. He rubbed her hand. "The magistrate is holding on to Roberts's ledgers until the murderer is identified and caught. I need to find out who killed Roberts so I can get the money from the insurance company. I'm stuck in London until this person can be found. With the help of Gabe, there are Bow Street Runners working on the case."

Lottie would not meet his eyes and instead stared at a spot on the counterpane. He was not surprised. He had just told her disturbing news. He continued to rub her frigid hand. "Since the investigation started, I learned that Roberts was an evil man. He managed the affairs of many noble families. When the Runners went through his ledgers, they determined he was skimming money from their accounts. I wanted to warn you, because your family was listed as one of his clients."

Lottie finally looked at him. Was that shock? Fear? "Thank you for letting me know," she replied softly.

"I'm sorry to give you such alarming news, but I didn't want to neglect to tell you what Roberts may have done to your family."

Her hand still felt cold, but she squeezed his back with what he thought was reassurance.

"There is one more thing. It seems that Roberts went by other names, aliases if you will. The Runners discovered that he previously worked for the Duke of Westcliffe under the name Nott. He's not a good man, and I don't know if His Grace is subject to any of his sinister dealings."

Her hand tightened further around his own as a multitude of emotions flashed across her face. But the final emotion was one James did not expect: anger.

She ripped her hand away from him and tore the counter-pane from her body. She jumped out of the bed, still naked, and gathered her clothing before hastily slipping it on.

"Lottie?" he queried, perplexed by her reaction. She ignored him and pulled on her short stays, tying them clumsily.

"What are you doing?"

She marched over to him and pointed her finger at his chest. "Was this all part of your plan to get me into bed with you? Force us to wed and take my dowry? You clearly are in need of money. I bet you wanted my aunt to catch us in the gardens." He could see her shoulders visibly shaking.

"We just have one night," she said in a mocking voice. "One night for you to take my virginity and make me tainted goods for the Duke. Well, guess what? I'll never marry you. And no man will ever get their hands on my dowry, because it's protected. So find some other virgin to fuck and force her hand."

James jumped out of bed without a stitch of clothing, fury rising within him. "Are you mad? I don't want your dowry. I want you."

He locked eyes with Charlotte. He had to make her understand. "Lottie, I love you. I would never do anything to hurt you.

Someone is after your life, and you're accusing *me* of being the bad man?" She lifted her head defiantly. "I'm just trying to help. You won't tell me who's trying to kill you. What are you hiding from me?"

"I don't believe anything you said," she said. Charlotte tugged on her dress without lacing it.

"I laid bare my heart and soul, and this is what I get for it."

She threw on her cloak and its hood. Without a word, she turned and left.

CHAPTER FIFTEEN

It had been three days of angst since Charlotte left Lord Carrington's town house and wove through the backstreets with a mixture of emotions. She worried the Bow Street Runners would uncover her identity as Mrs. Gibson, which placed a pressure on her to marry the Duke of Westcliffe as soon as possible. She was also upset that James had used her. During her entire journey, she had the odd sensation she was being followed and would pause every so often with her pistol raised before concealing it in her cloak and moving on. Eventually, she made her way back to her aunt's home. Once she was safely in her bedroom, Charlotte allowed all the emotions that had raced through her mind while navigating the backstreets to rush forth. She collapsed onto her bed and cried until she reached a point of utter exhaustion and fell asleep. The nightmares of the *Incident* returned, and she suffered through a tortuous slumber.

Charlotte rose from bed the next day with the sun high in the sky, but it went largely unnoticed aside from Bailey, since the household still believed her to be ill. James's revelations gutted Charlotte, and she fell into a melancholy she could not break. Although her group of friends visited and tried to cheer her up, she preferred to stay in her bedroom, which left her alone with her thoughts for too long.

She felt deceived by James, and it was akin to a dagger being thrust into her heart. He just wanted to take her virginity and force her to marry him. He was after her dowry—which was secretly protected by her grandfather from his grave—and no better than the debt-ridden lords who had pursued her.

Charlotte picked at the food on her tray while she sat by the fireplace and stared into the flames. Soon Bailey would come to prepare her for the masquerade ball. The costume Eleanor had put together in mere days hung in her armoire, ready for an evening of revelry, which no longer excited her. She did not know how she could ever trust another person or her own judgement again.

A knock on the door broke her maudlin thoughts, and soon Bailey was standing next to her.

"Lady Charlotte, are you ready to dress for the ball?"

"I suppose," Charlotte responded dismally.

Bailey marched over to the chair in which Charlotte was seated and crossed her arms. "Milady, I realize you may have me sacked for this, but you need to pull yourself together. You can't have some no-good man ruin you like this."

Charlotte raised her eyes warily as Bailey loomed over her with a stern expression that she must use for her errant, younger siblings.

"Up with you. Otherwise, I'll be getting you with a bucket of cold water. It's what gets the little ones out of bed."

Charlotte did not take Bailey seriously until her lady's maid returned with a bucket of water and eyed her with a look that would make any governess proud. Although Charlotte had sunk rather low, she still had her pride, and she was not going to let Bailey embarrass her.

Charlotte stood abruptly. "Fine!"

Bailey curtseyed with a glint in her eye and went to the armoire to retrieve the night's costume. Before helping her dress, Bailey eyed her neck where her wound had scabbed.

"It's healing."

She nodded in response.

Bailey coaxed her out of her dress and into the black tunic Eleanor created for her Persephone costume, to represent her life in the Underworld after Hades captured her. It draped at her shoulders, leaving her arms bare. Since Persephone was picking narcissus flowers when she was kidnapped, Eleanor provided a beautiful bouquet of daffodils for Charlotte to carry. The flowers were at the end of their season, but Eleanor had been relentless and found enough that were still in bloom. In order to cover Charlotte's scar, Bailey wrapped the wound with a bandage, then covered her neck loosely with vines as a sort of necklace to further symbolize that Persephone was in the garden prior to being captured.

"Sit down, milady," Bailey urged, so she could arrange Charlotte's hair. She sat at the vanity and turned her face to the left and to the right, noting her sunken eyes in the mirror. She looked awful, but she supposed the one saving grace would be that it was a masquerade ball, and no one would see the sorry state of her visage.

After Bailey created a braided crown with her hair, she handed her the remaining accoutrement to her costume, a black veil. Charlotte had argued with Eleanor that a black mask would suffice, but her friend would not relent. Persephone had to appear in mourning.

"Chin up, milady."

Charlotte forced a smile onto her face. "Thank you, Bailey."

"I will make sure no one is about." She waited for Bailey to check that the servants' stairway was clear.

The Duke had written that he would be at the Rowley Ball

the following night. He had given Charlotte the extra time she had requested before announcing their betrothal, but Charlotte knew she could not waste any more time given that the Bow Street Runners were searching for Mrs. Gibson.

She should have been savoring her last night as an unattached lady, excited for the scandalous masquerade ball. Instead, all she wanted to do was curl up into a ball and never leave her room.

Bailey's head popped into her doorway to let her know all was clear. Charlotte threw on her cloak and its hood, then made her way down the empty servants' stairs. She traversed the back garden and paused at the iron gate. She checked her surroundings. Her heart pounded in her chest as memories of the night of her attack raced through her mind. She glanced around nervously while trying to calm her nerves. After ensuring no one was lurking about, she walked toward the end of the alleyway until she reached the intersection with the main thoroughfare, where an unmarked carriage awaited. The door swung open, and the vehicle's lamp illuminated the blonde hair of Eleanor.

A footman helped Charlotte into the carriage, and she lowered her hood.

"You look divine!" Eleanor clapped her hands together. She and Beatrice looked at Charlotte expectantly.

"Your costume is perfect!" echoed Beatrice.

Charlotte smiled, though it did not reach her eyes. "You worked wonders, Eleanor. Thank you."

After Eleanor's initial excitement dissipated, her smile turned into a frown. "But you don't feel well, do you?" Eleanor glanced at an older woman snoring in the corner, whom Charlotte had not noticed.

"I'm afraid I do not."

Eleanor reached over and grabbed Charlotte's hands. "Let's

make the best of it. Bridget will meet us there. She sent a last-minute note that her brother found out she was going to sneak out, so he insisted on accompanying her. At least, the ball may be a distraction."

Charlotte nodded in acquiescence. Beatrice and Eleanor chattered about who they thought would be at the event and the scandal of it all. Soon, her heart raced, courtesy of being in a carriage and the *Incident*, and she searched the vehicle's interior for an object on which to focus. The woman's snoring provided a rhythmic distraction, and she stared at the rise and fall of her chest. She counted each of her breaths. Blood-red crept into the periphery of her vision, and she tried to push it away on her own, but could not.

Against her will, James barged into her thoughts and shoved the *Incident* aside like a vengeful marauder. As much as she wanted to hate him, she could not forget the moments of tenderness he had shown her, or how he had been her champion. She wanted to move on as she had intended, but she could not.

Her heart was broken.

Yes, she had to admit herself James had stolen her heart. But he had shattered it with his deception, which was the worst kind of pain. He had made her believe he cared about her. Then he had used her trust to sway her against marrying the Duke and position himself as the better choice. All for the dowry he thought would be his.

Through Bridget, James had sent letters to her since their tryst, begging for forgiveness. Yet, she could not trust him. It was all a façade. No one outside of Arthur and her grandfather had ever truly seen her, and she had been a fool to think James was any different. His apologies were false words to convince her to come running back to him.

The utter betrayal Charlotte felt from James exhausted her. Despite being in a carriage, she dozed off and before she knew it, she was awakened by her friends as the carriage slowed down in Richmond. An eight-mile journey had passed with her no closer to resolving her tumultuous feelings. The only positive was that the dominance of James in her thoughts had overridden the panic associated with carriage rides.

A movement in the corner caught her attention. The older woman opened her eyes. They mirrored Eleanor's, except for the wrinkled lines at the creases, showing a life full of laughter. Silver hair peeked out of her aubergine turban. The woman looked around the interior of the carriage, and her eyes rested on Charlotte.

"You must be Pulverbatch's daughter, Charlotte."

"How rude of me!" Eleanor interjected. "Charlotte, this is my grandmother, Aurelia Balfour, the Dowager Countess of Downham."

"It is an honor to meet you, my lady." Charlotte bowed her head in deference.

"Posh, no need to be so formal. You can call me Nan, like these two hellions," she said with a wicked gleam in her eyes as she looked at Eleanor and Beatrice.

"Oh Nan, you're the dearest. Without you, we would not be able to attend these events that are absolutely necessary in our education for navigating Society," Eleanor gushed.

The Dowager Countess clicked her tongue. "If you would have told me twenty years ago that I would be going to a Stanhope masquerade ball at my age, I would have told you that you were fit for Bedlam."

Eleanor's usual lazy smile widened into a grin. Her grandmother shook her head. "This one is trouble. God save the man you marry. He'll be following you around like a puppy dog," the Dowager Countess chided warmly. She then turned to Charlotte with a stern face. "Charlotte, you missed my diatribe earlier, but I told these young ladies that they must behave themselves. It's going to be tempting to engage in all sorts of wicked new moments that could lead to debauchery. You must show restraint. And I'm serious. You cannot ruin yourselves. I'm only allowing Eleanor's attendance, because she would have sneaked out anyway." She paused and lifted her eyebrows. "Even if I locked her in her room and had footmen stationed at all windows and doors. She has proven in the past to be a clever prisoner." Eleanor's grandmother pursed her lips.

Her granddaughter did not appear phased. "Now, Nan, you were once a debutante at the Stanhope Masquerade Ball."

"Ages ago, but some things never change. That is the reason I'm warning you to behave. Over the years, I've seen ladies ruined at this event, so don't put your futures at risk. I saw that black door invitation."

Eleanor raised her golden eyebrows in a similar manner to her grandmother. "No need to worry. I did just fine in Italy under Aunt Lydia's care. This masquerade ball, even the black door, must pale in comparison."

"You're going to be the death of me," her grandmother responded with a huff.

The carriage came to a stop and the door opened before the conversation could continue. The group of women donned their disguises.

"Don't stray too far," the Dowager Countess chided while they were still in the carriage.

The footman helped the ladies out of the equipage. Eleanor led the way, followed by Beatrice, then Charlotte, and finally, the Dowager Countess. Although Charlotte still felt melancholy, she could sense the energy and excitement pulsating in the queue of guests who waited to enter the ball. The queue, which snaked along the circular drive, slowly moved forward. In the middle of the drive, fittingly, a marble statue of Poseidon loomed over the guests with his trident. Torches lit the walkway of the stately home, allowing her to admire all the costumes as they stood in line. She forced herself to focus on the present with the hope it would distract her from the past.

When she was confined to her bedroom recovering and her friends had visited, Eleanor had regaled them about her vision for the ancient Greece costumes. Looking at their ensembles, Charlotte saw Eleanor had really outdone herself, and the designs outshone those of the other guests awaiting entry into the ball.

Beatrice was dressed as Aphrodite, the goddess of love and beauty, and donned a scandalously draped tunic that revealed the crease between her breasts. She wore red roses in her upswept hair and held a golden apple in her hand. Her costume was accented by a golden mask, which matched her earrings and numerous bracelets.

Eleanor chose the mischievous Até, goddess of delusion, rash decisions, and folly, who was known to ruin men. She was dressed in a black tunic with a black bandana, in which she had cut out holes for the eyes. She carried a small basket that contained irregular pieces of plaster and had a black cloth wrapped around her wrists. Blood-red rubies adorned her throat and ears.

The Dowager Countess wore one of her typical gowns for evening events, but held an aubergine mask adorned with feathers up to her face with a mask stick.

"Eleanor, the costumes are all stunning. What's in your basket? And what are those strips of black cloth around your wrists?" Charlotte asked.

The side of Eleanor's mouth quirked up. "I'm so glad you asked. I took some artistic liberties. These are my knuckle-bones." She jangled her basket. "The ancient Greeks gambled with them, so I thought this would be the perfect vice to lead unsuspecting men down the path of evil." Eleanor toyed with the cloth wrapped around one wrist. "As for this fabric," her grin widened, "there are many possibilities. It can be used to blindfold someone or tie someone's hands together, or even better, tie someone to something. All types of folly."

Although she was trying to forget her night with James, he had opened her eyes to what was possible with a man. From the look on Eleanor's face, Charlotte was pretty sure her friend referred to a particular style of bedroom activity. Beatrice's eyebrows were furrowed as she mulled over Eleanor's accoutrements in confusion.

"I heard that, Eleanor!" The Dowager Countess glared at her granddaughter. "I need to tie *you* to the carriage and not let you enter the ball," she threatened.

"Nan, you know I would never actually do any of this..." Her grandmother scowled and Charlotte was close enough to hear Eleanor mutter under breath "...and get caught."

Charlotte tried to ease the tension by turning to Beatrice. "What inspired your costume as Aphrodite?"

The moment she finished her question, she realized this topic was a mistake.

The usually unshakeable Beatrice looked down as her cheeks flushed bright red. "It's nothing," she murmured.

"Thanks to Eleanor, I think we have the best costumes," Charlotte offered. Eleanor, Beatrice, and her grandmother all nodded in response. Charlotte was thankful Eleanor rambled on about improving costumes. Finally, the group reached the door and gave their invitations to the costumed man who permitted entry. He wore a white linen cloak with a white mask, which provided a stark contrast to the dark-red brick of the mansion.

The women entered the stately home into a grand foyer, outfitted with a black-and-white checkerboard floor and a stunning black-marble fireplace adorned with gold accents. It was already a crush of tunics and cloaks of all colors, though predominantly white. There was more flesh on display than Charlotte had ever seen in one place.

Eleanor led the way, and they wound through the crowd with the Dowager Countess bringing up the rear. The masked men and women were in closer proximity to one another than was socially acceptable. They spoke with their heads bowed, but Charlotte did not witness any lascivious acts. She had been expecting a far more shocking affair, and was disappointed.

As they wove their way deeper into the house toward the ballroom, Charlotte detected a distinct scent in the air. Her stomach turned in response. Now that she was no longer an innocent, she knew it was the smell of sex. It immediately thrust James into her mind. More specifically, a naked James. She tried with all her might to dispel these traitorous images.

The group entered the ballroom befitting a country manor, with ceiling-high windows draped with rich brocade draperies and multiple chandeliers illuminating the space. Musicians played in the background, and Charlotte witnessed the source of that debauched smell. Scantily clad couples danced in abandon, their bodies gyrating to the music in a fashion Charlotte had never witnessed before. Some pairs passionately kissed while others...oh! Others fondled the private areas of their partners as if they were the only ones in the room. Her mouth fell open after she caught one man's hand stroking between the legs of a masked women while her head was thrown back in ecstasy.

The Dowager Countess had moved right behind Charlotte, and she heard her mutter, "Some things never change."

Charlotte whipped around. "Has it always been like this?"

"Yes, my dear. This is what happens when Society is too restricted. Everyone's just bursting at the seams to break free." The Dowager Countess shook her head and waved her hand in front of her, as if presenting a tableau. Charlotte rotated back around. Even though she was more knowledgeable about what the couples were doing, she was still utterly scandalized by the open displays of affection. Yet, she had no idea of the identity of the individuals, which she supposed emboldened them to act in such a way in the midst of a crowded ballroom.

Eleanor paused at the periphery of the dance floor and turned to face the others. She had a wide grin on her face, and her arms spread widely. "This is it."

Charlotte heard the Dowager Countess mumble under her breath before they formed a small circle around their fearless leader and awaited further instructions. Beatrice stood across from Charlotte with a calculating look on her face as she scanned the crowd. Between choosing Aphrodite and searching through the guests as if she planned an assignation, Beatrice was acting quite uncharacteristically of her usual decorous self.

"Let's grab drinks and find Bridget," Eleanor said. The women made their way to the refreshment table where there was a punch bowl. Charlotte was not used to serving herself at balls, but it seemed Society's rules had been tossed aside. As the ladies sipped their drinks, searching the crowd for Bridget, a tall woman walked over to them. She wore a tunic in which a slit was shockingly fashioned to expose her leg up to the thigh.

"Welcome, lovelies, are you enjoying yourselves?" the woman crooned.

The Dowager Countess spoke up, "Lady Stanhope, I see you've carried on the tradition of the masquerade ball."

Her eyes sparkled behind her silver mask. "How'd you know it was me?" she asked laughing. "I couldn't let the efforts of my predecessors be in vain, *Lady Downham*. I hope this ball lives up to prior ones."

The Dowager Countess shook her head. "For the sake of my granddaughter and these innocent young ladies, I hope it does not."

Lady Stanhope let out a generous chuckle that would be

shunned in any drawing room. "Well, I do hope you enjoy yourselves." She turned with flourish as her tunic spun around her, and she glided over to the next group.

"The wives of the Barons Stanhope have always been eccentric. This one's an actress," Lady Downham commented. She released an exasperated sigh.

"Beatrice, do you see any sign of Bridget? You're a bit taller than me," Eleanor asked. Charlotte applauded her friend for trying to cover up Beatrice's obvious perusal of the crowd.

"No, I don't see her or Lord Carrington."

"I'm surprised we haven't spotted her. I created glorious wings for Bridget's Nemesis costume." Eleanor led the group of women into the crowd around the dance floor in search of their friend. Charlotte thought more about Bridget's costume and drifted to the back of the pack. She did not understand why Bridget had chosen the goddess of retribution and vengeance. Bridget seemed rather timid and subdued. Nevertheless, "hell hath no fury like a woman scorned," and perhaps Bridget was a woman slighted. She adored her newly discovered friends, but she had the disconcerting feeling that each woman was hiding something. Charlotte shuddered as she recalled Beatrice's words when they first met.

We all have our scandalous secrets, and nothing in the ton stays hidden for long. The only safeguard is to keep it to yourself or rid yourself of anyone who would tattle.

Charlotte was so lost in her thoughts that she startled when a hand suddenly grabbed her wrist. She stopped walking and searched for the source of her detainment. A tunicked man with light-brown hair and cornflower-blue eyes, not dissimilar from her own, gazed down at her through a white mask.

"What do we have here?" the man asked smoothly. She jolted as the voice registered in her mind. It sounded eerily familiar.

"Nate?"

"Tut, tut. There's a mask for a reason. No guessing identities, sweetheart," he drawled. He tugged Charlotte closer to him. She was caught off guard, and her hands splayed across his chest to prevent herself from toppling over. She definitely knew this voice.

"Nate! It's Charlotte."

"Charlotte?"

"Your sister, you dolt!" The hands that had moved to her waist released her, and her older brother stepped back in revulsion.

"What are you doing in London? And what are you doing here?"

"I sent word to you, Henry, Arthur, and Father to let you know I would be in London for the Season! I assumed no one would care except Arthur, but I tried anyway. I guess I was right."

Nate puffed out his chest in indignation. "Dearest sister, you assume I read my correspondence. I do not."

"Regardless, you didn't even recognize me!" she hissed through her teeth.

"You are wearing a veil!"

"But I recognized you! I knew your voice," Charlotte argued while she tried to keep her words from trembling. She was absolutely crushed. She knew how little most of her family thought of her, but this was a low point.

"You sound different. You've matured." Nate moved his arm in a vertical motion, indicating her growth. Charlotte willed herself not to burst into tears.

"I just made my debut! Aunt Frances has been telling anyone who will listen about me, especially men of marriageable age. You have heard nothing?"

He shrugged with an annoying amount of insouciance.

"Honestly, Charlotte, I didn't. I try to avoid Society events at all costs, but I make an exception for the Stanhope Masquerade Ball. It's actually quite fun, which can't be said of all those dull events where marriage-minded mothers throw their daughters at me, even as a second son." Nate cringed.

"You should have recognized your own sister."

Nate shrugged his shoulders and raised his hands in defense.

She did not want to fight with her brother, so she turned on her heel and walked away before she said something she would regret.

Nate's behavior should not surprise her.

She was the *forgotten fifth*.

Charlotte looked around and realized she had lost her friends in the crowd.

Not for the first time, she felt utterly alone.

CHAPTER SIXTEEN

J ames stood next to Gabe at the side of the ballroom as they observed the debauchery unfold before them. His friend kept a watchful eye on his little sister. "I don't believe a masquerade ball was part of our agreement," James said.

"Neither did I, but what was I supposed to do? Bridget was going to sneak out on her own to come to this," Gabe responded grimly.

"You could have forbidden her from attending."

Gabe nodded. "I should have, but I was almost excited that she wanted to come to a social event on her own volition, even if it was a masquerade. You've seen how withdrawn she's been. I have been thinking perhaps she had made her debut too soon. Maybe she needed another year, but I don't think that's it."

"She is Nemesis," James offered.

"I noticed, but I don't know of any man who has hurt her besides our father. And he's thankfully dead."

Before they could discuss further, a deep voice rumbled from behind them, "Look who we have here." James spun around to find a hulking man with fiery hair in a black tunic and mask, sporting a stuffed crow perched on his shoulder.

"Jack?"

"Erebus to be specific. But if you're going to ruin the fun, then yes, the one and only."

"What are you doing here? I didn't expect you," James said.

"When you told me of the little issue with the insurance money and that you'd be stuck in London until a murderer was caught, I thought I'd keep you company." Jack shifted his gaze to Gabe in an assessing manner. "Plus, I've been looking to expand my business into London. I figured you might be spending some time with toffs, so it seemed a perfect opportunity."

James was surprised. He knew how much Jack avoided the *ton,* but James also knew Jack would do anything to make money.

James introduced Gabe and Jack.

Gabe raised his eyebrows. "This is your boss?"

"Yes, and my childhood best friend."

Gabe paused for a moment, then seemed to make a decision and nodded. "Doherty."

Jack eyed Gabe with a mixture of suspicion and loathing.

Gabe lifted his chin in the most aristocratic way. "You can call me Gabe. I would hate for us not to be on a first-name basis when you murder me in my sleep," he said dryly.

Jack's face transformed into a smile at the quip, and he laughed heartily.

"Thanks for the permission!" Jack smacked Gabe on his back.

Gabe shook his head good-naturedly, but James knew Jack could easily test Gabe's patience.

A group of women approached Lady Bridget, who stood at Gabe's right, but near the dance floor. As the goddess of revenge, her costume included an impressive set of wings, which to her benefit gave her a wide berth, even in the crush of guests. He studied the women and determined their identities, despite the disguises. He recognized the dark-brown hair and erect posture of Lady Beatrice and the fluid movements of the blonde-haired Lady Eleanor. An older woman trailed behind them, who appeared to be some sort of chaperone. Lady Bridget's face lit up as she saw her friends.

But one very important member was missing.

Was Lottie here?

James needed to see her. His remorseful letters had gone unanswered. These past few days had been some of the most painful ones he could remember.

He knew he had acted like a fool. He now felt like the scum of the earth for taking her virginity. Although her kisses had been innocent, the moment she went to her knees like a practiced courtesan, he had let his cock rule his mind and had told himself she was no virgin. He had wanted her so badly. All he could think about was making her his and sinking his cock into her delectable cunny.

If he had been truthful with himself about her likely virginity, he would have acted differently, he tried to convince himself. But he could not. He lost all reason when it came to Lottie.

He knew he deserved every minute of torture he had endured since that night. He did not think she would ever forgive him, and it tormented him beyond measure. He had barely slept. His stomach was perpetually tied in knots. He was disgusted with himself, but he also knew her treatment of him was ultimately for the best.

He had no right to her.

She was the daughter of an earl and was destined to become the Duchess of Westcliffe. Yet he had selfishly sought one perfect night with her that he would carry for the rest of his life, even if she became someone else's wife. Now, he had ruined everything that existed between them.

He had to speak with her. His eyes kept searching for her among the guests who stood near Lady Bridget and her friends. Even in a costume, he would recognize her chestnut hair and the confident way she held her shoulders back. James expanded the perimeter of his search.

His eyes suddenly detected a woman weaving through the crowd. James's stomach tightened. "Gabe, I'll be back."

He made his way through the throng of people, side-stepping anyone who got in his way. He needed to reach that familiar veiled woman, the same woman he'd seen in Roberts's office: Mrs. Gibson.

Luckily his height allowed him to keep his eyes trained on the black veil that wove in and out of the clusters of guests toward the doors that exited the ballroom.

It *was* her. The same color hair, the same height, and the same way she carried herself.

He ignored the protestations from a man he elbowed who did not move out of the way quickly enough. He arrived at the doors just before the veiled woman reached her destination and positioned himself in front of her.

This is it. I've finally found Mrs. Gibson.

The veiled woman stopped abruptly.

"James?"

His knees almost buckled beneath him.

Lottie? No, it couldn't be.

His mind spun. "You're Mrs. Gibson?"

He heard a gasp from beneath the veil, and Lottie tried to shove past him. He was so unsettled that he was caught unawares by her delicate frame colliding with him. He almost lost his balance as she moved away. Once he was steady, he turned and saw her disappear into the bottleneck of guests who were trying to enter and exit the ballroom.

He started after her, but a woman stepped in front of him. "Not now!" he growled.

"Oh, but you're so handsome and so...big."

He looked down to see a woman clinging to his arm, pushing her breasts against him.

"I'm not interested." He peeled her hands off his arm and stepped around her.

"Dammit!" he cursed under his breath, as he tried to muscle his way past other guests and through the doorway.

Once he finally made it out of the ballroom, his mind raced with possibilities. He ran toward the front of the home, reasoning that she was intent on making a hasty exit.

James darted outside the house and the cool, fresh air took away his breath momentarily after the stuffiness of the ball. He assessed the scene before him. Carriage after carriage lined up along the road in front of the property awaiting their owners. On top of that, vehicles were still entering the drive that led to the house to drop off arriving guests.

James sprinted to the line of equipages and proceeded to hastily check each one for a veiled head of chestnut hair.

He was such an idiot.

How did he not realize Lottie was Mrs. Gibson?

Infatuation, that's what it was. She had put him under her spell, and he had become blind to what was so obviously in front of him.

As he hurriedly moved from one carriage to the next, the yells of angered coachmen filtered through the night air. He eventually reached the end of the line, winded and frustrated.

There was no sign of Lottie.

He leaned over with his hands resting on his thighs while he caught his breath. He took a moment to process what had just happened and then buried his face in his hands.

Lottie was a murderess.

The carriage rattled along the streets of London. Charlotte kept looking out the window expecting James to be coming hellbent after her. She thanked her lucky stars that when she dashed out of the Stanhope estate, she was able to find Nate's carriage with the Pulverbatch family crest on the side. The coachman had previously worked for the family in Shropshire, so with her veil removed, he took one look at her panic-stricken face, and they were on their way back to the city posthaste.

She still did not see James trailing the vehicle, which gave her a small sense of relief; however, it did not assuage the overwhelming terror she felt.

He knew.

Just one word from him to the magistrate and she would be swinging from the gallows. Every worst-case scenario flashed through her mind. It did not help that she was in a carriage, which brought her back to that fateful day.

She had managed High Crest Hall's ledgers and discovered the new man of business, Roberts, was skimming money from her family. Claiming to be Arthur, she had forged a letter demanding a meeting. Roberts had denied her request, so she decided to go in person and confront the man.

Charlotte figured he would refuse to meet with a member of her family, given his earlier rejection of the letter, so she came up with the disguise of Mrs. Gibson. This poor widow had just lost her husband and was looking for a capable man to manage her affairs. Could she please meet with someone as highly recommended as Roberts to help her?

It worked like a charm, and she had gained entry to his office with a pistol stowed in her reticule as a safeguard. Being ignored by her parents as a child had an occasional perk, and had left her free to learn how to shoot like her brothers. Roberts quickly realized her identity when she accused him of stealing from the Earl of Pulverbatch. He attempted to kill her, and she reacted by shooting him in self-defense.

Charlotte fled.

She had clambered into the unmarked coach and ordered the driver to get her back to High Crest Hall as quickly as possible. She had been in survival mode, doing whatever was necessary to get out of Roberts's office alive, but once she was alone in the carriage, reality sank in.

She was a murderess.

Roberts had bled from the gunshot wound.

And she had been the cause of it.

As the carriage rattled away from the masquerade, as it had that horrible day, she used every ounce of energy left in her body to wrestle her thoughts from the past and focus on the present. Arthur always told her reason ruled the day. She focused on the black veil she held in her hands. It was a stark reminder of the day she had killed a man. She could feel the edges of panic and yanked the vine from around her neck and started counting each leaf. Her breathing eventually slowed, and she tried to think through her quandary. She needed to marry the Duke of Westcliffe soon.

Otherwise, she was out of options to save herself.

Charlotte did not trust anything James had told her about the Duke of Westcliffe being connected with Roberts. It had to be another ruse to get her dowry.

Return to reason.

Fact: tomorrow night, the Duke wanted to announce their betrothal.

Problem: how swiftly could she marry the Duke?

Solution: a special license.

Problem: how could she convince the Duke to obtain this sacred document?

Solution: she could feign excitement over the nuptials and proclaim she did not want to wait for the banns to be read.

Charlotte mulled this solution over while she toyed with the vines, the silkiness of the leaves providing a soothing effect. The Duke seemed to want to move forward with the marriage without unnecessary pomp.

Arthur was right, reason was a salve to her emotions. Her betrothal would be announced the next day at the Rowley Ball and then she would encourage the Duke to procure a special marriage license.

No.

Charlotte would write to the Duke in the morning so that he could begin the process of obtaining a special license even sooner. In the meantime, Charlotte would have to avoid James until she became the Duchess of Westcliffe and was protected.

She would send word to Arthur about their hasty nuptials, and ask him to ensure that their father signed the proper wedding contract. She would not bother notifying the rest of her family. If Arthur so pleased, he could tell them, but she did not have much faith they would care.

Charlotte closed her eyes. She felt calmer now that she had a plan of escape. Attending the masquerade ball had been a foolish idea. She should have backed out once Eleanor insisted she wear a black veil as part of Persephone's costume. Charlotte had argued with Eleanor that a black mask would be sufficient, but her friend would not relent. Charlotte had not known how else to persuade Eleanor without revealing her role as Mrs. Gibson, so she finally acquiesced and prayed for the best.

But the black veil had been a bad omen, and her prayers had not been answered. They had been thrown back in her face.

Now, James held her life in his hands.

All she wanted to do was live her life away from Society in Shropshire with her mare, Mirabel. Instead, she was rushing to marry a duke more than twice her age to save herself from the gallows.

Charlotte ordered the carriage to stop at the end of the street leading to her aunt's town house so she could alight in darkness and sneak in the back. She sent the coachman back to await Nate at the Stanhope Estate with a note to give to Eleanor that she had become too ill to stay and had left. Afterward, she climbed the servants' stairs without being noticed.

Inside her bedroom, she did not ring for Bailey. All she wanted to do was crawl into bed. Her tunic fell to the ground, and she slipped on her night rail. She climbed into bed, but the peace of sleep escaped her. She tossed and turned for hours until the light of dawn crept into her window and finally fell into a dreamless sleep, not knowing if she wanted to see another day.

It was well past noon when Charlotte finally awoke. She let out a long sigh. Her life was in shambles. She rang for Bailey, whose steps faltered when she saw Charlotte's face.

"How do you fare, milady?"

"I'm in trouble, Bailey. Deep trouble. I need to write some correspondence. I'm also cured from my 'illness' and will be joining my aunt."

Bailey looked concerned but held her tongue. She simply curtseyed and left the room.

Charlotte dragged herself out of bed. She was exhausted from her fitful night of sleep, and her legs felt as if they weighed at least eight stone. Her mind felt foggy, but she tried her best to focus on the notes she needed to write. She trudged over to her escritoire and started with the Duke. She hoped her desperation was not too evident in her wording. Next, she wrote to Arthur and pleaded with him to tear himself away from his Parliamentary matters to help her.

Once these tasks were finished, she picked at the tray of

food Bailey brought to her room. Her stomach was tied in knots from picturing herself swinging from the hangman's noose. She just needed two days, maybe three, to stay alive before she became a duchess.

What was James doing right now?

Was he banging victoriously on the door of the magistrate with the name of the killer so he could collect his insurance money? He was trading her life for a shipment of flax.

If she kept dwelling on what could happen any longer, she would either lose the contents of her stomach or her mind.

Charlotte stood.

Focus on the facts, you ninny.

She had to take control of her destiny and not leave it in James's hands, which meant plastering a bland smile onto her face that would make any lady of the *ton* proud, and preparing herself for the most important ball of her life.

Charlotte *would* become the Duchess of Westcliffe.

CHAPTER SEVENTEEN

J ames had not slept.

After losing Lottie, or should he say the murdering Mrs. Gibson, he returned to the masquerade ball feeling betrayed. All he wanted to do was leave, but instead, he found Gabe, who had been in a panic. Lady Bridget was missing, so he then spent the rest of the night with Gabe tracking down his sister. Although it was a trying few hours, it had provided a distraction for him. He had been too consumed with helping find Lady Bridget to be able to mull over the fact that Lottie was a killer.

They found Gabe's sister with her reputation intact and promptly left the ball. Once home, Gabe actually stayed and invited James to have a drink in his study. After a brandy and listening to his friend lament about squiring one's sister through the temptations of a London Season, James stood and said good-night. He needed to be alone.

Once James reached his bedroom, he paced relentlessly, trying to make sense of why Lottie would shoot Roberts. The best conclusion he formed was that it was somehow related to the money Roberts was stealing from her family. After accepting this theory, he finally collapsed onto his bed from sheer exhaustion.

James had slept so hard he awoke confused. For a brief moment, it was a blissful confusion, because his mind was disoriented and blank. Then, the past few days' events rushed into his brain, and he sank back into the mattress, wanting to escape it all.

You are an officer. Get it together.

James willed himself up and out of bed. Bright light assaulted his senses, and he heard the house abuzz with activity. He had never slept this late. One woman had turned his life upside down in more ways than he could count. On top of that, if he wanted to collect his insurance money, he was tasked with turning Lady Charlotte Tipton, daughter of an earl and the woman of his heart, in to the magistrate.

James felt a sense of guilt at the thought of revealing her identity as the murderess, but he quickly pushed that emotion aside. He had bared his soul to her and confessed his love for her. In return, she had lied to him by admission. Lottie had not said a word when he revealed to her that he was looking for Mrs. Gibson. Now he understood why she flew from the bedroom that night.

Downstairs, he found Gabe in his study.

"Well, this is a first." Gabe looked up from his ledgers. "I guess us toffs are really rubbing off on you. Sleeping well past noon, eh?"

"Something like that," James said.

"What's wrong? You seemed off last night."

James slumped into the chair near Gabe's desk and ran his hand through his hair. "You had more important things to worry about."

Concern shown in Gabe's amber eyes. "I'm all yours." He

leaned back in his leather desk chair and clasped his hands over his stomach.

James paused, questioning what to share with Gabe. However, given the turmoil in which he found himself, he needed someone else's opinion.

"Ever since our paths crossed that night at the docks, I knew you were different than other nobs. We have been friends a long time now. I trust you like a brother. What I'm about to tell you can't leave this room."

Gabe's face became serious, and he met James's eyes. "I swear it."

"Lady Charlotte is Mrs. Gibson."

A look of shock crossed Gabe's face. He whistled through his teeth in dismay. "You're sure?"

"Positive. I saw a woman at the masquerade ball wearing a black veil, looking identical to the woman in mourning I saw at Roberts's office. I followed her and addressed her as Mrs. Gibson, only to find out it was Lady Charlotte. She panicked and ran from me. I chased after her, but lost her in the crowd. By the time I got outside, she had disappeared."

Gabe shifted forward, shaking his head. "I can't believe it."

"It has to be true. Why else would she bolt when I connected her to Mrs. Gibson? Plus, she has nightmares. She told me she thinks someone is trying to kill her, and I thwarted an attack on her life."

Gabe's eyes widened. "She must be in over her head."

"She knew I was looking for the murderer of Roberts, and she revealed nothing."

Gabe leaned back in his chair and collected his thoughts. He spoke in a measured tone, "I realize there are a lot of emotions involved, but let us think of it from Lady Charlotte's perspective. She killed Roberts, who was a thief and worse. Perhaps it was self-defense, perhaps it was not. Regardless, she murdered someone. I wouldn't expect her to be sharing this delicate information no matter who you are to her. She has nightmares, you say? She must be scared to death."

"She's in danger, and I told her I would help. Yet she didn't tell me the truth," James said. "Instead, she is marrying Westcliffe."

"Ah, so you care."

"I told her I loved her, dammit."

A look of understanding dawned on Gabe's face. "It all makes sense now. She's in danger, you love her, but she's running to the Duke of Westcliffe for protection."

James dropped his head and cradled it in his hands. After a time, he lifted his gaze. "I don't know what to do."

"You do want her safe."

"Of course," James said.

Gabe drummed his fingers. "We need to better understand the danger to Lady Charlotte. Whoever is trying to kill her must be linked to Roberts and is seeking revenge."

"Roberts worked for the Duke of Westcliffe under a different name in the past," James told him.

"Oh, that's interesting," Gabe replied slowly, "perhaps he's not the knight in shining armor Lady Charlotte thinks him to be."

"I don't know what to think. I want to hate him, but Lady Charlotte will be protected by his title if they marry." James said.

"I thought he was a decent man though I don't know him too well. Just from the House of Lords. He only comes to London when absolutely necessary." Gabe tapped his fingers on the desktop while his mind worked. "What about his connection to Roberts? Skimming some money from aristocrats doesn't seem like the whole story. He's a duke. Why would he care about Roberts's death? You also don't know if he's connected Lady Charlotte to the murder."

James explained to Gabe what Morris told him. "The Bow Street Runner divulged that Roberts had debts under his current name all over the country. The Runners had found vowels hidden in a secret compartment behind a painting in his office with addresses from other cities, such as Liverpool and Newcastle. Apparently, Roberts had left the Duke of Westcliffe's employ over a decade ago, but had had only been in Shrewsbury for the past two years. He was known as Martin Nott when he worked for Westcliffe."

"How did they determine Roberts was linked to the Duke?" Gabe said.

"The Runners found a piece of yellowed vellum that was a receipt for three paintings by an unknown artist, George Heddon, purchased for the Duke of Westcliffe."

"Are the Runners suspicious of these paintings?"

"They're still trying to sort them out. The receipt is dated from 1805."

"If the receipt was that old, was it from the current duke or his father?"

"I'm not sure."

"That I can determine."

Gabe walked over to one of the many bookshelves in the study and ran his finger along the spines of the tomes until he pulled out a thick book with a red-and-gold cover titled *Debrett's Peerage, Baronetetage, Knightage, and Companionage*.

James looked at the book in confusion.

"It's a record of all the noble families with births, marriages, and deaths." Gabe sat back down at his desk and flipped through the book until he paused. His finger skimmed across a page. "Found it! The father of the Duke of Westcliffe died in 1807. It also looks like the current duke was a second son."

"So they need to find out how Roberts was tied to the duchy at that time," James said.

Gabe left the book splayed open on his desk. "It's very possible he was tied to Westcliffe, especially because the Duke's father would have been rather aged at that point. We need more information."

"Rumor is Charlotte's betrothal is imminent." James ran his hand through his hair. He was a man of action, and not having all the facts frustrated him endlessly. He wanted to make a plan.

"I haven't yet seen an announcement in the papers," Gabe said.

A disturbing thought passed through James's mind. "She's desperate. What if they elope or the Duke obtains a special license?"

"The Rowley Ball is tonight," Gabe said. "I heard Westcliffe is attending. I'll go and speak with him alone under the pretense of needing to discuss a political matter. This conversation will allow me to try to glean additional information."

"I can't stay home twiddling my thumbs awaiting your verdict," James insisted.

Gabe looked at James seriously. "I understand your frustration, but if you attend the ball, you'll need to stay away from Lady Charlotte. My sister mentioned she'd be there. Can you do that?"

James felt his jaw tighten. It would be infinitely better to watch the Duke parade Charlotte around than sit at Gabe's town house not knowing what was happening. He released his jaw. "I'll try." He could not make any promises.

Gabe stood from his desk, now eye level with James. "If you want to save her, you need...To. Stay. Away," Gabe punctuated each word in his most aristocratic tone, which brooked no argument.

"Fine!"

"Good. It's settled then. Do you want a brandy?" Gabe offered in a jovial tone.

"No. I need to clear my head," James said. "I'm going for a walk."

"Very well then." Gabe turned to pour himself a drink.

As James reached the door leading out of the study, Gabe's voice floated from behind him, "It will work out."

James paused with his hand on the doorknob and turned back toward Gabe. "I hope you're right."

Gabe glanced down at the still-open *Debrett's* and before James could turn back around, Gabe's face became pensive. "Wait."

James looked at Gabe expectantly.

His friend tapped the page. "I didn't think to make a connection, but are you a distant relation of Westcliffe?"

What an odd question.

"Good God...why would you ask that?"

Gabe pointed his finger at a spot in the book. "The current Duke of Westcliffe's full name is Theodore Frederick Adolphus Hughes."

James's full name was James Theodore Adolphus Hughes. His stomach lurched, but he shook his head. "There's no chance I'm related to the Duke. My uncle repeatedly reminded me that I was the bastard of a no-good guttersnipe who seduced my innocent mother, and that I was just as bad. My mother, on the other hand, swears she was married to my father. All she ever mentioned was that he was an officer in the military. I'm sure she would've told me if he had any notable connections. As for my mother, she was the daughter of a local baronet near Birmingham."

"I see. I suppose no one ever saw any similarities."

"Because I'm a common bastard? Rightly so."

Gabe glared at his friend. "Not necessarily. I *was* going to say it's probably because Hughes is a common enough name that people wouldn't make a connection."

"It doesn't matter. There's no relation," James responded sharply. He was already too emotional for his liking from the stress of Lottie's impending marriage, but now, Gabe was bringing up his childhood. James had buried that awful stage of his life long ago, and remembering it only made him feel worse.

But he paused again. Could he be entirely sure there was no relation?

His name was eerily similar to the Duke's. He knew nothing of his father. He only knew he was a bastard. There was nothing from his childhood that would explain a connection to the Duke.

His mother's story had been that his father was an officer in the British Army and was stationed in Birmingham. The two met at a local ball and fell madly in love. This officer—James could not think of him as his father—was able to procure a special license probably from some military connection. His mother married her beau soon after their meeting. Now came the part where his mother would get teary. Soon after they wed, the officer was called away due to a family crisis. His mother did not know where his family resided, but the officer swore he would return within a few days.

He never came back.

When James was older, his mother confessed what had transpired afterward. She found out she was pregnant, leading her to beg for charity from her brother, the vicar. The vicar's wife had died in childbirth, leaving him with a one-year-old son, so he readily took in his sister to manage his home. James's mother lived in the main house at first, but when she became swollen with child and could no longer hide her condition, his dastardly uncle moved her into the two-room old building on the vicarage property. Although his mother swore she was married and took

Hughes as her surname, his uncle did not believe her. He insisted there was no record of her marriage to an Officer Hughes. The vicar could not have a such a sinful woman, kin or not, living in his home. She was to be thankful he gave her a roof over her head. Even if that roof leaked in the rain and barely provided any warmth in the winter.

His mother gave birth to James, and to earn her meager keep, she acted as a servant in the vicar's house, while James did the same as soon as he was old enough. His job was to wait hand and foot on his spiteful cousin, Herbert. His cousin did everything he could to make James's life more miserable. One of Herbert's favorite tricks was dumping his chamber pot onto the floor of different rooms of the house. If James got to the disaster in time, Herbert would sit and taunt James as he scrubbed his cousin's feces off the floorboards. If James did not find the contents of the emptied chamber pot soon enough, his uncle would drag him out back by his ear to a hidden area of the vicarage property and whip him.

James learned the hard way to stay silent. He had cried after the first whipping, and the next time it happened, his uncle put a sack over his head and gagged him to muffle the sounds. Being in darkness and not knowing when the next lash would come almost broke him. After that, he kept quiet, even as the tears ran down his face, and his skin burned from the whip.

His mother never knew the truth. His uncle threatened to toss James and his mother on the street if he ever said a word. Instead, the vicar would make up stories and tell his mother that James was caught stealing or intentionally breaking items in the house. His mother would look at him with imploring eyes when his uncle made the accusations, but all he could do was lower his gaze and stare at the ground powerlessly.

His mother had been raised a gentleman's daughter, so she taught him what she could in their squalid home. His uncle and

Herbert would force him to sit next to his cousin while he was being tutored so James could sharpen his quill, fetch any needed materials, and keep the fire lit. They assumed James was too daft to understand anything. What they did not realize was that he lapped up every morsel of education he could glean from Herbert's lessons as he awaited his cousin's next command.

James knew he had to educate himself in order to be free of his uncle and save his mother. At night, when the main house slept, James would sneak into his uncle's library and read as much as he could before the dawn broke. At the earliest age possible, he enlisted in the Royal Navy and clawed his way up the ranks. When he saved enough money, he bought his mother a tiny cottage away from her brother, which allowed her to leave the vicarage and live as a "widow." She still fervently believed James's father, her husband, would have returned to her if he could. Once, she professed to James that she would feel it if the love of her life died, and so she knew with certainty he was alive. His poor, disillusioned mother.

James closed his eyes. That was his earlier life in a nutshell.

"James?" Gabe's voice inquired.

James opened his eyes with a storm raging in their depths and met Gabe's gaze. "As I said, there's no chance I'm related to the Duke." He turned on his heel and left the house.

CHAPTER EIGHTEEN

Charlotte walked into the Rowley's elegant home and stood next to her aunt, waiting to be announced. Her heart was still racing from the carriage ride. On top of this, she was in a constant state of agitation, wondering how soon she could wed.

The Duke was her only hope for protection from a death sentence. Arthur had stopped at their aunt's home after she sent him the urgent message, and he agreed that Westcliffe was still Charlotte's best course of action. If Arthur did not identify any other feasible options, then there were none.

Better to marry the devil you know or something like that.

But could Charlotte convince the Westcliffe to speed up their nuptials?

Eligible dukes did not grow on trees. The fact she had snared one at all was a miracle.

Charlotte's and her aunt's names were announced, and they entered the inevitable crush of yet another ball. Charlotte realized that very soon, she would no longer be Lady Charlotte Tipton, but instead, Her Grace, the Duchess of Westcliffe.

She paused. What would her surname be? Perhaps she

really did not know the Duke, but there was no turning back now.

Charlotte scanned the room for Arthur, who promised he would make an exception for her and attend this ball as a sign of support. She needed him by her side to calm her nerves. With thoughts of her betrothal being announced imminently to more of a stranger than she would like to admit, her palms moistened, and she felt lightheaded. She needed a breath of fresh air before her aunt found the Duke. She turned to her aunt, who led them through the crowd.

"I'm not feeling well. I need to go to the balcony for a moment. The crush is stifling."

"This is the most important day of your life," Aunt Frances said.

"I know. I'll return shortly."

She did not wait for an answer and made a beeline for the doors that led outside. She let out a gasp as cool air assaulted her lungs, and she gripped the railing at the edge of the balcony to support herself. Her chest heaved while she tried to steady herself. She did not know how long she stood there, but finally, she felt more stable, despite the tension pulsating through her body.

She opened her eyes and looked around quickly. Luckily, she was alone. Nevertheless, the din from the ballroom carried out the open doors to where she stood and frayed her nerves even further. She felt like a cornered animal.

She had to collect herself.

Charlotte lifted the hem of her light-pink ball gown and descended the stairs to the lush garden below. She maneuvered the rolled gravel paths as quickly as her slippers would allow, hoping to find a bench on which to sit in solitude. Gooseflesh covered her arms from the cool air, but she welcomed the chill and hoped it would numb her body and her mind. After she turned a corner, a bench came into view, thanks to the lanterns illuminating the pathway. With a sigh of relief, Charlotte sat down and took off her satin gloves. She stowed them in her reticule, and her hand brushed against the pistol she learned never to go without.

She cupped her face with her bare palms. Despite the cold, her cheeks felt flushed. She closed her eyes once again, trying to calm the rioting thoughts in her mind. She had to focus on her goal: marrying the Duke. It did not matter whether or not she truly knew him. She just needed the protection of his name.

Charlotte tried to picture Westcliffe, but of course, her traitorous mind only generated a stern face with a pair of stormy eyes and raven-black hair. She let out a sigh and froze when the sound of crunching gravel caught her attention. She slowly turned around to locate its source. A figure was hidden in the shadows at the bend in the path where she had turned to reach the bench.

"Finally, we're alone," an unfamiliar male voice spoke.

Charlotte's hands thrust into her reticule. "Who are you?"

The figure stepped out of the shadows. The metal of a pistol trained on her caught the flickering lantern lights.

"You killed Simon Roberts and John Powell. You made a very powerful man angry."

Charlotte's heart pounded in her chest. From overhearing her brother Will talk about his experiences in the army, she knew not to make any sudden movements that would cause a man to reactively pull the trigger. Her trembling hands were in her reticule, but they fumbled with her gun's safety. She had to keep him talking.

"I did nothing of the sort and know no John Powell. I'm freezing and must put my gloves back on. I'll be on my way, sir." It was bad enough that she murdered one man, but now she was accused of murdering two?

She needed to figure out a way to escape without turning her back to the man. Before she could come to a conclusion, his eerie voice broke through the quiet of the gardens.

"You're not going anywhere," the man threatened.

Charlotte heard the click of his safety release.

Yet again, James caught sight of Lottie rushing across a ballroom. She dashed through the open doors that led to the balcony. He had to speak with her before she announced she was betrothed or would marry the Duke of Westcliffe. James did not know what he would say to her, but he knew he had to see her.

By the time he made it across the ballroom and through the throngs of people to reach the outside, she was already gone from the balcony. He looked out over the gardens and saw the back of a feminine figure on a bench.

It must be her.

He noticed a man creep along the path toward her and pull a pistol from his greatcoat.

His heart stopped.

Lottie's life was in danger.

She had her hands in her reticule as her voice drifted up to him. He could not discern exactly what she was saying, but he heard the word gloves. She fumbled in the purse, which seemed exaggerated.

The man continued to face Lottie and seemed unaware of his presence on the balcony. Her hands remained in her reticule. He thought her head turned toward him, but he could not be sure.

James pulled out his own gun, released the safety, and aimed at the man. One glove emerged from Lottie's reticule, and her head darted in his direction. She dramatically slipped her glove on her hand then returned to searching in her purse for the other one.

A flashback from the alleyway appeared in his mind when she had gloriously aimed a pistol at the blackguard. He prayed she carried a firearm with her again, but there was no way for him to know for sure. She was at a ball.

He was a good shot, but he worried he was too far from the ruffian and was hesitant to fire. He could not risk the attacker reflexively pulling the trigger and hitting her. The garbled voices of Lottie and the man continued while she kept her hands in her reticule. Her arms suddenly stilled, and she gave the slightest nod of her head. She must have her gun.

An unspoken message filtered into James's brain, and he knew exactly what she was going to do.

"Hey! You there! What are you doing?" James bellowed from the balcony. Startled, the man glanced at him.

She pulled out her pistol and fired.

But James heard a second shot and saw Lottie's body crumple to the ground.

He did not even realize he screamed as he sprinted down the stairs to her. He prayed to the God in which he did not believe and to the devil, whoever would answer him.

I'll do anything to keep Charlotte alive.

Anything.

He jumped over the gunman's corpse and rushed to her side.

"Lottie, are you there?" James pleaded.

A moaning sound emerged from her body.

She's alive!

James grabbed her empty pistol and shoved it into his pocket while throwing away his own gun across the gardens. Surely someone had heard the gunfire and would be outside soon.

He needed to take the blame. He gently moved Lottie onto her back.

That's when he saw the injury.

Blood seeped from her left upper arm. He cursed and ripped off fabric from her petticoat and tied it around the wound. It was like *déjà vu* from the alleyway, but this time, it was a bullet and not a dagger.

"Lottie? Can you hear me? It's James."

"It hurts," she groaned, then her body became limp.

Lottie will live.

Lottie will live.

James scooped her into his arms and ran toward the balcony. He bounded up the steps as quickly as he could while he held one hand over the bandaged wound. Once again, he felt an overwhelming sense of guilt. Maybe it was Lottie's association with him that caused all this bad luck.

He was a bastard after all.

He reached the top of the stairs and was surprised none of the guests awaited him. The noise inside the ballroom must have been enough to muffle the sounds of the gunshots. James rushed through the door while the guests danced a quadrille, oblivious to the mayhem that had just occurred outside. Suddenly, a man of similar height to James stood before him.

"Is that Lady Charlotte?" the stranger demanded.

"Yes, she has been shot."

"Good God, this way," the man ordered. James followed him along the edge of the ballroom while the guests realized he carried a bloodied woman. Their whispers grew until the buzzing made James feel as if he were trapped in a beehive. Although he had tied the fragment of petticoat around Lottie's arm, he could feel the moisture of the blood seep through the fabric. Gentlemen caught swooning ladies while James followed the stranger to the private rooms of the house, where a servant stood, monitoring the entrance.

The stranger barked orders to the man. "Call for Dr. Stone and tell him the Duke of Westcliffe needs him immediately."

James's stomach clenched when he realized this man was whom Lottie would wed. His Grace ushered James into an empty room. He seemed genuinely concerned. Servants followed them into the chamber, and the Duke ordered the staff to bring supplies for the wound.

James delicately placed her on a settee. His Grace continued to command the room.

A new, worried voice entered the fray. "Charlie!"

James turned to find a lean, young man rush toward Lottie, with light-brown hair and spectacles covering his hazel eyes.

"Who are you?" James demanded.

The man kneeled beside the settee and ran his arms up and down Lottie's body to check for additional injuries. James was going to throttle this pup. He grabbed the young man's shoulder. "I said, who are you?" James growled.

The man's mouth dropped open, and he pushed up his spectacles in an affronted manner. He stood and James realized his lanky frame was taller than he thought. "I'm Arthur Tipton, Lady Charlotte's brother. And who the hell are you?"

"I'm Captain Hughes. Your sister was shot in the garden."

James looked back at Lottie lying there with the blood-soaked petticoat fabric. Servants dashed in and out of the room with items. A pile of linens suddenly appeared by the settee with alcohol. James stepped around Arthur and secured more fabric on her arm.

The Duke approached the settee. "What do you think you're doing?" came his imperious voice.

"I'm an officer. I know how to handle gunshot wounds. The bleeding needs to be stopped."

"We need to talk once you're done," the Duke ordered. James held pressure over Lottie's upper arm. Once she was stabilized, they could talk as much as *His Grace* wanted. James had some questions of his own. He pushed firmly until finally the bleeding slowed, which felt like ages.

"Help me shift her so we can see if there are any more injuries," James barked in his best officer voice. Now was not the time for formalities, and he did not care if he was speaking to a nob. The Duke and Arthur turned Lottie, while James held fabric over the wound.

He scanned her body. "I don't see anything else. You can ease her down." Surprisingly, the Duke and her brother lowered Lottie without a word.

She moaned from the movement.

An additional voice arose behind James. "I'm Dr. Stone, what's happened?"

James turned to see a man similar in age to himself peering down at them.

"You're the doctor?"

"I served in the war. I know a thing or two about bullet wounds," Dr. Stone tartly replied.

James moved aside for the doctor, who carefully unwrapped the bandages.

"She's lucky the bullet just grazed her arm." The doctor's voice softened. "You did a good job stopping the bleeding. Soldier?"

"Captain in the Royal Navy."

The doctor nodded then rifled through his bag. "I need to clean the wound and stitch it up." He pulled out a bottle of laudanum and eased some into Lottie's mouth. Dr. Stone then instructed the men to hold her. He handed a piece of leather to James for her to bite.

"I can hold it," Arthur said. "I'm her brother."

"No, I'll do it," the Duke demanded in his most aristocratic voice. "We were to announce our betrothal today."

"I don't care who holds it, it just needs to be done. Now!" the doctor ordered the bickering men.

James, who was still holding the leather, eased Lottie's mouth open and placed it between her teeth. The intrusion caused her eyes to flicker. Dr. Stone poured alcohol onto a piece of linen.

"Keep her still," he instructed. The Duke and her brother positioned themselves while James manned the leather. The doctor wiped down Lottie's bloody arm with the linen.

When the alcohol touched her wound, her eyes flew open, and she tried to sit up from the pain. His Grace and Arthur held her down, and James kept the leather in place.

"Shouldn't the laudanum be working?" James growled.

"Shortly," Dr. Stone answered. He poured more alcohol onto the linen.

"If you touch her again before the laudanum takes effect you will answer to me," James threatened.

The doctor eyed James. "Captain, the wound needs to be cleaned quickly. I don't tell you how to do your job, so don't tell me how to do mine. Hold her still. The laudanum should be working soon," Dr. Stone commanded.

Before James could speak the Duke cut in, "Be quick about it."

Dr. Stone cleaned the arm once again. Lottie winced but did not bolt upright. Her teeth ground into the leather.

After the doctor finished, he threaded a needle. James waited with bated breath while the doctor inserted the needle into her skin. Lottie did not react, and James realized the tension in her body was gone. Her mouth had also become slack.

He let out a sigh of relief and removed the leather from her mouth while the doctor continued stitching. The Duke and

Charlotte's brother left their positions but hovered around the settee throughout the entire procedure.

Finally, the doctor finished and leaned back. "I can see you all care for Lady..."

"Charlotte," His Grace said.

Dr. Stone continued, "I'll leave laudanum for the pain, but she shouldn't be moved right now. When she awakens, give her fluids, and I will come to check on her first thing in the morning."

The three men murmured their acknowledgement of the instructions.

The doctor stood, packed his bag, and then left.

A woman rushed into the room. "I was waiting for the doctor to leave. I didn't dare come in before then. We have kept all the guests' prying eyes away. What happened?"

James realized it was Lady Rowley, the hostess of the ball.

"Yes, *Captain Hughes*," the Duke taunted, "tell us what happened." The eyes of the Duke of Westcliffe, Arthur Tipton, and Lady Rowley all stared at him expectantly. If he did not answer their questions properly, he could ruin Charlotte's future.

"I'm close friends with the Earl of Carrington and was introduced to Lady Charlotte at the beginning of the Season," James began.

Start with a nob, always start with a nob, he told himself. This group of judgmental aristocrats could not balk at him becoming acquainted with a lady of the *ton* if it was through the Earl of Carrington.

"At tonight's ball, I saw Lady Charlotte rush to the doors leading to the balcony, and she looked distressed. I went to check on her, and she was already in the gardens," James paused for effect, "with a man pointing a gun at her."

Lady Rowley gasped.

James continued, "I was armed myself, but I was too far for a good shot. Lady Charlotte kept the man talking, so I sneaked down into the gardens. I crept up and killed the man, but his gun released as he fell to the ground."

"Oh, my heavens," exclaimed Lady Rowley. James glanced over to ensure she did not need smelling salts. Lady Rowley was fanning herself, but she appeared rather stable for a lady of the *ton*.

"Is this man still in the gardens?" Tipton asked.

"His body is," James answered.

"A dead body in my gardens? The magistrate must be called." Lady Rowley whipped her head toward James then to the Duke. "Don't you agree Westcliffe?"

"Yes. Immediately." The Duke nodded to Lady Rowley, who turned to James.

The chignon holding her raven-colored hair streaked with gray did not jostle one bit. Although she was quite short compared to him, she still managed to look down her aristocratic nose at him as if he were an errant schoolboy. "Captain Hughes, come with me. I will need you to speak with the authorities."

James nodded but took one more look at Lottie on the settee. With the laudanum, at least she appeared to be resting more comfortably.

He did not want to leave her for even a moment, but he had no choice.

CHAPTER NINETEEN

Lady Rowley dragged James through the ballroom to reach the gardens. He heard all the guests atwitter, speculating about what had just transpired. Once they exited the home, she banished him outdoors to guard the dead body until the magistrate arrived. Lady Rowley stationed footmen at the balcony doors to keep curious guests away, which added to the drama.

James thought this was an unnecessary precaution. The *ton* may gawk at a murdered body from a distance and gossip endlessly, but they would never sully their pristine reputations by getting too close to such a gruesome sight. However, his hostess had no qualms about sending James to this sort of scene.

After the authorities arrived and James recounted the night's events with painstaking detail, including the parts he fabricated to protect Lottie, he was finally allowed back inside. James rushed to the room where she lay. The brown head of Arthur was bent over his sister, and he rubbed her hand lovingly. It did not matter that the man was Lottie's brother. James wanted to be the one comforting her. It took every ounce of self-control to not throw him aside to make room for himself next to Lottie.

But he could not.

He had to keep up the ruse that he barely knew Lottie, in order to protect her.

The Duke of Westcliffe marched into the room, no doubt after ordering more people around.

"You've finally returned," he said, and eyed James warily.

"It was deemed necessary by Lady Rowley that I guard a corpse," James replied. *"Your Grace,"* he added as an afterthought. He still did not care that he was a duke. He was the man she was to wed. James wanted to be that man.

The Duke's eyes narrowed, and he stepped closer to James. His intimidation tactic did not work, because they were of a similar height. James stared back into the Duke's hazel eyes unflinchingly.

"How do you really know Lady Charlotte?" the Duke demanded.

"I told you, Your Grace, I was introduced by the Earl of Carrington."

"A brief introduction, as you call it, would not warrant you to rush after a young lady who was distressed. You could have compromised her."

"And what bothers you more? The fact that Lady Charlotte would have been ruined by me, or that she might have liked it?" James had just drawn a line in the sand. He was not intimidated by Westcliffe.

The only sign of agitation in the Duke was the pulsation of his jaw muscle. "Captain Hughes, I'm normally a pleasant man who tends to avoid conflict. But you have pushed me beyond my limits. One more insufferable comment out of your mouth, and you'll be naming your seconds."

"Very well then. I'll stick to the facts. Does the name Simon Roberts mean anything to you?"

The Duke's brow furrowed. "No, it does not."

"How about Martin Nott?"

The Duke's lips pursed for a moment before returning to his judgmental façade. "Are you trying to insinuate something? I warned you, Captain—"

"Stop!" Arthur wedged himself between the two men. "I cannot take this any longer."

"Explain yourself," the Duke said to Arthur.

Arthur pushed his spectacles farther up his nose and let out a breath. "You both know my sister Charlie, I mean, Lady Charlotte." He glanced at the fuming men. "And I believe you both care for her."

The Duke and James glared at each other, then turned their heads back to Arthur, who looked back and forth between the men who stood identically with their legs braced and their hands behind their backs. He cleared his throat. "I believe Captain Hughes is referring to Roberts because of an incident that occurred several weeks ago. He recently became my family's man of business in Shrewsbury. His predecessor, who had managed our affairs for years, died unexpectedly. Roberts took over all of his accounts."

The Duke interjected, "How does this involve me?"

Arthur adjusted his glasses once again. "You'll see, Westcliffe. As I was saying, Charlotte lives at our country seat in Shropshire with our mother, and manages the household ledgers of High Crest Hall. She realized Roberts was skimming money from our family. You may have noticed that my sister is not one to back down. She wrote Roberts a letter under my name, demanding we meet."

Both men watched him intently. "Roberts denied the request, so she traveled to Shrewsbury incognito as a woman in mourning named Mrs. Gibson. When Roberts learned she was a Tipton, he pulled a gun, threatening to kill her. Charlotte had her pistol with her as a precaution and shot Roberts in self-defense. She fled the scene, and then soon came to London to escape Shropshire and Shrewsbury." Arthur appeared as if he was about to cast up his accounts.

The Duke's scowl had fallen, and sincere worry etched his face. "That poor girl." He shook his head. "Now I understand why she wrote me that she was so eager to marry."

He turned to face James. "But I know nothing of this Roberts fellow. Whatever possessed you, Captain, to accuse me of being involved with this?"

"You're somehow connected to him though. Roberts is, or was, the man of business in Shrewsbury for my shipping job. A shipment of flax from Ireland was on a ship that sank, and I had to meet with Roberts to go over the ledgers. When I reached his office, a veiled woman in mourning was waiting to see him before me. I didn't want to wait, so I went about the rest of my business in Shrewsbury. When I returned, there was a huge commotion because Mrs. Gibson had just shot and killed Roberts."

This time, James focused on the Duke. "I came to London for the insurance money. The company refused to release it until they possessed the original copies of the ledgers, which were being held by the magistrate until Mrs. Gibson was found. I've had the Bow Street Runners working on the case, and they found old documents in Roberts's office tying him to the Duke of Westcliffe. Perhaps now you can explain the connection, Your Grace."

"I'm warning you—"

"Did you know Nott?"

"I did not," the Duke snapped.

"From what we found, he worked for your father until he left a decade ago and changed his name to Simon Roberts."

His Grace remained tightlipped, so James continued, "Since his death, someone has attacked Lady Charlotte twice. You claim to know nothing? Who is trying to harm her?" James challenged.

"Fine. I knew Nott years ago. After my father died, he disappeared, and I never heard from him again. I have no idea who is after my future wife," the Duke responded.

James didn't believe him.

Arthur stood between them and said reasonably, "We have a sordid mystery to unravel, and my sister is caught in the middle."

"The Runners I hired found a receipt Roberts had stashed away from 1805 for three paintings by George Heddon, purchased for your father. They think the name is fake and is being used to hide something."

The Duke shook his head, a weariness overtaking him. "I'm unaware of any of this. My father and late wife shared a passion for art, but it was lost on me. They would rotate different paintings throughout our estate, but that is the extent of my knowledge. I didn't pay the artwork much mind."

Arthur stroked his chin, deep in thought. "The attacks on Lady Charlotte's life must be linked to Roberts's death. If Your Grace has not heard from him in a decade, Roberts must have become involved in something bad."

The room fell silent as the three men replayed the recent events in their minds. Soon Arthur's eyes once again darted between James and the Duke. He pushed up his spectacles, clearly a nervous gesture. "You have never met before?"

James and the Duke responded simultaneously with a resounding "no" and looks of disgust on their faces.

"There's no relation?" Arthur asked, with an inflection at the end of the sentence.

"Absolutely not. It's impossible. My father was an officer," James said.

Arthur cleared his throat. "I see. I suppose Hughes is a

common name. I know the Duke of Westcliffe's family has long been established in Kent, but what about you, Captain Hughes?"

"Birmingham. Not even close to Kent. My mother insisted on keeping the name of the good-for-nothing officer who deserted her soon after they married. I've never met the knave, so I would never claim to be any distant relation of His Grace."

The Duke stumbled backward, and his eyes swept up and down James's body. All the color rushed from his face. "What's your mother's name?"

James's emotions were roiling inside him from the day's events, which had led him to disclose too much about his unsavory background. He could not comprehend why the Duke would care about his mother's name, but at this point, he just wanted the conversation to end. "Rose Clarke."

The Duke made a choking sound and looked at James as if he had seen a ghost.

"Why?" James barked.

His Grace let out an almost inaudible whisper, "When were you born?"

James crossed his arms. "1787."

He did not think it was possible for the Duke's face to become paler, but yet it did.

"No, no, no, no." His Grace shook his head back and forth.

James's patience finally snapped, and he threw up his hands. "What is it?"

"You're my son."

James stared at the Duke in disbelief. "Impossible."

"No. Very possible. Is your mother alive?"

"Of course she is," James retorted.

The Duke of Westcliffe ran his hand through his sandy-blond hair. "That can't be."

"Well, she is alive." James tried to look at him objectively.

He was tall like James, yes, but he had light hair and hazel eyes, which was a stark contrast to James's features. Moreover, he looked like the epitome of an aristocrat with his square jaw, straight nose, and sharply delineated cheekbones.

The Duke regained some of his composure and gestured toward a group of chairs that were across from the settee. "Let us sit."

"Sit?" James responded incredulously. "I'm not your son, and we should be focused on Lady Charlotte."

"I gave her extra laudanum while you were speaking with the magistrate, because she became uncomfortable and was agitated. She'll be comfortable for a while," Arthur reassured James.

James ran his hand through his hair while emotions further tumbled inside him. There was no way *this* duke could be his father.

"Sit down," the Duke said. "Please," he added as an afterthought. James stared back at him.

Arthur intervened. "I understand the discomfort of this situation, but I see a strong resemblance between you two. A standoff is not going to get us anywhere. We should discuss this calmly," Arthur mediated, his nervousness gone and his political acumen now at the forefront.

"Fine," James huffed, and he went and sat on one of the chairs. The Duke sat in the one facing him, while Arthur sat to his left. To his right, Lottie was sleeping soundly on the settee, breathing even.

"Your Grace, please start from the beginning. Captain Hughes, try not to interrupt until he is finished speaking."

"Is this some kind of legal proceeding?" James asked.

"Well, no, though I suppose it would become a legal matter if you truly are his son." Arthur stroked his chin contemplatively.

James let out a sigh. "Get on with it then."

Arthur continued in an even tone, "Your Grace, please explain."

"Your mother is truly alive?"

"Yes."

The Duke shook his head in disbelief. "I cannot believe this. After so many lost years... And your name?"

"James."

The Duke mouthed James's name. He shifted in his seat.

"Your Grace, please proceed," Arthur said.

The Duke struggled to settle down, but finally, he rested his forearms on the armrests of the chair and began. "You see, I was a second son. I bought a commission in the army, never expecting to inherit. My older brother was healthy, and my father had groomed him to become the next duke since the day he was born. While I was in the military, I was stationed in Birmingham. One of my comrades was from Yardley so we traveled the few miles there for a local ball. I met two lovely women, identical, with hair as black as ravens and eyes the color of silver," he fondly reminisced. The corners of his mouth curled up.

James straightened in his chair, forgetting his annoyance at the Duke. "You knew Aunt Julia?"

His Grace placed his forearms on his thighs and leaned forward, looking James in the eye. "I did. Although the two women were twins, your mother had this mischievous look that her sister did not."

James eased himself back into his chair, entranced. He could not believe he was hearing this story, and from the Duke of Westcliffe of all people?

"The moment I spoke with your mother, I fell in love with her and knew she was the only woman I could marry. I was nervous that she would only like me due to my connection with the Duchy of Westcliffe, so I didn't mention it at first. After Rose expressed her interest in me, I immediately approached her father, who was a baronet. I asked for permission to ask her to marry me. I told Sir Reginald that I was the second son of the Duke of Westcliffe to help persuade him to agree, but he scoffed at my request. He thought the chances were low I would inherit, and he had his eye on a particular baron for his daughter."

The Duke proceeded with the tale in a foreboding voice. "I rushed back to tell Rose that her father rejected me, but still did not tell her about my father, the Duke. I wanted her to make an unbiased decision. She professed her love to me and agreed to marry without her father's permission. I obtained a special license. We ran off and wed shortly after. Then, the day after our wedding, I received an urgent missive to return to Westcliffe immediately. The rider said it was dire but wouldn't reveal any details. I had to leave forthwith and didn't have a chance to tell Rose about my background. I was going to explain everything when I came back."

Although James had been listening intently, the spell broke at this part of the story. He eyed the Duke accusingly. "But you never returned."

The Duke's head fell. He took a deep breath before he raised his head again. When he lifted his eyes, they were laced with anguish, but James did not have any pity. "You deserted my mother."

"James."

"Don't call me that. It's Captain Hughes to you."

"Let me explain."

James stood abruptly. "You don't know how much my mother was tortured, how much I was beaten by my ruthless uncle. Decades of suffering because you never came back!"

Arthur jumped up from his chair before James could storm toward the door. "I understand your anger, but this is the one chance you have to hear the full story from Westcliffe's point of view.

James eyed the Duke. Arthurs softened his voice. "You don't want to look back on this moment years from now and wonder 'what if I had listened?'"

The Duke dropped from the chair to his knees. "Please, let me explain." James looked down at the Duke disdainfully. He didn't care that he was groveling, and surprisingly felt no satisfaction from having a nob beg before him. James could still feel the pain between his shoulder blades from his uncle's whip and see the suffering in his mother's eyes.

Arthur looked anxiously between the two men. "I can't watch this collapse." He squared his shoulders and used his most commanding voice, which was a stretch for the thoughtful academic. "Westcliffe, off your knees. Captain Hughes, back to your chair."

The Duke and James looked at him in surprise.

"Now!" Arthur ordered.

The two men trudged back to their seats.

"Your Grace, please continue," Arthur said.

The Duke proceeded in a tortured voice, "I returned to Westcliffe to learn my dear brother had died in a carriage accident and that I was the heir to the Dukedom. I loved him and was crushed by the news, but was relieved to tell my father I already had a wife who could be pregnant with the Westcliffe heir." Pain flashed across his face. "I never saw my father so angry. My brother had been betrothed already, and he expected me to marry my brother's intended, Miss Antoinette Waycott. Her father was a wealthy baron who neighbored our estate and had married a French *émigré*. I refused and told him how much I loved Rose. My father accepted my decision, which should have made me suspicious, but I was grieving and not thinking properly. I sent a letter to your mother explaining everything and that I would return as soon as possible."

"She never received a letter," James said.

The Duke shook his head. "My father forced me to stay in Westcliffe to learn about my future responsibilities. I begged him to return to Birmingham. He said I could go back in six weeks and that Nott would check on Rose in the meantime. I had no choice but to acquiesce. Before the time was up, Nott returned and gave me the devasting news that Rose had died."

James was out of his chair again. "My mother was alive. Aunt Julia was the one who died. She supposedly drowned before I was born, but my mother didn't believe it. She was convinced someone murdered her."

The Duke put his face in his hands. "I was young and naïve. I believed Nott when he said your mother was gone."

"You were wrong, and she suffered for years!"

The Duke lifted his head and looked absolutely defeated. "Knowing what I do now, he must have murdered the wrong sister."

James stood. "Your family killed my aunt!"

Arthur sprang from his chair, and despite his slender frame, he demonstrated surprising strength. He grabbed James's coat and dragged him back before he could reach His Grace.

"James, I mean Captain Hughes, I'm so sorry. I had nothing to do with this horror. I was too trusting. I'm only to blame in that I believed Nott and my father. In truth, he was a monster. He tried to force me to marry Miss Waycott immediately upon learning of Rose's death. I refused because I was heartbroken. The most I could do was push it out six months, and then she became my wife." The Duke ran his hand through his hair the same way James did.

"You never came back," James choked out, with tears

welling in his eyes. He never thought he would see the day he would feel this magnitude of pent-up emotion.

The Duke leaned forward with a pleading look in his eyes. "James, if I had any idea, I would have come back. This was my father's doing, and I was duped. He was an evil man. I know you'll never forgive me, but please, at least know that I would never do anything to intentionally hurt you. I loved your mother, and I would have loved you, too, had I known you existed."

James jerked himself out of Arthur's grasp. He slumped into his chair and buried his face in his hands while tears streaked down his face. He swallowed a sob and rose from the chair.

He had to leave.

James rushed out of the room in search of a place for solitude. He could not stomach seeing anyone at the moment, especially not a herd of bloodthirsty nobs with a tear-streaked face. The guests were surely reveling in being present at what would be the most scandalous ball of the Season. The gossip in drawing rooms and gentlemen's clubs tomorrow would be unrivaled.

The animals.

James hurried farther into the Rowley's private quarters. He jiggled a few door handles, only to find the rooms locked. His face felt cool from the dampness of his tears. If he did not find a room where he could be alone soon, he would knock down one of these locked doors.

Frustration building, he continued on his until finally a door eased open. He poked his head inside the room, a library, and let out a sigh of relief as he noted a single candelabrum on a table, providing a soft glow to a room of books. He closed the door behind him and flopped onto the library's chesterfield sofa. He lay back and covered his eyes with his arm. The momentous information he had just learned from the Duke, no—his father—sank in.

James had no idea who he was.

CHAPTER TWENTY

James did not know how long he remained motionless in the library, but he finally dragged himself up from the sofa. He did not feel any closer to reconciling his feelings toward his absentee father, but at least he had taken time to be alone with his thoughts. He spied a decanter near the lit fireplace and walked over, his shoulders slumped. He poured himself a brandy and drank it in one gulp. He needed fortification for what lay ahead.

James was an officer. He never backed down from a challenge, including one involving his long-lost father. He took a deep breath and squared his shoulders before he left the library and went back to the room where Lottie recovered and where he met his father, the man who deserted them. As James approached, the voices drifting from the ballroom sounded softer. They must have headed into supper.

The Duke and Arthur were bent deep in discussion, heads bent, with Arthur gesticulating. James approached the two men and cleared his throat.

Arthur looked up. "I'm sorry about your aunt. We were trying to understand the meaning of the receipt for the paintings by the mysterious artist. We think Roberts and perhaps West-cliffe's father may have been hiding something else, though we can't determine what that may be." James did not have the patience to hypothesize at the moment. He had just learned so much emotionally-laden information, so he just nodded with his customary stern look.

"Right." Arthur clasped his hands together. "We were waiting for you to return to address the more important task at hand. Who is after my sister?"

James walled off his emotions as best as he could to focus on Lottie. "It must be related to Roberts, Nott, whatever you want to call the bastard. And maybe it's related to the Duchy of Westcliffe."

"I know of no present connection with Roberts and the duchy, so the Runners you hired need to keep searching for an answer," the Duke responded.

"They will," James said.

The Duke looked intently at him. "I must see your mother. I never stopped loving her, and she is still my wife."

"That would mean Captain Hughes is your rightful heir and your daughters are illegitimate," Arthur said. "Though your first wife was believed dead, so I'm sure the courts would look favorably on the matter with your daughters. The more pressing issue is proof that you were married to Captain Hughes's mother."

James interjected, "This is the problem. When I was young, I went to St. Paul's Church to find documentation of the marriage because I wanted to believe my mother when she swore she was married. Our lives were that of servants under my tyrannical uncle, the vicar." The Duke flinched, as he should, before James continued, "When I went to the church, there was no record of it. It solidified the unrelenting reminders from my uncle that I was a whore's son, a worthless bastard."

The Duke shook his head in disgust.

Arthur looked over his spectacles at the Duke. "Do you recall signing the church's registry?"

"Rose and I both signed it. If it wasn't there, it must have been removed."

Arthur pursed his lips and tilted his head while he thought, then said, "If Roberts intended to murder James's mother, one would assume he accepted that you were married. Otherwise, why do such a thing? He may have removed the marriage record to hide any evidence."

"Or my uncle could have done it. He reveled in the power he had over my mother and me."

The Duke shook his head. "This is all too much."

"How do you think I feel?" James said.

Charlotte's mind was muddled. A fog drifted through her brain, and the moment she thought she recognized a thought or a sound, it floated back into the mist and was lost. Other times, she would resurface from darkness and catch a snippet of a familiar voice, then dive back into a featureless abyss. This time, there was still fog and confusion, but it was not quite as thick. She heard voices and tried to turn her head in the direction of the sound. A stabbing pain shot from her arm. She grimaced.

Why does my arm hurt?

This one cohesive thought was too much for her addled brain, and she submerged herself in darkness again.

"Lottie."

A voice intruded into the abyss. She tried to ignore it. It was actually quite comfortable to have a blank mind.

"Lottie." This time, she felt her body move slightly. She flung her good arm up to stop the pain.

"Bollocks. Sorry, Lottie."

Who's Lottie?

Whoever she is, she is not here. Charlotte tried to return to the darkness.

Leave me alone.

There was pressure on her right hand. "Charlotte, it's me, James."

Charlotte sounded familiar.

I'm Charlotte, now this voice can go away.

Her mind began to wander.

"Charlotte, please. It's James."

I don't know a James.

She drifted off again.

Charlotte remained in blissful oblivion for an unknown amount of time, but finally the shadows lifted. Her senses detected stimuli. Voices, pressure on her arm, pain...lots of pain.

Her eyes flew open. Candles shed light on an unfamiliar chamber.

"Lottie, I'm here. It's James." She turned her head to the voice, and recognition dawned upon her when she noted the concerned gray eyes gazing down at her. She knew James. She knew him quite well. The usual storm brewing in him was absent. Instead, he looked exhausted and despondent. Dark circles lined the eyes on his usually handsome face, and stubble covered his angular cheekbones and square jaw.

Charlotte tried to sit up, but that only worsened the pain. "Ow," she moaned. Her right hand flew to her left upper arm.

James caught her hand and gently lowered it.

"You were hurt very badly."

She squinted at him as fragments of memories tried to form in her mind. She thought she had heard *Lottie* in the darkness.

"What happened?" her dry voice croaked.

James soothingly rubbed circles on the top of Charlotte's hand with his thumb.

"You went out to the gardens where a man shot you."

Charlotte eased herself back against the headboard and tried to piece together her memories.

"What happened before that?"

"I saw you rush across the Rowley's ballroom, but I didn't know why. It looked as if you were running away from something."

Rowley Ball, Rowley Ball, Rowley Ball.

She furrowed her brow. "There was something important about the Rowley Ball."

James stroked her hand. "Did it have to do with the Duke of Westcliffe?"

The name of her almost-betrothed triggered a flood of memories and images from that night.

A crowded ballroom.

Fresh air.

The gardens.

A man in the shadows.

A gun.

Her stomach dropped. "I shot him."

James glanced around the room and lowered his voice. "I told the magistrate it was me," he reassured her and continued to rub her hand.

"But did I?" her voice cracked.

"Yes. You looked distressed in the ballroom, so I followed you outside. You were already down in the gardens with a gun trained on you. I distracted the man, and you got off your shot. His gun went off as he fell."

"Is he dead?" Charlotte whispered.

"Yes."

"Good."

James chuckled. "Lady Charlotte Tipton, this is the second time you have approved of a killing."

Charlotte felt his hand on her chin. She had been looking at the wall while she sorted through her muddled mind, but she now felt her head being turned. Sable hair and silver eyes dominated her vision.

"You're amazing," James murmured.

"I knew you were on the balcony. I could feel you, and then I sneaked a glimpse, and there you were."

A smile spread across his face. His handsomeness when he was not scowling still made her breath catch.

"I have a lot to tell you. Arthur has been staying with you at night for propriety's sake, but I have been allowed to sit with you during the daytime with Bailey present."

Charlotte's eyes roved around the unfamiliar room, catching sight of her lady's maid dozing with her sewing on her lap. "Where are we?"

"One of the Rowley's bedrooms. After you stabilized, Dr. Stone said we could move you from the drawing room to a more comfortable situation."

"How long has it been?"

"Several days. Arthur and I have been easing you off the laudanum as quickly as we can. I saw too many sailors chase the dragon and didn't want you to become addicted. How's the pain?"

She tried to adjust herself and flinched. "It hurts, but I'll get through it. You must tell me everything."

"Are you well enough?"

"The suspense would be infinitely worse."

Charlotte let out a hiss of pain when James adjusted her against the pillow that was propped up behind her.

James raised his eyebrows. Still, he did as she asked, and he told her all that had transpired. It was more than Charlotte could ever imagine. How her life had become intertwined with a long-lost son of the Duke of Westcliffe was almost too much for Charlotte to handle in her laudanum-induced state.

"You're actually the heir to the Duchy of Westcliffe?" Charlotte could not fully wrap her mind around this development.

James shook his head. "The only fact I know is that I'm his son, but there's no record of his marriage to my mother. We can't prove that I'm the heir."

Charlotte was curious. "Does that upset you?"

"Not particularly. You know what I think of the *ton*. The only thing that matters to me is having you by my side. Lottie, I want to marry you. I know I may not have the protection of my own title, but I'll fight with every breath I have left in my body to keep you safe. You are my everything. Losing you would have killed me. I need you."

Tears streamed down her face. This was too much, but it felt so right.

"Yes, yes, YES! I love you, James." She snuffled in the most unladylike fashion. After all that had happened and still with a touch of laudanum in her system, Charlotte was finally acknowledging her true feelings for James.

"You don't know how much that means to me. I have loved you this whole time, but I knew I was never worthy of you. I still am not, but I don't care anymore."

Through her sobs, Charlotte choked out, "You silly man." She tugged her hand from James's clasp and slapped his arm.

"Charlie! You're awake."

Charlotte tried to stop the tears, but they kept coming. "Arthur." She started to turn toward his voice but stopped herself as a jolt of pain shot through her arm.

Her beloved brother rushed to her side and leaned over the bed. His hair was a mess as usual, and his spectacles were falling down his nose. She loved Arthur beyond belief.

"Thank heavens—you had us all worried."

"I'm sorry. I always seem to get myself into scrapes."

Arthur shook his head. "Some things never change."

"I'll not be your responsibility anymore."

"Oh?" Arthur responded with a knowing look in his eyes.

"James has asked me to marry him, and I said yes." A grin spread across Arthur's face, and he clapped James on the back.

"Good man. But could you not have waited until she could sit up unsupported? I'm afraid you have her at a disadvantage."

Charlotte laughed tears. Arthur was always so serious and scholarly that many did not realize he was actually quite witty.

James responded smugly, "I was in the military. You always attack when your opponent is weakest."

The two gentlemen chuckled. They both looked down at Charlotte with relief. Her sobs diminished, and she collected herself. "What are we to do next?"

"Dr. Stone has been checking on you each morning and evening. He'll be delighted that you're awake. Hopefully, you can move back to your aunt's home soon," James explained.

Charlotte assessed his stubble, tussled hair, and disheveled appearance. "Have you rested?"

James sheepishly looked down at his hands before he raised his head to look at her. "No, I couldn't leave. I came too close to losing you. I wasn't going to let it happen again."

Fresh tears welled in Charlotte's eyes. It must be the laudanum, because she had never been this emotional. Or maybe it was because she loved this man so much it hurt.

After realizing she was the *forgotten fifth* as a child, Charlotte had always walled off her emotions. Emotions made one vulnerable, and she refused to let herself be at the mercy of others. Now, she was letting in her emotions for James. Instead of feeling exposed, it felt wonderful. There was a power in knowing that James loved her just as much as she loved him.

Charlotte reached out for his hand with her good arm and gave him a squeeze.

"Lady Charlotte," a voice bellowed from the other side of the room. The Duke walked purposefully toward the group.

"Your Grace," Charlotte said. She tentatively smiled. She did not know how he would react to the news that she was to marry James.

He glanced down at James and Charlotte's entwined hands. "Ah."

She eyed him nervously.

"I see my son has spoken with you."

James glared at him. "Yes, *Your Grace*."

The Duke clasped his hands behind his back and stared down his aristocratic nose at James. "I realize it would take me more than a lifetime to atone for my mistakes, but you have to give me a chance."

Before James could retort, Charlotte chimed in. "You'll give us your blessing to be married?"

"Undoubtedly. I enjoy your company, Lady Charlotte, but I believe you're much better situated as my daughter-in-law than as my wife. And I already have a wife whom I must see."

Charlotte grinned. "I entirely agree."

He looked at James. "Before I take my leave, I want to let you know that I wrote to your mother. I hope she will accept my invitation to come to London. Being a duke, I'm not used to apologizing, but I groveled quite thoroughly, if that's any consolation."

Charlotte saw the corner of James's mouth twitch.

Perhaps there was a chance at reconciliation.

CHAPTER TWENTY-ONE

F amily.

James stopped dreaming at a young age of what it would be like to have a mother, father, and maybe even siblings. But now, he looked around the dining table and saw that previously unattainable image before his eyes. Although he was still angry at his father, he could not help his heartstrings from tugging as he shared a meal with his parents and his half-sisters.

His mother had accepted the Duke's letter begging for forgiveness and the ducal carriage that had accompanied the note. His mother wrote to James that she was making haste to London to see for herself if her beloved husband truly lived.

James was with the Duke when his mother arrived and alighted from the carriage. He witnessed the mix of emotions that crossed her face. Her mouth fell open, then she began to cry before she rushed into her husband's open arms. His petite mother sobbed into the Duke's jacket, the top of her head not even reaching his shoulders. Her sobs quickly morphed into screams, and she proceeded to punch him furiously. James smiled as he recalled the deluge of expletives with which his normally mild-mannered mother assaulted the Duke.

"James, you appear quite amused," his mother inquired from her position next to her husband, eschewing Society's expectation for her to sit at the opposite end of the table. The two could not keep their eyes off each other. He felt as if he intruded upon a young couple in love.

"You look happy, Mother," James responded, covering up the true nature of his grin.

His mother blushed like a schoolgirl and glanced at the Duke under her dark lashes. "I never thought this day would come."

"I will spend the rest of my life making up for every day we were apart," the Duke vowed. James's coldness toward his father had thawed slightly. He could only hold on to his anger for so long now that he saw how much the Duke truly cared for his mother. However, James clung to his spite as much as he could. Letting down his guard entirely would make him exposed, and James's life had taught him that the only person upon whom he could depend was himself.

Moreover, he still had trouble thinking of the Duke as his father. James never knew how to imagine his missing parent, but it had never crossed his mind that his real father would be one of the highest members of the aristocracy. After James's deprived childhood, it was hard for him to reconcile this fact. Nevertheless, he could not deny he did resemble his father in some ways, and he was trying to think of him as such.

"Father, it seems you are asking for immortality," James's half-sister Genevieve quipped as she raised her left eyebrow and gave her father an impudent stare.

Sister! Never in James's wildest dreams would he have not one but four sisters. Genevieve must have taken after her mother with her thick, curly mahogany hair and dark eyes. His other sister who was in Town, Celine, mirrored the Duke with her sandy-blonde hair and hazel eyes. He had not met his other two sisters, since they were married and in the countryside with their families.

Besides never imagining he would have four siblings, James did not think he would hear one of them challenging a duke at the dinner table. He was realizing that his newly discovered family did not act like most of the *ton*, despite being in their upper echelon. He was also coming to terms with the fact he was a part of—no, peripherally related to—the social class he despised. Proof of his parents' marriage had not been found, so he remained the bastard that his uncle accused him of being.

His family's voices faded into the background while James ruminated over what Lottie would think if he remained born on the wrong side of the blanket. He tried to convince himself that she would not mind, but the fear that he would significantly lower her station nagged at him. They had not discussed such hypothetical situations just yet.

Lottie had been convalescing at her aunt's town house for the past several weeks, and when he visited, chaperoned of course, he tried not to bring up any of the recent frightening events. She luckily had her courses, so they could have the formal courtship they had skipped at a more leisurely pace. However, it was still not the standard wooing of a typical debutante. No, James's bride-to-be was recovering from a gunshot wound. He ran his hand through his hair, despite being seated at the table, and chided himself again for not protecting her. The *ton*, on the other hand, did not see their situation in the same light. The gossipmongers were beside themselves with the romantic story of a naval hero who was the long-lost son of a duke, rescuing a damsel in distress.

If only they knew.

Charlotte gazed out the window of her aunt's drawing room. She was improving, and moved around the town house without excruciating pain in her upper arm. Although Dr. Stone had removed the stitches from her wound, he continued to order her to rest and stay indoors. It was becoming harder and harder to do so as Charlotte became more restless. The only time she felt a sense of calm was when James came to visit. Those stormy gray eyes were not so stormy anymore. She liked to tell herself it was all because of her, but she knew finding his family played a large role as well. She was sure of this since the Duke no longer had the melancholic look in his eyes. Making their family whole had been a boon to everyone.

She and James talked about nothing and everything at the same time. They had skipped so many steps in getting to know each other that it felt as if Charlotte was discovering him anew. James told her about the attack on his ship and the cannonballs that had splintered the deck's wood and injured his arm, leaving the gruesome scars. He recounted his oppressive childhood under his uncle, but also how he met Jack Doherty when his now friend tried to steal a loaf of bread from him. In return, Charlotte opened up about feeling like the *forgotten fifth* throughout her life and the bravado she used to hide it. She regaled James with her exploits as a rambunctious child, trailing behind her older brothers.

Once they had bared enough of their souls to each for the time being, the pair stayed on lighter topics. Charlotte was learning all of James's favorites. His favorite color was the blue of the ocean when it was tinged with gold from the rising sun. His favorite food was anything that was fresh and not salted, due to his years at sea. His favorite season was one where he could be on the deck of a ship and neither freeze nor be fried by the sun.

Charlotte smiled at his practicality. He had lightened up

significantly, but he was still too serious for his own good. She would have to find a food he truly enjoyed, ones that made him moan with delight. Her cheeks heated as she thought of what else could satisfy James. With their chaperoned visits, they did not have any time alone, which had not bothered Charlotte right after her injury. But now that she was on the mend, being in the same room as James without the ability to touch him was pure torture.

Her chastity was not the only thing that bothered Charlotte. As she became more mobile, Charlotte noticed there were men outside her home whenever she looked out the window. She brought it up with James the day prior, and he shrugged it off. After all the recent attempts on her life, he would not act this nonchalantly unless he knew exactly what was afoot. He must be hiding something from her, and Charlotte did not like it one bit. She was not some helpless miss, and she needed to be apprised of what was going on, especially with regard to her own life. She had never let a man control her before, and she was not going to start now. A knock on the drawing room door interrupted her thoughts.

"Come in."

Robinson opened the door. "Captain Hughes seeks your audience."

"Bring him in and call for Bailey."

"Yes, Lady Charlotte."

Despite Charlotte's frustration, her breath caught when James crossed the threshold into the room. He was dressed like a proper aristocrat with his smartly tied cravat, fitted coat, and snug breeches that accentuated the muscular definition of his legs. His black top-boots gleamed in the sunlight that filtered through the windows. This cultured look was his new uniform since he had resigned his naval commission. The Duke had insisted that James learn how to manage the ducal estates instead of continuing his military career. Even if Westcliffe's marriage to James's mother was not proven, the Duke intended to bequeath his unentailed properties to James. James had fought the offer at first, not wanting to be part of the despised *ton*, but he finally acquiesced. He admitted to Charlotte that the driving force was wanting her to have the life to which she was accustomed, despite the glaring fact that he was still a bastard.

Silly man.

Charlotte was the *forgotten fifth*, and James's love was all she needed. She tried to convince him that she did not care about titles or material goods, but he would not budge.

James purposefully crossed the room toward where Charlotte sat near the window.

"Lottie, what troubles you?"

Charlotte paused. No one, not even Arthur, had ever been so attuned to her emotions.

"I…"

James knelt next to the chair where she sat and clasped her hands.

"Tell me."

Charlotte was torn between being angry at him, and her heart melting at his concern.

"You must know the identity of those strange men outside."

He shrugged his shoulders just as he had done the day before.

She stood abruptly.

"Your arm!"

"I don't give a fig about my arm right now. You know who those men are, and you aren't telling me."

James slowly rose to his feet so that he towered over Charlotte. He looked down his nose at her. How she did not guess that he had noble blood coursing through his veins was beyond her. "It's nothing for you to worry about."

Charlotte tipped up her chin. "It's not up to you to determine what I should concern myself with. You can't make these decisions for me." Charlotte poked his chest with her finger.

"You're still healing."

"I'm improving. What do you think the stress of not knowing what's going on is doing to my healing?" Charlotte retorted.

James crossed his arms and glared down at her. Charlotte lifted her chin even higher.

"The truth is much worse."

"You infuriating man. If you truly want to marry me, there can't be secrets. I will not wed someone who is not honest with me." Charlotte sat with a huff while guarding her left arm.

The muscle in James's clenched jaw pulsated. "You're not going to marry me, because I'm trying to protect you?"

Charlotte shot to her feet again and neglected to take care of her arm. "Ouch!"

James immediately moved toward her with his arms outstretched.

"Don't touch me. You just admitted that you're withholding information from me."

James ran his hand through his hair and took a step backward. He let out a prolonged sigh. "Please sit down, Lottie."

Charlotte eyed him warily but gingerly returned to her seat. Her arm throbbed. James positioned himself on the edge of the adjacent settee. He leaned forward, resting his forearms on his thighs and clasped his hands. "God, you're a stubborn woman."

"You're just noticing that now?"

James chuckled and shook his head. "Not at all. I love your passion, in all forms." His eyes raked over her body and lingered at her chest.

"James!" Charlotte's cheeks flushed. She scanned the room and made note of Bailey, who dutifully sat in the farthest corner immersed in her sewing. She must have slipped in while Charlotte's mind was consumed with the man before her.

James's face became somber. He leaned back and tried to make himself comfortable. Whether it was the information he was going to impart or his military training, James did not look one bit relaxed. Charlotte fiddled with her fingers while she waited for him to begin. Before he started, he glanced at Bailey, then asked, "Perhaps you would like some tea?"

He made a good point. "Bailey, fetch us tea and biscuits. You can leave the door cracked open for propriety."

"Yes, milady." Bailey curtseyed. Charlotte could see her lady's maid bite her cheek so as not to respond with a quip. It was always an effort on both their parts to maintain the strict roles of mistress and servant that Society made them play.

"As you are aware, the Bow Street Runners and my father's solicitors are looking for irrefutable proof of my parents' marriage. In addition, the Runners are trying to determine who Roberts and those hired killers worked for." James paused.

"And?" Charlotte inched to the edge of her seat anxiously.

"They found paperwork hidden by Roberts. It seems he would hide one or two pieces of information in various locations with the hope of making it more difficult to discover all the pieces. The Runners searched his office and his private quarters, took apart furniture, and looked behind walls and under floorboards. They found pieces of hidden evidence. Who knows what else is hidden elsewhere. From what they have found thus far, it confirms that he had a long history of criminal dealings. It's shocking no one discovered this until now."

"What is it?" Charlotte champed at the bit.

"I'm getting there. On one of the discovered papers, the Runners found a flame stamped on the paper without a signature. When the magistrate looked over the body of the man who tried to kill you at the Rowley Ball, he found a small flame tattoo on his wrist. At the time, I thought nothing of it. Once the Runners discovered the symbol on the paper, I had them show it to the magistrate, and he agreed it was identical to the man's tattoo. Apparently, the Runners have been tracking this flame symbol for years because it's been associated with many criminal activities, including during the war with Napoleon. They think it represents *le Diable*.

"The devil?"

"Yes, the King of France's underworld."

Charlotte's eyes widened.

"Can you see why I was waiting to tell you about this? *Le Diable* is the reason I have men stationed around the house, watching you constantly."

Charlotte nodded in disbelief while panic spread through her body. She finally found her voice again. "What else do you know?"

"Not as much as I'd like." James's eyes darkened. "I did learn *le Diable* was busy during the war. *Les flammes* were found in any country Napoleon touched and in England as well."

"The flames?"

"His followers are *les flammes,* and they are part of his *l'Enfer...*his Inferno, hell, Hades. Whatever you call it, it's *le Diable's* diabolical following. I don't know how long Roberts was involved with *les flammes.*"

Charlotte's mind had been more at peace since she and James reconciled, and she had been cleared of murder when it was accepted it was self-defense. Subsequently, memories of the *Incident* haunted her less. But talk of such frightening matters transported Charlotte back to that fateful day in Roberts's office.

Escape.

I need to escape.

Charlotte's heart pounded in her chest. She scanned the room for keys. She knew the door was locked. Her eyes fell on the corpse sprawled on the floor. Blood crept through the linen of Roberts's shirt from her bullet. Bile rose in her throat and Charlotte forced it down.

No time for hysterics, she told herself while trying to think clearly. She would be discovered any moment if she did not escape quickly. She scanned the lifeless body. His gun lay next to his hand.

"Dammit," Charlotte muttered. She had seen Roberts lock the door to his office, so the key must be nearby. Her eyes flitted around the room once more for what felt like minutes but was only mere seconds. She returned to the corpse and saw a bulge in his trousers.

She rushed to his lifeless body and fell to her knees. Charlotte shoved her hand into the pocket of his trousers, and the coolness of metal struck her skin. She yanked out a ring of keys and dashed to the door, fumbling with them until she found the correct one. She ran out of the office and toward the rear exit, too panicked to check if anyone saw her escaping. Charlotte spilled into the alleyway and sprinted until she reached the main thoroughfare. She slowed down to a brisk walk, so as not to appear suspicious.

"Charlotte! Charlotte!"

Something tapped her right hand, and she was forced back into the present. She took a gulp of air and was about to bolt from her chair when firm hands applied pressure to her right arm and left hip to keep her still. Charlotte's eyes blinked several times, and the familiar furnishings of her aunt's drawing room came into focus. Her heart still beat a staccato and sweat dripped down her corset.

A storm raged in James's eyes. "What's wrong?"

"I'm fine...just fine," she choked out, and tried to settle herself.

He released her body and ran a hand through his hair.

Despite his new debonair appearance, some habits could not be squelched.

"This is why I didn't want to tell you."

"No." Charlotte paused and closed her eyes, controlling her breathing. She concentrated on the pain in her arm to distract her from the memories. Her eyes opened slowly, and she carefully continued, "I need to know. I'm not some cossetted miss. I'm not a coward and will face my enemies." Charlotte tilted her chin up with bravado for which she fought, and locked eyes with James.

The storm did not thrash in his eyes as much, but it still simmered. "You were thinking of that day in Shrewsbury."

Charlotte nodded.

"You need to tell me how to help you. I can't just watch you suffer," James said.

While Charlotte put her mind to rights, a question formed. "How did *le Diable* know that I was Mrs. Gibson?"

"I don't know. Perhaps someone followed you that day. But now *le Diable* should also have me as a target, since I've been deemed responsible for the murder at the ball. I hope that will deflect his attentions from you."

Charlotte furrowed her brow with worry. "James, I would never want you hurt."

He grabbed her hands and ran his thumbs soothingly along the tops, despite the fiery look in his eyes. "I want him to come for me so that I can slit his throat and stomp on his cruel heart."

"James!"

"No one hurts those I love."

Charlotte worried her lip. "Do you think *le Diable* was responsible for your aunt's death?"

He let out a long sigh. "The Runners haven't found any evidence of when Roberts became *une flamme*. I believe Roberts killed my aunt, thinking she was my mother, though it may have been on the order of my grandfather. My father said my grandfather was a cruel man, and thinks he ordered Roberts to make my mother disappear by any means necessary in order for him to pave the way to marry Miss Waycott."

"Oh, how awful. How could your grandfather act so terribly?"

James shrugged his shoulders. "The marriage to Miss Waycott must have been of utmost importance to my grandfather. I asked my father, and he told me she was the daughter of a wealthy local baron who married a French aristocratic woman whose family had been displaced during the French Revolution. He suspected the baron's family benefited from the wars with France through smuggling, but he never pried and turned a blind eye. As I come to know my father, I'm realizing he prefers not to look for trouble."

James ran his hand through his hair. "I have a nagging suspicion that there is much more to the story."

CHAPTER TWENTY-TWO

Charlotte's mind raced to process all the new information, but she continued to return to one salient point. "Is *le Diable* still after us?"

"I suspect as much. I'm working with the Runners to find out more about him. I'll not let you leave this house until I know it's safe."

"You'll not let me?"

"Lottie, please don't start this again," he begged. "I would not *like* you to leave this house before then."

"That's a start." Charlotte leaned back on the settee and forwent the perfect ladylike posture that was expected. She could not believe she was entangled with one of the most dangerous men in France, and likely England as well. Of course, she did not want to leave the house until she knew it was safe, but she had to remind James he could not dictate her every move.

"What do we do now?" she asked.

"It looks as if you are not quite ready to leave the house anyway, so I'm going to do everything in my power to find out more and keep the men stationed outside."

"Captain Hughes!" Aunt Frances floated into the drawing room. Charlotte let out a groan. James purposely called as early as was acceptable, hoping that her aunt would still be abed. Given his connection to the Duke, James now stood on a pedestal in her aunt's eyes, and she fawned over him as such. However, Charlotte wondered if Aunt Frances's flattery would vanish if James was not proven to be the Duke's legitimate heir.

James's stern visage returned. He stood before he executed a bow. "It's always a pleasure to see you, Lady Hardwicke. I just finished my visit with Charlotte, because I have important business to attend to for my father."

"Oh! I'm sorry that you can't visit longer, but the duties of a *duke* never end." James's gaze flickered to her own, and Charlotte rolled her eyes. James was a quick study in knowing how to placate her aunt while finding a reason to make a swift exit.

He said his goodbyes, then briskly walked to the door in order to avoid any last-minute remarks from her aunt.

Aunt Frances took his seat. "Any updates?" she asked eagerly.

"I'm afraid not, but both the Bow Street Runners and the Duke of Westcliffe's solicitors continue to actively search for the marriage license. They have not lost hope."

Her aunt let out a dramatic sigh and braced herself on the cushion. "Thank goodness," she exhaled. If she became this melodramatic about whether or not James was the heir to the Duchy of Westcliffe, Charlotte could not imagine how she would respond if she knew that someone was trying to kill her niece.

Charlotte paused. Her aunt would likely be more concerned that a murder would dirty her Axminster rug. Charlotte was glad she had chosen not to reveal any details regarding the danger she faced to her aunt, and instead fed her tidbits about James's potential rightful place in Society. This topic was the perfect material to keep her aunt occupied.

"I'm glad to hear they are still on the search." Her aunt, now satisfied with the latest update on the search for James's dukedom, sprang up from her seat. "I must get ready for today's calls." She swept out of the room with her head held high.

Before Charlotte could get settled, Robinson appeared in the drawing room doorway to announce Beatrice, Eleanor, and Bridget. Charlotte's mood lightened, and she instructed the butler to show them in. Bailey's figure appeared behind Robinson.

"Bailey, it looks as if there will be three guests for tea." Her lady's maid nodded and headed back to the kitchens.

The women filed into the drawing room. Beatrice at the front, as usual, followed by Eleanor, and then Bridget. Beatrice held herself regally, being the daughter of a marquess, after all. Eleanor held herself properly for all intents and purposes, yet she had a mischievous look on her face like she hid the most fascinating secret. Bridget brought up the rear with her shoulders drawn forward and a forlorn look in her eyes. Charlotte still could not figure out what made all the Lockharts have that sad aura about them, but Bridget was by far the worst. She always looked as if she wanted to curl herself into a ball and hide from the world. Bridget opened up somewhat when she was with their group of female friends, but Charlotte still suspected she was hiding a terrible secret.

Charlotte greeted the ladies and answered their inquiries regarding her arm before they seated themselves around the settee upon which Charlotte was perched.

Beatrice arched her eyebrows. "We passed Captain Hughes leaving the house as we arrived."

"Oh?" Charlotte attempted to respond nonchalantly, but her cheeks flushed anyway.

"No need to be embarrassed, you're betrothed," Beatrice reassured her.

"I know, but it still feels, well...odd." Charlotte had lived her life in the periphery as the *forgotten fifth*, so becoming the center of attention was a new and unsettling experience.

"How magnificent to be head over heels in love with someone," Eleanor exclaimed with a glint in her eye. She clasped her hands together.

"Eleanor, we swore never to marry. You can't wax poetic about love," Beatrice responded.

"Who said anything about marriage?" The corner of Eleanor's mouth quirked upward. "You can have love, or lovers for that matter, without nuptials."

"Eleanor Balfour," Beatrice chided.

Eleanor rolled her eyes. "Stop being so stuffy."

Beatrice shook her head. "I have no idea what you were doing in Italy."

Eleanor waggled her eyebrows. "Neither did my chaperone."

Charlotte let out an unladylike bark of laughter. After what she had just learned from James and the turmoil she was feeling, the ridiculousness of this conversation was the levity she dearly needed. "You just brightened my day."

"We're flattered of course, but we thought you would be in a wonderful mood after seeing Captain Hughes. You love him, do you not?" Eleanor asked earnestly.

Charlotte felt her cheeks heat up once again. She straightened the nonexistent wrinkles in her skirt and took a moment to compose herself. She slowly raised her eyes and looked at each of the ladies in turn. "I'm afraid that I do. A year ago, I was home in Shropshire. I, too, was not looking to fall in love, or get married for that matter, but I suppose love came looking for me. Now here I am."

"What troubles you then?"

Charlotte turned to the quiet voice of Bridget and saw concern etched on her face.

Although Charlotte was hesitant to open up to her friends about all her insecurities, she had confided in them about everything related to the *Incident* and its repercussions. Well, everything except the intimacy she had shared with James.

"Did Captain Hughes learn something new?" Beatrice queried in her direct manner.

"Yes." Charlotte took a deep breath. "He found out that the king of the French underworld, *le Diable*, has been the one after my life."

Charlotte heard a gasp and turned toward the sound, but she could not tell if it came from Eleanor or Bridget. Her eyes roamed over the faces of her friends. Beatrice and Eleanor looked appropriately concerned, whereas Bridget appeared shocked, and her face had lost all its color.

"I've never heard of such a man. Who is he?" Beatrice asked.

"He's apparently very dangerous and not to be crossed. James is trying to find out more about him. He has followers, *les flammes*, in both France and England. They've been associated with some of the murkier situations during the war and continue to be active. They're part of *le Diable's l'Enfer,* and they have flame tattoos to mark their allegiance. The man who shot me at the ball had that tattoo, and it matched the symbol found on one of Roberts's documents."

Beatrice and Eleanor appeared understandably uncomfortable while they digested this new information, but Bridget was visibly trembling.

"Bridget, are you quite all right?" Charlotte said.

Bridget swallowed several times, trying to clear her throat. She choked out a response, "I'm fine. It's just startling news."

Charlotte nodded and studied Bridget further. She must be hiding something. Whatever it was, it must be horrid for Charlotte's situation to elicit such a response.

"What's the plan?" Beatrice quickly recovered and was back to the matter at hand.

"The doctor has not cleared me to leave the house yet. James has men guarding the property while he continues to work with the Runners to learn more about *le Diable*."

"How terrible," Eleanor exclaimed. "If there's anything we can do to help you deal with this, please let us know."

Charlotte looked at her newfound friends and was beyond grateful to finally be part of such a supportive group. "Thank you. You ladies mean the world to me. Coming to visit while I'm trapped indoors is the best thing you can do."

"Let us talk about other subjects. No need to dwell on murder attempts and death and what not," Eleanor said.

Charlotte smiled. If death and murder did not ruffle Eleanor's feathers, she was not sure what would.

Beatrice and Eleanor proceeded to update Charlotte with the latest gossip, while Bridget appeared withdrawn and shaken. Charlotte's heart broke for Bridget due to her distress, and wished she would confide in their group. Charlotte understood, however, why her friend did not reveal what troubled her. As Beatrice had said when they first met, "We all have our scandalous secrets and nothing in the *ton* stays hidden for long. The only safeguard is to keep it to yourself or rid yourself of anyone who would tattle."

How right she was.

James sat in the corner booth of a pub in one of the shadier parts of London. Jack Doherty sat across from him, dwarfing the seat with his hulking size. James was a large, well-built man, but the only time he ever felt small was when he was around his best friend. Even though the establishment was dimly lit, Jack's fiery hair was unmistakable. He kept it short because long hair could only be a vulnerability in a fight. Jack's whiskey-colored eyes glowed under the flickering light from the single sconce near their table.

"You're not dressed like a toff," Jack said.

James glared at him. His friend always knew the best way to rile him up. "I'm more comfortable dressed this way."

"Thank you, *Your Grace*, for sparing a commoner like me a moment in your busy schedule." Jack dramatically bowed from his seated position at the table. James shook his head. He knew Jack jested, but he also knew Jack's contempt for the *ton* ran much deeper than his own.

"Since I have graced you with my presence, you'd best make it worth my time," James retorted.

Jack's face spread into a wide smile, and he took a gulp of his ale then slammed the mug on the table. "Glad I didn't lose you!"

"You're never going to lose me, even if you tried."

Jack let out a hearty laugh. He leaned back and crossed his arms.

"I know you love to spend time with me, James, but there must be a reason we're here."

"There is, but before I start, what are you really doing in London? You didn't mention this trip before I left Birmingham."

"After you left, I got word that the owner of Roulette was in money trouble. You know I've been looking to expand into London."

James nodded in acquiescence, despite suspecting there was more to Jack's motives for coming to Town. "Who's running everything in Birmingham? Your sister?" James took a sip of his ale and eyed Jack across the rim of the mug.

Jack let out a belch before answering. "You bet. I wouldn't trust anyone but Helen."

"She's well?"

"Well as ever. She has a mouth on her though, even with your mam teaching us our letters and how to talk like toffs. She likes to do everything her own way." Jack shrugged his shoulders and finished his ale. He held out the mug to a passing barmaid with his left hand, his second finger visibly absent from a factory accident, and ordered another.

James had had an idyllic childhood compared to Jack, so that was saying something about what his friend had gone through. Helen was the only family Jack had left, and was not his sister by birth, but by circumstance. His friend would kill anyone who touched a hair on her head.

"Enough about what I'm doing here. Tell me what's going on," Jack said.

James took a bigger gulp of his drink, then gave Jack the abridged version of all that had happened since coming to London.

Once he was done, Jack eyed him warily. "Bloody hell, James. This is a mess."

"I know. I don't think even you could have gotten yourself into as much of a pickle as Charlotte has."

Jack shook his head. "Maybe as a scamp, but now? Never. I know everything and everyone. She sounds like a tough chit, though." Jack rapped the fingers of his right hand on the worn table. "Perfect to work for me."

James narrowed his eyes at Jack. He knew Jack was taunting him again, but he could not suppress the anger that welled up inside him at the thought of Lottie being in danger once more. "You're lucky we're in public, so I don't throttle you."

Jack chuckled. "You haven't been able to beat me since I was a scrawny whelp on the streets."

"I may not be as big as you, but I'm wily and was in the Royal Navy too long to lose."

Jack appeared amused. He opened and closed his monstrous fists. "Think what you want, you know I'm right. I could beat you with one hand tied behind my back, Jamesy boy," Jack challenged.

Before James could offer a rebuttal, Jack continued, "Who's behind these guys?"

"*Le Diable.*"

Jack's eyebrows shot up. "Really?" he said slowly.

"You know him?"

His friend's face became serious for once. "He was my top competitor in the smuggling market."

"You smuggled?" James asked.

"Don't be daft. How else would I get brandy and silks out from underneath Napoleon's nose? I figured you would have caught wind of it eventually, but I guess I'm that good at what I do." Jack smirked. "You probably don't know half of my other *businesses*. Now that the war is over, I've had to look for other ways to make money."

James eyed his best friend, not believing he had been that oblivious to Jack's other dealings. But then again, he may not have wanted to know what else he was doing. James had enough to worry about in his own life.

Jack continued, not noticing James's dismay. "You're too good of a man, too *honorable*," he said the last word with chagrin. "Truthfully, I kept you in the dark because I didn't want to have you feeling all righteous or guilty or whatever a good man would feel. I, on the other hand, have no qualms with using underhanded means to get what I want," Jack finished flippantly.

"What do you know of *le Diable*?" James asked. He needed to get to the heart of the matter and help Lottie.

"I've never met the bastard, but he fights dirty. He also has something of mine, so I want to take him down." Jack's tone became spiteful. "Attacking a lady is just what *le Diable* would do."

James ran his hand through his hair. "Charlotte is confined to her aunt's home while she's healing, but she should be well soon. I'm scared for her to leave the house. I have it surrounded night and day with guards." Although fear for Lottie's safety still gripped James, he felt the slightest sense of relief at being able to confide in his friend.

Jack looked at James resolutely. "Leave it up to me. Give me some time and she'll be able to leave the house without anyone touching her."

"How?"

"The less you know the better." Jack signaled to the barmaid, and she brought over another mug of ale. The two men sat in silence, sipping their drinks, each alone in his thoughts.

CHAPTER TWENTY-THREE

C harlotte sat in front of the mirror of her vanity.

"You look beautiful, Lady Charlotte." Bailey was a woman of concise words, so her ebullient praise touched Charlotte's heart. Her lady's maid had fussed over her hair, and Charlotte now had diamond pins arranged in her upswept coiffure. These accoutrements complemented the sapphire-and-diamond hair combs from her aunt's sapphire parure that she had lent her.

Charlotte had to admit, the precious blue gemstones brought out the color of her eyes. Between her hair accessories and jewelry, Charlotte sparkled with every movement. "It's all thanks to you, Bailey."

"Nonsense, milady." Her lady's maid surveyed her work and tucked a nonexistent tendril of hair into Charlotte's chignon for good measure. The bullet wound in Charlotte's arm had significantly improved, but it was still tenuous and healing. Luckily, infection had not set in, and the burning pain had lessened. Bailey fashioned a thin bandage to cover the wound for protection that fit perfectly under the sleeve of Charlotte's gown so the guests would be none the wiser.

Who was she kidding, though?

All the *ton* was still agog of Charlotte's dramatic injury and her naval knight in shining armor. Today's wedding of Lady Charlotte Tipton to Captain James Hughes was going to be the event of the Season.

At first, Charlotte had tried to fight the *ton*'s frenzy surrounding her life, but she gave up and was now trying to ignore it. That did not mean she was impervious to the attention and knew that the *beau monde* would scrutinize all aspects of her big day. Charlotte could not help but be thankful that her wedding gown was impeccable, and that the *ton* could not criticize her wardrobe, courtesy of His Grace. Her former almost-betrothed and now soon-to-be father-in-law, the Duke of West-cliffe, had insisted that he gift her a dress for her wedding, as a show of goodwill.

Charlotte adjusted the spider-gauze that covered the smooth, white silk of her gown, which was adorned with pearl floral embellishments, lace trim along the hem, and a ruffled neckline.

"The Captain is going to fall all over you," Bailey stated matter-of-factly.

Charlotte tilted her head back and forth, allowing the light that streamed in through her bedroom window to catch the sapphires and diamonds in her hair.

"I hope so," Charlotte responded nervously. She had waited for this day that she still could not believe she was truly marrying James, the love of her life. Charlotte was convinced yet another catastrophe would come between them. She would not relax until they had said their vows and were married before God.

The bedroom door flew open, and her aunt glided into the room. "Oh, Charlotte, you look a dream!"

Bailey gave a curtsy and left the two women alone.

"Thank you for lending me the jewelry." Charlotte smiled at Aunt Frances, surely appreciating that the sapphires truly suited her complexion best.

"You will soon have a collection of your own." Her aunt let out a sigh. "Even if Captain Hughes doesn't inherit, Westcliffe will ensure you two are well-situated. No need to worry."

As was often the case with her aunt, Charlotte forced herself not to roll her eyes, but she could not hold her tongue. "There is more to life than jewels and titles."

Her aunt looked at her, genuinely befuddled, then a thought crossed Charlotte's mind. "Did you look at the marriage settlement?"

Her aunt did not even feign innocence. "Of course, I did. You know your father would sign off on anything. Arthur discussed the matter with Westcliffe, but I just wanted to be sure you were compensated appropriately."

"Compensated? I love James."

Her aunt waved her hand in dismissal. "If the worst-case scenario happens and Captain Hughes doesn't become titled, you need to ensure you have enough financial means besides your dowry. I see what that trade grandfather of yours did for you. The dowry is a boon, but you can never have enough funds. Money and the connection to the Duke will allow you to remain in Society." Her aunt let out a dramatic sigh.

Then her aunt turned her attention to the next pressing matter. "I've yet to understand why you didn't want a large wedding. You're the talk of the *ton*. How could you let this opportunity pass by?"

"We made a compromise. I'm recovering from a gunshot wound. I would hate to swoon in the church and embarrass the family." The only way to connect with her aunt was through Society's opinion, not the fact that Charlotte and James did not want to be paraded about at their own nuptials.

"The wedding will be a small, private affair. This way, you'll be one of the few people to witness this momentous occasion." In the reflection of the vanity mirror, she saw her aunt's eyes widen and an almost gleeful look formed on her face. "Plus, Eleanor has kindly agreed to sketch James and me for the papers, so the *ton* can corroborate your firsthand account."

Her aunt clasped her hands together excitedly. "Excellent point, Charlotte. I'm going to be one of the only people with this coveted information. Now then, stand up for me. I must make note of everything you're wearing." Charlotte acquiesced and eased herself up from the cushioned vanity stool, careful not to wrinkle her dress. She wanted to save her energy for the actual wedding.

Her aunt's eyes roved Charlotte's figure in an assessing manner. "Turn around." Charlotte rotated as commanded, wanting the evaluation to be completed. She finished her spin and faced her aunt. While her back had been turned, her aunt's facial expression had changed. Was that a tear in the corner of her aunt's eye? Charlotte never thought she would see the day.

"You look beautiful, my dear niece. I'm proud of you."

Charlotte was shocked.

A single sniffle emerged from her aunt before her typical façade returned. The moment was gone before it began. "The carriage waits to take us to the church. Your father and Arthur are downstairs."

Aunt Frances swept out of the room and Charlotte was left to look at herself one more time in the mirror. She felt like a princess with her shimmering jewelry and gorgeous gown. Her cheeks possessed a healthy glow from the excitement of finally marrying James and starting the next chapter of her life. She picked up her bouquet of pink peonies and white roses from the garden that were tied with a white ribbon. Charlotte stood and turned toward the door. She took one last glance over her shoulder to catch her reflection in the mirror before walking out the bedroom door and into her future.

She was descending the stairs and saw Arthur standing at the bottom. He looked up lovingly at her before his face broke out into a wide smile. Charlotte wanted to run down the steps, but she maintained a steady pace and did not trip over her gown.

"Wow, Charlie, you look stunning," Arthur exclaimed. He covered her gloved hands with his own. Arthur knew her as his tomboyish younger sister, not a full-grown woman. From the look on his face, he was just realizing this now.

"Thank you," she replied.

Arthur pushed up his glasses and cleared his throat. "Shall we?" He offered Charlotte his arm to escort her to the town coach.

Charlotte linked her arm with her brother's, "Where's Father?"

Arthur raised his eyebrows. "He's waiting in the carriage."

Charlotte knew she should not feel a pang of disappointment that her own father did not care enough to catch a first glimpse of his only daughter on her wedding day.

Arthur sensed her discomfort and gave her arm a squeeze. He bowed his head to speak softly into her ear. "Charlie, this is your day. Don't let him bother you. I love you dearly."

Charlotte lifted her gaze to look at Arthur and gave him a reassuring smile. He was right. Wishing for things that would never be had no place on her wedding day. Her future was with James.

Charlotte and Arthur entered the carriage and sat across from their father.

"Daughter." He glanced at Charlotte before turning his attention back to looking out the window.

The equipage jolted and headed to the church. Charlotte

studied her father and felt a sense of liberation. He was actually a pathetic excuse for a man. He had ruddy cheeks, a bloated face, and a distended abdomen, all from overindulgence and laziness. She did not need his approval. In fact, she did not even want it. After all that had transpired, Charlotte was now a more confident woman who no longer needed to act out to gain the attention of her family as she had done in her youth. She had the brother she adored seated beside her, and the man she loved waiting for her at the altar.

That was all Charlotte needed.

The coach stopped rocking, indicating they had reached the church. Charlotte felt butterflies in her stomach while she waited for the footman to open the door. She noted the heavy breathing of her father before he waddled out of the carriage. Arthur alighted next and held out his hand to help her down. Her aunt waited in the atrium of the church. She had taken a different carriage with her husband. Her aunt had decided her spouse, who lived a separate and happy life, should attend their niece's wedding.

"Most people are seated," her aunt announced. She eyed Charlotte's father. "Peter, you have one job. Walk Charlotte down the aisle and deposit her in the front." She was about to turn when she paused. "Oh, and look happy about it."

Her father gave an insouciant shrug. In the light, Charlotte noticed the wrinkles on her father's face and the thinning of his hair. He looked years older than his true age. Her eldest brother Henry resembled him and also lived an indulgent life. The last she had heard, Henry was out in the country at one of the earldom's estates with his latest mistress. He was eating and drinking to his heart's content with several other bachelors who did not want to be bothered by the Season. If Henry did not change his lifestyle, this was the future that awaited him.

Aunt Frances shifted her attention to Charlotte and

assessed her appearance once more. "You look perfect." With that declaration, her aunt slipped into the narthex, leaving Charlotte with her father and brother.

"I'll be right back." Arthur followed his aunt and then returned shortly after.

"I don't see your betrothed, but Carrington was near the altar. Let me check if we can get this wedding started. Wait here."

Her father quickly found a bench in the atrium on which to sit. He rested his clasped hands on his protruding abdomen and leaned back against the wall. He was already fatigued, despite the short walk from the town coach to the church.

"Will you be all right?" Charlotte looked at her feckless father.

"Quite," he responded. He closed his eyes to rest before the arduous task of walking his only daughter down the aisle.

Charlotte could not sit down and wait. She paced in nervous anticipation, her bouquet hanging from her hand. She simply arrived before James. After a few moments, she could not lie to herself. Charlotte was worried. She had become too accustomed to expecting the unexpected and now feared the worst. Did *le Diable* attack James? Was he in some horrible carriage accident? Was he crying off their wedding? Her pacing quickened as she ran through all the possibilities.

Return to reason.

Charlotte was in the midst of ranking her worries by probability of occurring when a snort broke her train of thought. She turned toward the source of the sound and found her father snoring with his mouth gaping open. He really was an impossible man.

Before she could dwell on his failings further, the door between the atrium and narthex flew open. Arthur strode toward her with his brow furrowed.

Charlotte knew something was wrong. "What is it?"

"James is missing."

Charlotte's heart sank. She tossed out all the hypothetical reasons James was not at the church and focused on the most likely. He had cried off the wedding. She was destined to always be the *forgotten fifth*. "I can't believe it!"

Arthur was taken aback. "I'm worried something has happened to him."

"What?" It was as if someone had dumped a bucket of cold water on her head. "You really think so? He didn't finally realize he'd be better off without me?"

Now Arthur appeared upset, which was a rare occurrence. "Charlotte Tipton, I have seen the way James looks at you. The devil himself could not keep that man from this wedding." He stood over her with his hands on his hips just like when she had gotten into scrapes as a child. "All I know is that James left a brief missive for Carrington that he would meet him at the church instead of riding over with him from the town house."

Arthur's eyes quickly glazed over while his inquisitive mind turned over possibilities. Charlotte did the same. Per the note, James had not forgotten about the wedding but had been called off for some reason.

But what? Was it a trick by le Diable to get James alone?

Charlotte's heart raced as genuine fear took hold of her body.

"What if something happened to him? We must find him."

Arthur responded calmly, "We need to think about his absence methodically. I'll send one of the footmen back to Carrington's house to determine if any of the servants know where James headed, or at least in what direction."

Arthur's logic made perfect sense, but it would take time. Charlotte felt helpless. "We must do something now."

"Let me check with Carrington once more and ensure there's no critical information he forgot to mention."

Arthur exited the atrium, leaving the door open, and Charlotte paced again.

It must be le Diable, Charlotte reasoned.

James had told her Jack was going to take care of this particular threat to her life, but he never said if the protection encompassed James as well. She could not lose him...she just could not.

Although there were only a small number of wedding guests, Charlotte could hear the din of their voices from the main part of the church. The sound grew louder and louder until suddenly...was that a cheer?

Arthur rushed inside the atrium. "He's here!"

Relief flooded over Charlotte, but that was short-lasting. "I'm going to kill him for scaring me like that!"

A lopsided grin spread on Arthur's face. "Charlie, don't let marriage change you too much. Your combination of pragmatism and impulsiveness is incomparable. Just remember, in order to get married, your groom has to be alive," he jested.

Charlotte could not help but smile. "Let's get married then!"

Arthur forcefully nudged their father's foot, and their father awoke with a confused look on his face. "Father, you need to walk Charlie down the aisle, remember?" he asked sternly.

After a few moments collecting his thoughts and a couple of glances around his surroundings, their father hoisted himself into a standing position. "Yes," he muttered.

Her father walked toward Charlotte, his breathing labored. He stopped before her and seemed to see his daughter for the first time that day. "It's your wedding day, Daughter."

"How kind of you to remember."

CHAPTER TWENTY-FOUR

She's going to kill me, James thought, while he waited at the altar for his bride to walk down the aisle.

He stood resplendent in a black, superfine long-tailed coat, gray waistcoat, and black breeches buttoned just below the knee, with white stockings and black shoes. James now had a valet who had dressed him up finer than usual, it being his wedding day and all. James felt like a dandy with his cravat meticulously fashioned into an Osbaldeston. Gabe stood beside him in his formal dress, looking dapper as usual.

The doors of the church opened, and James's breath caught as the most beautiful image appeared before him. Well, almost the most beautiful. Charlotte was gorgeous in a white gown with an astounding number of sapphires and diamonds glistening upon her, but her brow was furrowed. Was she truly angry at him? He had hoped he would have a happy bride on his wedding day, in spite of his tardiness.

He saw her glance at the portly gentleman leading her down the aisle, whom he assumed to be her father, Lord Pulverbatch. Her brow furrowed more deeply. Ah, perhaps James was not the cause for her disdain.

Charlotte pushed her shoulders back and tilted her chin up like the empress of his dreams and looked down the aisle. Charlotte's eyes locked with his and her brow relaxed. A smile spread across her lovely face. As she walked down the aisle, James could not tear his own gaze from those two cornflower-blue eyes that were fixed upon him. He was the luckiest man in the world. He did not know what he had ever done to deserve such a breathtaking woman as Lottie.

When his soon-to-be bride reached the altar, her eyes were misty. James grinned like a fool, because he was so happy. Lord Pulverbatch left her side without so much as a glance. James would never be able to stop looking at Lottie. He would make up for all the times her family ignored the treasure that was Charlotte Tipton. He smiled even further. She would be Charlotte Hughes from now on, and be all his to worship for the rest of their lives.

James took hold of her hands, and the bishop began the ceremony. He was too busy memorizing Lottie's every detail to pay attention to what the clergyman was saying. He noticed that one tendril of chestnut hair had escaped her chignon and curled near her right ear. He realized her eyes appeared a deeper blue than usual and matched the color of the Strait of Gibraltar as the Atlantic Ocean and Mediterranean Sea became one. He had to remember every single part of this day.

James realized belatedly that the wedding guests had emitted a collective gasp and that Lottie's mouth had formed a delectable O. He blinked and looked around, trying to understand what had happened. The guests spoke excitedly with each other.

The bishop looked down his nose at James. "Lord Thornbridge?"

Now James understood. The morning had been a blur. He had received an urgent summons from Morris just as dawn was breaking. James made haste to the docks, but was waylaid by his hackney throwing a wheel. He had to search for another one at such an early hour. Finally, he made it to his meeting spot with Morris, where the Bow Street Runner triumphantly held a piece of vellum they had found underneath a floorboard in Roberts's apartment. James quickly learned that it was from the registry of the church in which his parents were married. James rushed back to Mayfair to swiftly change for his own wedding. He did not have time to notify anyone aside from dispatching an urgent message to the bishop.

James glanced to the front pew and saw his parents embrace with joy, despite the impropriety of the gesture. He turned back and found Lottie recovered from the initial shock. She quirked an eyebrow, and James shrugged his shoulders. Her chest vibrated with a silent chuckle. Meanwhile, the bishop tried to quiet the guests to resume the service.

The Duke's voice boomed over the crowd, "Ladies and gentlemen, the Marquess of Thornbridge needs to marry his marchioness." The guests laughed and settled down. His father ensured everyone's attention was directed to the front of the church before he took his seat. The bishop cleared his throat and continued through the ceremony without further inter-ruptions.

When the service reached the final segment, Gabe handed James the gold posy ring that had been worn by generations of Marchionesses of Thornbridge. The exterior had delicate floral engravings while the inside was inscribed with the words, *My Heart is Yours*. James's father had given him the ring, not knowing if he would ever truly become the marquess.

James looked down at his beautiful bride and tears welled in her eyes once more. He recited the age-old pledge to forever love and cherish the woman before him.

"With this ring I thee wed, with my body I thee worship,

and with all my worldly goods I thee endow. In the Name of the Father, and of the Son, and of the Holy Ghost. Amen."

James slid the ring onto the fourth finger of Lottie's left hand. After what felt like eons, the ceremony finally ended.

James looked at the woman he loved whom he could finally call *wife*.

Husband.

Charlotte could not believe she was married to James. She arranged the silk skirt of her dress on the seat of one of the ducal coaches to prevent wrinkles from developing before the wedding breakfast at the Westcliffe manse. James climbed in after her, and his imposing form seemed to take up the entire opposite side of the carriage.

He leaned forward and tucked an errant lock of hair behind her ear. "I'm so happy."

Charlotte smiled widely back at him. "I am too, but why did you almost miss the ceremony?" She was no longer angry but curious as to what happened. James proceeded to explain the emergent missive that delayed him earlier that morning.

"I thought you had simply forgotten about me just like most of my family. But then, Arthur suspected something terrible had happened to you. I was sure it was *le Diable* and feared for your safety. I can't lose you."

James reached out and grabbed her hands, his large palms easily surrounding her own. "I would never forget about you. I'm sorry I wasn't able to give a warning in advance. Morris summoned me so urgently, and I assumed I would be able to make it back in time."

"I forgive you, *husband*." Charlotte's cheeks flushed, and she gazed hungrily at the virile man before her.

"I accept your apology, my wife, my lady, my marchioness." The side of his mouth lifted. "I didn't need the title, but you deserve to have what you're accustomed to and more."

"I would have married you no matter what the circumstances. Our love is worth more than all the titles, all the gold and diamonds in the world."

Charlotte tilted her head and raised her eyebrows. She added teasingly, "Or insurance money."

James looked down abashed. "You know I really wasn't going to turn you in," he muttered.

"I'm grateful your father made the case disappear."

James lifted his eyes. "I hate to admit it since I still don't like the *ton*, but I'm glad he has some powerful friends."

"You're one of us now," Charlotte jested.

James let out a disgruntled sigh. Before he could lament his new place in Society, the carriage jolted as it made a turn. Charlotte, who had already leaned forward while James held her hands, lurched toward him. James caught her before she could fall and swiftly scooped her into his lap. He took care not to jostle her left arm.

"Well, this is convenient." His mood changed and his eyes darkened. He looked like he would devour Charlotte.

"Is that so?" she responded playfully.

"The supervised visits these past few weeks have been torture. Knowing what it was like to be inside you and then having it taken away was a cruel punishment."

Charlotte's heart beat faster at James's dirty words. She squeezed her legs together to curb the pulsation between them.

She wrapped her right arm around James's neck. "It's been torture for me too. But we have the wedding breakfast, and we can't arrive disheveled."

"It's our wedding. We can arrive any way we please." James's arousal nudged her bottom.

"I wanted us to have a proper wedding night, but I don't think I can keep my hands off you until then." One of James's hands toyed with her breast as he spoke. Even though there was a barrier of fabric, her nipple hardened immediately, and moisture pooled between her legs. Charlotte did not think she could fight the need she felt for James.

"Then ravish me," Charlotte challenged. She grabbed James's head and pulled his mouth toward her own.

The moment their lips connected, everything felt right in the world. James thrust his tongue into her mouth, and Charlotte eagerly responded. This was not a slow seduction. It was a pent-up desire that had grown over the past few weeks and was suddenly unleashed.

James broke the kiss, and Charlotte felt the sudden void, only to be replaced by a tingling feeling as his lips traveled down her neck to her collarbone. Although he was careful not to disturb her wound, he took no time in pulling down the front of her gown, allowing her breasts to spring free from their constraints.

"I've been waiting too long." James looked up at Charlotte for a moment, long enough for her to see the hunger in his silvery eyes before he returned his attention to her breasts. He devoured them as if they were a delectable dessert. His tongue lapped her left nipple that hardened in response and a jolt of sensation traveled from her breast to her core. He sucked her nipple with just a little bit of teeth. The heady mix between the nipping and soothing motions of his tongue made it even more pleasurable. Charlotte wiggled her bottom over James's arousal, wanting more. His member hardened further, adding to the unmet sexual tension in the carriage.

James moved to her other breast and gave it much of the same attention. She heard a moan and realized it had escaped from her mouth. She threw her head back from the overwhelming passion that coursed through her body. James's hand crept up her leg and reached her garter, but he kept going. She felt his calloused fingers delicately trace her inner thigh. Charlotte shivered.

James raised his head from her breast. "Are you chilly?" he murmured.

"No," Charlotte responded breathlessly, not able to formulate much of a response. James returned to her breast while his hand continued its journey toward her center.

He reached his target and looked at Charlotte once again. "You're so wet for me. Only for me."

"Only you," Charlotte moaned. James let out a groan and then two fingers entered her core and thrusted in and out. He spread her juices over her pearl and used his thumb to stroke her most sensitive area. Sensations swelled in Charlotte, and she writhed in James's lap, trying to handle them all. Despite the frenzied feeling within her, something was still missing. James thrust inside her and rubbed her pearl, but the feeling did not grow quickly enough.

"More," Charlotte demanded. James chuckled, though his voice sounded distant because she was so consumed with reaching her ultimate pleasure. James lowered his head and sucked her nipple while he continued his ministrations lower down. Charlotte breathed rapidly, and she rode James's hand shamelessly. James gave another swipe of his thumb, and everything exploded. Charlotte yelled out his name, and her whole body shook uncontrollably. The most heavenly sensations permeated her.

James eased his thrusting but continued to attend to her pearl. Despite reaching the peak of her bliss, each wet stroke of James's thumb on her nub caused ripples of her orgasm to continue. She kept calling out his name, not wanting this feeling to ever end.

When all her pleasure had finally been spent, Charlotte's head dropped onto James's chest from sheer exhaustion. Her eyes closed while her breasts remained exposed and uninhibited. James eased his hand out from under her dress. Charlotte heard a sucking sound as James licked her juices off his fingers. Charlotte was too tired to open her eyes, but she quickly formed an erotic image of her husband savoring her. While Charlotte drifted off to sleep, she distantly noticed that James's arousal was still protruding into her bottom. Before she could think more about it, her mind went blank.

CHAPTER TWENTY-FIVE

"Lottie, Lottie." James gently shook Charlotte's good shoulder. They were close to his father's stately home. James's member was so tightly wound that he felt as if he was about to burst. In spite of the unbearable discomfort, James refused to take Charlotte for the first time as his wife in a bloody carriage. He just had to survive the wedding breakfast and then he was locking his wife in their bedroom and showing her how many ways he could make her scream his name.

She begrudgingly opened her striking eyes and took a moment to become aware of her surroundings. She looked down and saw her perfectly rounded breasts on full display.

"Oh!" She quickly sat up and rearranged her dress. Her cheeks blushed becomingly.

"How long have I been asleep?"

"Not long."

"I feel so...relaxed."

"I'm glad," James said evenly, using all his energy to play the gentleman, when all he wanted to do was tear Lottie's gown off, throw her down on the seat, and fuck her until his name was coming out of her delectable mouth. Instead, James had to shift his position to keep the discomfort of his raging erection at bay.

"It's still there." Lottie shifted on his lap. "Does it hurt?"

"Like the devil."

"I could help you. How much time do we have?"

"No more than ten minutes."

Lottie furrowed her brow. James knew she must be performing calculations in her clever mind.

"If you're already so, um, excited, would it take that long?"

"It wouldn't, but I'm going to give you the wedding night you deserve."

"There has to be a different way." Lottie slid off his lap and before he could protest, she pulled down his breeches and smallclothes. His member eagerly sprung free, engorged and close to the point of release. Lottie reached out and encircled it with her right hand, rubbing her fingers around it, as if she was taking stock of his manhood.

"Lottie," James groaned.

"Right." She gave a slight nod of her head, almost to herself, and moved her hand to his base. James let out a hiss from a mere stroke. His wife made him feel like an untried youth. James remained tense while he waited for her to continue. Instead, Lottie dove down and took him in her mouth.

"Oh!" James grabbed on to the edge of the seat with both hands. In spite of Lottie's initial gusto, she now gingerly eased his member into her throat before pulling back and repeating it again, but deeper this time. James was about to explode.

Lottie paused for a moment and looked up at him with those big blue eyes. "Is this all right?" James would never forget the image of his wife staring at him while his cock rose in front of her face. James used every last ounce of control to not spend this instant.

"Yes," James answered through gritted teeth.

She licked the head of his member before she took him again with her mouth. James could not take the torment much longer. He reached out to her nape, careful not to tussle her hair and guided Lottie with the pace and the depth. She sucked on him more vigorously and took him deeper into her throat. James had never felt anything so exquisite in his life. Well, except when he was actually sinking into her cunny, but this was damn close. Lottie became more comfortable with every movement back and forth, and soon, her tongue circled him while she sucked. James teetered on the edge as he felt the pressure build until a darting of her tongue over his tip sent him all the way.

James let out a yelp, and he pulled his member from her mouth and released on the seat. His head fell back, and all the energy drained out of his body. James stayed like this with his eyes closed until his erratic breathing calmed down. With the little wherewithal he had left, he reached into his pocket and pulled out a handkerchief. He handed it to Lottie, who wiped her mouth before he used it to clean up the seat.

"That was fun." Lottie looked at him wickedly, knowing she held all the power.

James let out a groan. "You minx. You'll be the death of me."

The coach slowed, and James mustered the energy to quickly shove his satisfied member back into his clothing. Charlotte also righted herself and attempted to smooth the wrinkles from her gown. The guests were not going to have guess hard to figure out how the newlywed couple passed the time between the church and the breakfast, but James did not care.

They were married.

~

Charlotte sat next to James on a settee and looked around at the friends and family who had gathered for their wedding breakfast. She was beyond happy. As she gazed contentedly at the guests, she noted the groups that had formed in the drawing room after the meal.

Her aunt spoke animatedly to the Countess of Carrington and James's mother, the Duchess of Westcliffe. Eleanor, Beatrice, Bridget, and James's new sisters all sat together with their heads bent, likely gossiping or creating some kind of mischief. Jack Doherty sat on the opposite side of the room, looking deceivingly bored while the Earl of Carrington carried on a conversation around him. The only movements that gave away that Jack was not entirely unaffected were when his eyes darted to the group of Charlotte's friends. Since the young women were together, she could not tell who caught his eye, or perhaps Jack's case, offended him. She had noticed his vocal distaste for the *ton*. Near the windows, Arthur spoke with the Duke of Westcliffe, probably about Parliamentary matters, given the passionate look on her brother's face.

Charlotte placed her hand on James's forearm, "It looks like most everyone is having a good time."

"I entirely agree. I think our presence here is no longer needed." James waggled his eyebrows at Charlotte.

James's mother broke away from the other ladies and walked toward them. Charlotte was still amazed that this petite woman could have given birth to such a magnificent and large man. The Duchess's raven hair and silver eyes, though, gave no doubt about her relation to James. Her Grace approached the newlyweds with a knowing look on her face.

"I have the coach waiting out front for you," she stated, and then smiled while she eyed her son and new daughter-in-law. James had confided in Charlotte that he had never witnessed such lightheartedness in his mother until she was reunited with the Duke.

"Have I told you that you are the best mother in the entire

world?" James replied innocently. Charlotte loved this playful side of him that must have been buried deep down inside his hardened exterior.

"You may have mentioned it, but it needs to be repeated frequently to truly resonate." The Duchess smiled lovingly at her son.

She made a shooing motion. "You two go and celebrate your wedding."

James grabbed Charlotte's hand and stood. They hurried to the door, hoping not to get waylaid by a well-wishing guest. They escaped uninterrupted and slipped into the awaiting town coach, with outriders.

Charlotte felt relieved for more than one reason. First, she no longer spiraled into a panic episode when she was enclosed in a carriage. She attributed this to feeling more at ease with James by her side, even though there was still the nagging sense that *le Diable* was always watching. Jack had told James he had taken care of the threat, and her husband trusted his best friend with his life. That trust would have to be enough for now. Second, Charlotte was en route to consummate her marriage with her delectable husband. It had been a long and arduous road to reach this point, filled with scrapes and scars, but she would do it all again if it meant being with James. Third and finally, Charlotte and James were embarking on the next chapter of their lives. For both of them, they now had each other and a sense of belonging. Although it would be difficult at first, she was ready to discard the epithet she had mentally carried throughout her life, *the forgotten fifth.*

She was now found.

Charlotte looked over at her finder, the man who truly saw her for who she was. Her usually upright husband was a vision of repose as he sprawled his muscular frame against the squabs opposite her. A few strands of sable hair fell over his forehead, giving him a roguish look, despite his perfectly tied cravat and fitted jacket and breeches. His face became lax, and he closed his eyes. The tension released from his body. Charlotte understood. It was the happiest day of her life, but it took fortitude to appear poised throughout the ceremony and wedding breakfast.

When James opened his eyes, Charlotte studied him. When they had first met, she saw only storms, but then the turmoil lessened. Now, his eyes were placid like the surface of a still pond on a wintry day reflecting the gray sky.

She watched these same eyes darken as they roved up and down her body. "Thankfully we only have to travel a stone's throw away."

"You promised me a proper consummation of marriage."

"Oh, you'll get it and more."

Charlotte shivered from the carnal desire evident in James's hungry gaze. Suddenly, his face took on a worried look.

"What is it?" Charlotte's stomach dropped. It seemed that something good never lasted for long.

"You are satisfied with the town house my father gifted us?"

Charlotte let out a guffaw and relief coursed through her body. "You silly man. Of course! That was very kind of your father. Why would I not be?"

James looked a bit sheepish. He glanced around the carriage. "It was the house my grandfather bought for his mistresses. My father never had use of it, but still, it was a place for dalliances."

"You of all people should know I'm not a naïve miss fresh out of the schoolroom. I could not care less. It's a home for us to make our own, and we can make it as scandalous as we want."

James smiled. "I really am the luckiest man in the world. My father told me about his different estates outside of Westcliffe. I can't wait to show them to you. We have time to choose where we want to settle."

"As long as we're together, I'll be excited for you to show me anything."

James reached across the aisle, lifted Charlotte effortlessly, and straddled her legs around him without jostling her left arm. He could not keep his hands off her.

"Anything?" He bowed his head to where her neck and shoulder met and showered her with kisses. The deluge tickled her skin. Charlotte threw back her head and laughed.

"I thought you were going to behave yourself in the carriage!"

"I am, but it doesn't mean I can't have a little fun." Charlotte loved this relaxed side of James. They both paused as the realization of their intimate position became evident.

"I love you," James said in a husky voice.

"I love you too," Charlotte whispered. She admired the glorious man before her.

Their lips slowly met. This kiss did not have the urgency of their earlier embrace before the wedding breakfast. Instead, it was a kiss to seal their union and a kiss for their future together.

The carriage slowed, and James leaned back. A wide grin spread across his face. "It seems you're ready for me to carry you across the threshold, my dear."

James hoisted Charlotte up from his lap and placed her on the seat. He opened the door to the coach himself, ignoring all propriety. James stepped down and held out his hand for Charlotte. Instead of leading her out of the carriage, he scooped her into his arms. The town house's staff was outside to meet the new marquess and marchioness. They were too well-trained to do anything but keep stoic looks on their faces as James approached them, carrying his wife.

The butler stepped forward. "My Lord and my Lady Thornbridge, I'm Collins, at your service," he said, and gave a deep bow. He swept his arm out. "This is your household staff. We welcome you home."

"It's a pleasure to meet you. You can see my hands are full at the moment." There were twitches of lips as James continued, "My first request is that you leave us some food and take the rest of the day off."

Without waiting for a reply, James walked up the house's front steps with the swagger of a commanding officer, but with a look of pure boyish delight on his face. He carried Charlotte across the threshold of their new home and gently lowered her. She took in her surroundings. The wall coverings were dated, but the home had good bones. She and James would make it their own.

Collins rushed in behind the couple and hurried to stand in front of them. "That is most kind of you, my lord. Your rooms are prepared, though we have not seen a valet or lady's maid."

James grinned. "We gave them the day off as well. I must show my wife her duties as a marchioness. That will be all."

Collins's eyes widened momentarily before he schooled his face into a blank tableau.

"You are most kind, my lord." He pivoted on his heel and went to inform the rest of the staff that these were, in fact, the orders.

James took Charlotte's hand and guided her toward the stairs.

Charlotte paused at the base and said in a seductive voice, "Duties, Captain? Or should I say *my lord*?"

James's pupils dilated. "If you speak to me like that, my lady, I'll have to ravish you on the stairs."

"Is that a challenge?"

James growled and led her up the steps by her right hand. Charlotte laughed as she grabbed her skirt, careful not to irritate her injury too much.

"This better be it," James mumbled as he flung open the door of what she hoped would be the master's chambers. They were met with a bedchamber decorated in dark green and gold, with an imposing canopy bed accented with fabric from the last century.

James slammed the door shut and lifted Charlotte once again. She let out an uncharacteristic squeal as James brought her to their marriage bed. He gently placed her on the counterpane. Charlotte's hair was mussed, and her chest rose and fell rapidly in anticipation while she lay waiting.

He peeled off his jacket and made quick work of his cravat and waistcoat. "I'm going to bed you properly, my wife."

"I'm ready," Charlotte responded breathily while she gazed at his muscular torso, peppered with dark hair.

"Come here, my marchioness." James crooked his finger.

Charlotte sat up, and James crawled onto the bed toward her. He rotated her body and undid the buttons on her dress with nimble fingers. She heard him grunt in frustration as he moved down the column. "I could murder whoever decided to put this many buttons on a damn dress."

Lottie chuckled in response to his exasperation. James did not find undressing her a laughing matter. Despite bringing her to release in the carriage, which was most ungentlemanly, he felt like he was still acting admirably, because he did not completely ravish her. After weeks of chastity during Lottie's recovery and chaperoned visits, James determined he was an absolute saint when it came to keeping his hands off her. Now, all that stood between him and his delectable wife was a multitude of buttons and layers of fabric. He wanted to tear the dress away but knew his father had done everything in his power to give Lottie the perfect wedding gown.

James cursed under his breath when he finally reached the bottom and was presented with a new challenge. A petticoat and stays lay before him. He quickly removed the items of clothing with astounding dexterity. When he reached Lottie's chemise, his patience was gone, and he tore the fabric off her body, leaving her in just garters and stockings. She turned around and sat on her knees with her bottom resting on the soles of her feet. A shy look crossed her face.

"You're so damn beautiful," James growled. Lottie should never feel embarrassed. She put every other woman to shame. Her chestnut hair fell out of its chignon while her face had a delightful glow. The freckles that he loved dotted her nose and shoulders. Her pert breasts stood proudly, while her trim waist widened into rounded hips. The dark thatch of curls between her legs teased him. He could not wait any longer. He had to claim the perfection that was his wife.

James eased her into a lying position before he hungrily kissed her. His tongue thrust into her mouth, as if he were a starved man. After a brief hesitation, Lottie met him thrust for thrust and their tongues intertwined. He kissed her neck, then moved his attention to her breasts and paid each one the reverence it deserved. Lottie threw back her head and moaned while she ran her hands through his hair as he sucked on each nipple.

It was not enough. He wanted more. "I need to taste you."

Lottie's breaths came out erratically. His arousal pulsated in his breeches. He spread her legs and dove between them. He lapped the juices from her folds that tasted of musk, salt, and something uniquely Charlotte. Lottie wriggled in response to his caresses, and she moaned his name. He grabbed those rounded hips and swirled his tongue to tease her pearl.

Lottie grabbed at the counterpane. "James!" He reached up

with one hand and played with her nipple and continued his lingual ministrations. Suddenly, she came undone. He felt her body shake while she climaxed. His name came out of Lottie's mouth, mixed with groans, while he licked her pearl so that she could have every last ounce of pleasure.

James used all the self-control he could muster to not spill in his breeches. His member pulsated with need. Eventually, her body quieted, leaving Lottie panting with her eyes closed. He lifted himself up and licked his lips to savor the taste of his wife.

Lottie's eyelids fluttered, and she opened them sleepily. "Oh, James."

He kissed her forehead. "Rest a moment." She closed her eyes again, and her breathing slowed, appearing satiated.

James took this opportunity to ready himself. He hopped off the bed and discarded the remainder of his clothing. Once he was completely nude, he crawled back onto the bed and kissed her gently on her forehead, then cheeks, then mouth.

He leaned back and hid none of himself. Lottie's eyelids opened, and two blue eyes stared back at him. She quirked up the side of her mouth and perused his naked form. Her gaze stopped at his throbbing member, and her tongue darted out over her lips.

"If I wait any longer, I'm going to explode."

"I'm always ready for you." She motioned for him to come closer. Lottie wrapped her good arm around his neck and pulled James down. He kissed her and positioned the tip of his cock at her entrance, coating it in her juices.

"You're still wet for me."

Lottie let out a sigh. "Always."

James entered her to the hilt.

"Your cunny is so tight."

"Give me more, James," Lottie moaned.

"I don't know if I can be gentle."

Lottie raised her eyebrows and locked eyes with him. "Who said anything about being gentle?"

"God, I love you," James said. He withdrew slightly then began to thrust in and out of her perfect cunny. Lottie learned his rhythm and matched with the rocking of her hips. He drove deeper and deeper as pleasure built up further inside him. Lottie's breathing quickened as she begged him for more. He felt her body hum with tension again. She was so close to her peak, and he wanted to get her there before he could let himself go.

Lottie screamed his name, and he felt her body pulsate. Her cunny tightened around his cock and provided the pressure that took him over the edge. James let out a yell and spilled his seed into her womb. The most exquisite pleasure washed over him. He collapsed next to Lottie and pulled her close so that she lay on top of him. He held her tightly to his body, waiting for their breathing to slow.

She lifted her head from his chest and looked down at him. "I love you, Captain."

He kissed her deeply and pulled her closer. Both exhausted, they drifted off to sleep.

The last thing James remembered was never wanting to let her go.

EPILOGUE
ONE WEEK LATER

S unlight filtered through a crack in the drapes and projected a sliver of light onto the bed. James traced his finger down Charlotte's back and over her rounded bottom.

"I never want to leave this bed," she proclaimed, as she lay on her stomach with her head turned toward James.

"We have done a good job of doing just that." He chuckled and gave her bottom a little slap. "I wish we could stay here forever too." He positioned her so that her bare breasts rested on his wide chest. "At this rate, we'll be filling the house with children in no time."

"I grew up in a big family, but it often felt like it was just Arthur and me. I wasn't sure what I wanted, but now I know. I want little boys running around with black hair and silver eyes."

James kissed her lips tenderly. "What if I want little girls running around with brown hair and blue eyes?"

"We can compromise and have both." Charlotte kissed him back and let out a contented sigh.

"We'll have to go back out into Society soon, but only for a little while. Parliament should be done shortly and then we can go back with my family to Westcliffe. Our real honeymoon can start once we travel to the other estates to check on them."

"That will be wonderful," she responded. She could not ask for anything more than excuses to spend all her time with James.

"We'll start north in Scotland." James kissed her forehead. "Then travel to the west of England." He kissed her cheek. "Then journey south." He kissed her lips.

She traced the dark hair on his chest and looked back at him coyly. "I assume that we'll have to consummate our marriage at each home. It's the only way it's valid, is it not?"

James looked seriously at her. "I'm afraid you're incorrect."

She was crestfallen. "No?"

"The houses will not be enough. Surely there are woods, gardens, a caretaker's cottage or two. All of these must be given our attention as well."

She slapped him playfully.

A wide grin spread across his face. "I feel like a new person with you. It's as if a giant weight has been lifted off my shoulders."

"You make me feel complete. I love seeing you infinitely happier than the grumpy man I met at the Markham Ball."

"I was not grumpy," James said.

She raised her eyebrows.

"Fine. Maybe a little."

She chuckled and gave him a slow kiss. Then she looked up at him, and her brow furrowed.

"There's one thing that's been bothering me, but I haven't wanted to bring it up."

"What's that?" James asked.

Charlotte trailed her fingers along James's chest. She met the silver eyes she knew so well and asked for an answer she was not sure she wanted to hear.

"I know we're safe from *le Diable* because of Jack's help, but how did he get us this protection?"

James rubbed her back and paused for a moment. "With Jack, I try not to ask too many questions, because he's involved in many things that aren't exactly savory." Charlotte remained silent and nodded, urging him on. "He and I are like brothers. We would do anything for each other. He's been at odds with *le Diable* for some time, so he said he would take care of it and not to worry. Afterward, he reassured me that it was done."

She could tell her husband was skirting around the crux of the matter. "I understand, but please tell me. What guarantees that we're safe?"

James let out a sigh.

"He traded a life for a life."

Find out about the deal Lady Beatrice Walford and Jack Doherty strike that will change both of their lives in Book 2 of the Scandalous Secrets series, *A Lady's Ruinous Secret*.

ACKNOWLEDGMENTS

Thank you to my amazing husband. In anything I have pursued, he has always been there to ground me, provide encouragement, and offer endless support. He did not even blink when I told him I was writing a book, and was immediately ready to help me figure out how to make it happen. Thank you to my darling son, who joined the journey on the home stretch and provided me with love and snuggles as I wrapped up the final version. Thank you to my wonderful family, who have always been my biggest supporters in everything I have done, and who have taught me the importance of hard work and dedication.

Thank you to my dear friends, who helped me along the way. To Regina, who is my fellow romance novel enthusiast and who read through my manuscript early on. To my childhood friend Katie, who is a sounding board for all things in life, romance novels included.

Thank you to Grace Bradley, who was the first person to review my manuscript and provided me with the feedback, confidence, and mentorship to pursue publication.

A huge thank you to Tanya Crosby-Straley, Jill Stadler, and the Oliver Heber Books team for believing in *A Lady's Dangerous Secret,* and for your phenomenal support as a burgeoning author. This dream would not be possible without you.

SUBSCRIBE TO HAZEL'S NEWSLETTER

Come say hello! You can connect with Hazel and subscribe to her newsletter at: www.hazelhaas.com

ALSO BY HAZEL HAAS

ABOUT THE AUTHOR

Hazel Haas did not grow up wanting to be an author despite being a voracious reader and creating stories in her mind. Once she had a successful career, she realized something was missing. Hazel decided to write down the stories that danced in her imagination, and her creativity was unleashed. Tales of historical romance and intrigue followed, and the result was pure joy. Hazel had found the missing piece to the puzzle.

When Hazel is not meandering through the woods and envisioning her stories, she loves to read, hike, garden, go to the beach, and travel. She always prefers the unmarked paths. Hazel has a soft spot for exploring castles and country houses, where you will find her gazing adoringly at their plasterwork ceilings. She lives on the East Coast of the United States with her husband and son.

Hazel loves hearing from readers. You can connect with her and subscribe to her newsletter at: www.hazelhaas.com.